Spelons

ARPress
45 Dan Road Suite 5
Canton MA 02021

Hotline: 1(888) 821-0229
Fax: 1(508) 545-7580

Ordering Information:
Quantity sales. Special discounts are available on quantity purchases by corporations, associations, and others. For details, contact the publisher at the address above.

Printed in the United States of America.

ISBN-13: Softcover   979-8-89389-217-8
          eBook   979-8-89389-218-5

Library of Congress Control Number: 2024905938

Spelons

The Hidden People

RICK MOLES

TABLE OF CONTENTS

DEDICATION

I would like to dedicate this book to my family. My wife Veneshia, who has been with me for over 52 years. During that time she has encouraged and supported me in whatever endeavor I attempted. That includes writing this book. I would go to her with different ideas, and she would be happy to discuss the good and bad parts of each chapter. She is not an author, but she is a good judge of a story line. Therefore, I valued her input totally. I also want to dedicate the book to my daughters, Lisa and Lori. I would send a copy of each chapter to them and wait for their critique. All too often the chapters were returned with a supply of suggestions. Some I listened to and some I didn't.

On one occasion, I had sent Lori a copy of the chapter where Daniel is trapped in the cage. The copy I sent to her had Daniel getting shot and killed by the man with the gun. I immediately got this phone call with Lori on the other end frantically screaming at me. She kept saying "NO NO NO, you can't kill Daniel. You can hurt him really bad, but you can't kill him." Needless to say, I accepted her constructive suggestion. She saved Daniel's life.

These are only some examples of the support and encouragement I received from all my family. That includes not only my wife and children, but my grandchildren also. That was another reason for the book, was to leave something behind. I wanted to leave something that my grandkids and great grandkids can say someday, "My Poppy wrote this book."

Thank you all.

ACKNOWLEDGEMENT

The way I look at an acknowledgement is to bring to light the person or persons who directly or indirectly influenced me to write this book. I have been an avid reader for many years. The author, whose books I read most often, is Stephen King. At the time I began writing Spelons, I had read almost every book Stephen King had written. It was his style of writing that encouraged me to write. I know inside, that I would never become the level of writer as Mr. King, but the book was still inside me waiting to come out.

So, with the books of Stephen King as my guide, I sat down to write Spelons. The idea for Spelons actually came to me on a hunting trip. I used to bring King's latest novel with me into the woods. As any hunter knows, deer hunting involves a lot of sitting and waiting. As I would sit either in a tree stand or on the ground. I would read the latest novel.

My mind began to wonder, and the idea of small people living in the cave systems of Middle Tennessee began to grow. While reading the latest King novel, my own mind began to create characters for the book, both big and small.

After many failed attempts and scores of writings and rewriting, I finally finished Spelons. I hope you enjoy it, and I hope Mr. Stephen King gets to read it.

CHAPTER 1

Steve heard the shot early in the afternoon. It came with a thunderous boom that seemed to shake the very air around him, a boom that woke him from the drowsy stupor brought on by the warm afternoon sun. The sound seemed to come from everywhere, but he felt sure that its approach was from the general direction in which Tom Gregg was hunting. Tom was his best friend and quite the experienced hunter. Steve, on the other hand, knew very little about the business of stalking and killing the ever-elusive white tail, and really had no desire to learn. He sat perched in his tree stand with gun in hand only to quell the persistent nagging of his friend Tom.

I'll bet he's shot a deer, Steve Mason thought. Now he will have to blood trail it, field dress it and drag it back to the truck. That's going to take a good two hours, he grumbled. In the meantime, here I am stuck in this lonesome tree waiting for that big buck to come by, the buck that I probably won't shoot, if he does dare to show his antlers.

His thoughts were interrupted by the sound of rustling leaves coming from behind his left shoulder. Steve slowly turned his head and waited for his eyes to focus in the distance. There, not fifty feet from him stood a large deer with antlers that seemed to mingle with the underbrush. The deer was massive. Steve's heart began to pound, as he raised the rifle to his shoulder. His gaze traveled the length of the barrel, as he brought the front sight into the 'V' of the rear sight.

The weapon was centered directly on the shoulder of the approaching animal. The pounding in his chest began to echo in his head. Louder and louder until he finally lowered the rifle from his shoulder and cradled it in his lap.

I just can't do it, he thought, he is just too beautiful. This guy belongs in the woods running free, not in my freezer wrapped in paper, or hanging on the wall in my den watching the evening news. He sat and watched the magnificent animal for several minutes, as it wandered about the forest searching for acorns and other browse to eat. Finally, as the deer disappeared into the forest underbrush, Steve released a heavy sigh. "I sure hope no one kills that guy this year," he said, "I think next time I go hunting, I'm going to bring a camera instead.

His thoughts were shattered by the sound of the rumbling in his stomach. "Umm," he said, "I didn't realize just how hungry I was. I'd better get down from here and find something to eat." Steve sat precariously atop the Apache Port-A-Stand, trying to determine the best method of getting to the ground without breaking something important. The port-a-stand was nothing more than a ladder with a seat, which is leaned against a tree and chained there securely. Steve unloaded the hunting rifle he had borrowed from Tom, and tied a length of rope to the muzzle. He carefully lowered the weapon to the ground. Now, he thought, I've got the gun on the ground, if I only had me down I'd be happy. Balancing himself on the top rung of the ladder, he stood and turned around. His arms instinctively wrapped around the large oak tree to which the stand was secured. A strong breeze moved through the woods causing the tree to sway. Steve swayed with it. "Good grief," he mumbled, "I've got to get down from here now." Carefully he released his grip from the tree, while holding onto the sides of the ladder. He was then able to step down each rung of the ladder and plant his feet firmly on the ground.

He looked up at the spot he had just left, and a mournful "Oh No" formed on his lips. The ladder was still chained to the tree. He knew he had to climb back up and remove the chain before the tree stand could be lowered and disassembled. With trembling knees, he managed to make his way back up the ladder and bear hug the large oak when he reached the top. He reached around the tree and found the small nut and bolt that secured the chain to the tree. From his position it was all but impossible to remove the nut. He knew that he would have to lean around the tree in order to get his hands on the nut and remove it. With his left foot planted securely on the top rung, Steve leaned over the edge of the tree stand until he was able to effectively remove the nut.

Another gust of wind caused the tree to move just enough to make the stand slip no more than an inch. But, that inch was enough to cause Steve to lose his foothold. His body weight forced him over the edge of the stand, and gravity did the rest. As his reflexes took over, his left hand grabbed the edge of the ladder seat. In the blink of an eye, he found himself hanging by one hand from the port-a-stand. His feet were only a few feet from the ground. Rather than trying to pull himself back up, he simply let go and fell to the ground, landing in a soft bed of leaves and rolling onto his back.

"Whew, I made it," he said, but looking up he saw the tree stand still attached to the large oak. "Oh great," he said, "I've still got to get that thing down." Grabbing the ladder by both sides he began to shake it vigorously. The chain rattled, and the bolt that held the two links of chain together came tumbling to the ground. The chains slipped free from the tree and the stand came loose. Steve eased it to the ground and shouted, "Ha! That's the way you get an Apache Port-A-Stand down from an oak tree," and he began to laugh. The sound of his laughter echoed through the silent woods bouncing from tree to tree and eventually coming to rest on a pair of ears nestled in the brush only a few yards away.

Once the stand was safely on the ground, he had to disassemble the ladder into its parts and ready it for carrying. An experienced hunter could have probably accomplished the task in a matter of five minutes, but Steve was no expert in any sense of the word. Fifteen minutes and several foul words later, the ladder was ready for transport.

"Now, what should I do?" he muttered to himself. "If I go back to the truck, I'll just have to wait for Tom to return, since I don't have a key. Besides, I'm not totally sure I could even find the truck."

Another cold breeze embraced the back of Steve's neck and a chill began to crawl down his back sending a shiver through his body. A fire, he thought, that's what I need now. Something to keep my buns warm until Tom gets back. Lets see, he thought, I'll need some firewood. "I'll just get a few sticks and arrange them in the basic Boy Scout tee pee fashion, and I'll have a blazing fire in no time," he mumbled to himself, as he wandered off into the woods. His intent was on finding the firewood and not on paying attention to the direction in which he was traveling. Steve was totally unaware of everything, including the pair of eyes that watched from a distance. The crosshairs of the Weaver scope followed him as he walked.

Tom Gregg was an experienced hunter. From late September until the middle of December, Tom spent most of his waking hours in the woods hunting for deer. He could not understand why any grown man would not want to be outside in the midst of nature enjoying the fresh air and searching for the ever-illusive white tail deer.

Tom had left his tree stand with Steve, which left him hunting from the ground. It was not his most favorite method of hunting, but under the circumstances, it would have to do. He certainly did not want Steve traipsing around in the woods with a loaded gun and no idea where he was. A large white oak tree had fallen over from old age, and the trunk and roots had left a nice hole in the ground. The hold had been filled in somewhat with leaves and branches shed from the other trees over the past several seasons. Tom nestled himself comfortably in the hole so the roots and trunk were behind him. The arrangement of the tree trunk and roots provided him with both cover as well as protection from the cold wind.

This wasn't the greatest location from which Tom had ever hunted, but at least he was protected from the elements. He had found two 'rubs' and one 'scrape' not more than fifty yards from where he sat. There was also a small trail leading past the scrape. Tom recognized the scrape as a mating area for the deer. The large buck had scrapped the ground with his hooves, then urinated on the bare ground as a signal to the females, that this was his mating territory. This was the type of sign that most deer hunters looked for when hunting, and this was exactly what Tom had found. He sat quietly waiting and listening for any sounds or sights that might indicate his quarry was approaching.

The first sound to break the silence was the familiar snort of the buck. It came from behind the tree over Tom's left shoulder. The big deer was not yet visible, so Tom sat quietly and waited. He heard the rustle of leaves as the cautious mammal slowly made its way down the hill toward him. Quiet, wait, don't move, he thought. Come on big fellow just a few more steps and you are mine. Just step out from behind that tree, that's it, two more steps and. Three thousand feet per second is the speed the bullet from Tom's Winchester 30-06 was traveling as it left the muzzle. In less than a heartbeat, the lead projectile had found its mark. The entrance point was just behind and slightly above the left shoulder. As it struck the hard sinewy meat of the fully-grown deer, it began to mushroom. The bullet swelled and spread out to twice its original size, taking with it shoulder muscle, heart tissue and lungs. Vital arteries and nerves were mangled as it made its way through the soon to be dead animal.

By the time the bullet left the body, it had grown to more than twice its original size and was carrying with it a massive amount of the animal's vital tissue. The exit hole was quite a bit larger than the entrance hole and left its victim limping away in search of a place to die. The deer was not going to lie down and die without trying to escape. With most of its lungs and shoulder missing, he still managed to limp into the woods for several yards. Finally the loss of blood and oxygen proved to be too much for the large buck, and he quietly took his last breath lying against a small dogwood tree. As his body fell against the small tree, a single leaf was shaken loose and floated down. It landed on the big deer as though nature were trying to bury her dead.

As the smoke cleared, and the ringing in Tom's ears began to fade ever so slightly, he saw the fatally wounded deer fall to the ground in a small stand of loblolly pines. I'll just wait here for a few minutes, he thought, and give the poor fellow a chance to die with honor. If I go after him now, it will just cause the adrenaline to start pumping and he'll jump and run for miles. Don't want the meat to have that gamy taste.

Tom leaned back against the stump of the hug3 white oak and lit his camel cigarette. Nothing like the taste of a good smoke while you wait, he thought, as he exhaled the first puff. He had passed up several chances to light up earlier, while waiting for the big buck, but the smell of smoke would have certainly frightened him away. The wait was worth it. That buck was a real beauty.

As Tom expected, there was a spot of blood on the ground at the exact point the deer had been standing when he fired the shot. Judging from the size of the blood pool, it wouldn't be too difficult to trail this big fellow. He found the blood trail leading into the pine thicket and began his search. The thicket extended for about three hundred yards before emptying into a field of weeds and blackberry briars. The deer had decided to spend his last few moments of life in the confines of the briar thicket. Tom knew that he had to get the deer out before nightfall, and that meant fighting the briars to get him.

He wondered if the final thoughts of the deer might have been something like, "if I'm going to die, I might as well take somebody with me, or at least make it as hard on them as possible." That had to be what this deer was thinking, when he decided to run through these briars, Tom thought, as he inched his way along the trail left by the dieing buck. Finally, there he was about fifty feet in front of him. The big deer had decided to give up his struggle in the dead center of the briar patch. How fitting.

Getting to the deer was much easier tan trying to drag him out. He tied a short piece of rope around the front legs and secured them to the head. This prevented the head from dragging the ground and damaging the trophy. The problem, however, was not the head dragging the ground, but rather the huge rack of antlers snagging on the thick stems of the briars, to say nothing of the thorns that kept snagging his hands and face. "Can't field dress him in this thicket," Tom mumbled to himself, "got to get to the pine trees. Just a few more feet." The sweat poured from Tom's face and the muscles of his legs and back began to ache, as he pulled the dead weight through the maze of thorns. With one final tug, he freed the deer from the grasp of the unyielding briars.

The sun was settling low in the sky as Tom plunged the four-inch blade of his Shrade hunting knife into the soft fur on the belly of the deer. The smell of warm blood filled his nostrils. Tom liked the smell of blood.

CHAPTER 2

"Mommy, when will daddy be home?" asked five-year-old Jennifer Mason, as her mother, Sheila, began to peel the last potato to put into the pot. "He said he would be home about dark," Sheila replied, just as the potato she was peeling slipped from her hands and landed on the floor. "I'll get it," yelled Jennifer, as she raced for the potato. "Never mind," said Sheila, "you go into the living room and pick up your toys before Daddy gets home. You know he won't like to see them scattered all over the place."

"O-k-a-y," Jennifer moaned, as she stomped from the kitchen into the living room. The large yellow ball lying beside the couch caught her eye. The anger that she carried with her from the kitchen came to rest in her foot, as she kicked the ball across the room. Fortunately for Jennifer the ball struck the side of the recliner and rolled passively into the corner.

Sheila was beginning to get upset – no, mad was more like it. It was almost six o'clock and Steve hadn't even called. "Its like this every time he goes out somewhere with Tom Gregg," she grumbled. "He has no concept of time or space and is totally oblivious to everything except having a good time. He had better be having a good time now, cause he'll not be having one when he gets home. She sat the large pan down on the stove top with such force, that water splashed out and onto the floor. That didn't help her anger much.

She placed the cover on the large pot of vegetables that was to be their dinner then turned and walked toward the living room. It's terribly quiet in there, she thought, the young lady had better be picking up her toys. As Sheila rounded the doorway into the living room, she saw Jennifer lying on the floor in front of the couch. Her head was on a large stuffed animal and her eyes were closed.

"Oh no you don't, young lady," she said. "You're not going to take a nap now. You will never fall asleep tonight. C'mon, lets get these toys picked up." Sheila helped her small daughter to her feet and helped her get started on her clean up job. Jennifer was picking up the toys as Sheila walked into the den.

The stereo was always tuned to her favorite oldies rock-n-roll station. She pressed the 'ON' button and the sound of the Beatles wanting to hold your hand filled the house. "There," she said, "that ought to keep us awake while we finish our work." She returned to the living room to find Jennifer dancing to the tune, as she picked up the toys. "That's my girl," Sheila bragged, "that makes Mommy so proud of you. You're such a big girl. Lets dance and pick up the toys together." The two ladies worked together and finished the job. Sheila returned to the kitchen to check on the pot of stew. She glanced at the clock. It was 6:45, " He'd better be here soon," she mumbled under her breath, "this is the last time he's going to be late." She had no idea just how late Steve was going to be.

CHAPTER 3

Just a few more sticks should do it, Steve thought, as he continued to gather the necessary firewood. "There, that should do it. Now to head back to the tree stand, build a fire, and wait for Tom to come back. Now, lets see, tree stand, which way is the tree stand? I came from …… Well, wait a minute, which direction did I come from? How am I supposed to tell one tree from another, they all look the same. Hold it, stay calm, don't panic. I know, I came down that hill because I almost tripped over that log. Steve reached into his pocked and pulled out the small compass that Tom had given him. "Now lets see, how do I use this thing." He knew the needle pointed north, but that was about all he could remember, and that information was totally useless. "Why can't I remember how to use this thing? We learned how to do it in boy scouts."

The sight of the compass stirred his memory, and suddenly Steve was in the North Ridge High School gymnasium, at one of the few Boy Scout meeting he was ever able to attend. Steve's dad was a factory worker during the day, and worked evenings at Ray Dodd's service station and grocery store. His nighttime and weekend job left little time to spend with Steve doing those father-son things that most kids remember. For Steve, the special evenings that he did get to spend with his father were special, and the boy scouts was one of those special things that he shared with his dad.

Steve remembered that particular evening, because it was the one devoted to the use of the compass. He remembered being in the meeting with several other young scouts, and they all had their compasses. As the instructor began to explain the finer pints of degrees and true north, someone tapped him on the shoulder. Steve looked around to see the unmistakable face of Horace Farley.

In 1982 when Steve and Horace were twelve years old, the word nerd had not yet become widely used. Horace Farley, however, was the personification of everything that was a nerd. He was the original ninety-seven pound weakling that always got sand kicked in his face. Horace was the kid that the body building magazines were always talking about. He wore dark rimmed glasses with thick lenses. Some of the kids called the coke bottle glasses.

Most kids tried to look cool and wear the latest clothes, parachute pants or something like them, but not Horace. Someone, and rumor has it that it was his weird mother, used to place a large bowl over his head and cut around it with a pair of scissors. There were always rumors of people having this type haircut, but no one had ever seen it until Horace came to town. Everyone laughed at his haircut, his glasses, and his clothes. Steve did too, but not as much. He was probably the closest thing to a friend that Horace ever had.

As if the glasses and hair weren't enough, there was the matter of his clothes. His weird mother probably got them from the good will, and the only good will in North Ridge was the basement of the local Baptist church. His trousers were barely long enough to reach the top of his mismatched argyle socks, leaving the same strip of skin with everything he wore. His shirts were always a size too big and always had at least one button missing. Most often it was the one right in the middle of his skinny belly. It would always gap open every time he sat down, and his belly wasn't always clean.

All this abuse didn't upset Horace very much, since most of it was verbal and not physical. I guess he just learned to live with, or at least not show any ill affects from it. Horace, however, was exceptionally smart. He made 'A's in every subject, and didn't have to study. It was his superior intelligence and willingness to share his knowledge with the more Neanderthal football players that kept him alive through most of his elementary and junior high days.

Horace was constantly looking for something mischievous to do in his spare time. He learned things so quickly, that it left him hopelessly board. Steve was not so fortunate. He had to work hard and practice often in order to learn something moderately complex and using the compass was no simple task. Horace mastered the art of compass reading quickly and promptly focused his attention on Steve, who was at best struggling with the prospects of establishing a true northerly bearing.

"C'mon, " Horace said, "I've got something really neat to show you." "I can't," Steve said, " I have to learn how to read this dumb compass." "Forget that thing," Horace replied, " I'll teach you how to use it later. Besides, when will you ever need to use a compass anyway? What are the chances of you ever getting lost in the woods? You hate the woods, besides, I told you, I've got the neatest thing in the whole world to show you."

"What is it," Steve asked, "what's so all fired neat that it can't wait?"

"Girls!" Horace whispered, with a smile on his lips that spoke of something sneaky and sure to get everyone in big trouble.

"Girls? What girls?" Steve asked. "There's no girls in here, this is a Boy Scout meeting."

"What's tonight," Horace asked. "Thursday," said Steve, "so what?"

"Exactly," he answered, " and I happen to know that the high school cheerleaders practice on Thursday nights downstairs in the girls locker room."

"So," Steve asked, "what's that got to do with us?"

"I also happen to know that one of the windows to the dressing room has a tiny hole in it and you can see right into the locker room. But, that's not the best part. Right about now, those beautiful cheerleaders are changing clothes and taking showers. How about that? Have you ever seen a naked girl take a shower?" Horace asked with an evil grin?

"Well no," said Steve, "not exactly, at least not a real girl in real life, but I have seen some magazines. I've seen plenty of naked girls there."

"Well my friend, forget about those books, forget about the compass, forget about everything else and come with me." Horace said," I'm gonna show you the real thing."

They slipped out of the gymnasium without the scoutmaster noticing and made their way in the direction of the boy's bathroom, but made a dash for the side door when no one was looking. The girl's locker room was in the basement of the gym, and the windows were at ground level. This made the plan much easier.

It was just as Horace had said. There was a small hole in one of the windows. It was about the size of a quarter. It looked as if someone had probably thrown a rock through it, but it was just the right size for looking into the dressing room without being seen.

"Go ahead," Horace urged, "you go first, I've seen this hundreds of times." As Steve peered through the tiny hole, he was sure his heart was going to explode. It was beating so fast he could feel it pounding in his chest and hear it in his head. It was the most amazing thing Steve had ever seen in his twelve short years in North Ridge. Cheerleaders were running around in there underwear. They were the most beautiful teenage girls he had ever seen, and to see them in just bra and panties was almost more than he could stand. He was sure that everyone could hear his heart beating, and he knew that he was going to have a heart attack. That's all I need, he thought, drop dead hear with a heart attack right here outside the girls locker room. I can just see the headlines now. " TWELVE YEAR OLD PEEPING TOM DIES FROM HEART FAILURE."

" They're not taking showers," Steve said, they are just changing clothes." "I know," said Horace, " I think girls are ashamed to take off all their clothes in front of each other. They don't want anyone to see anything, but this is good enough for me. Here, move over. Let me see. You've been there long enough besides; it might make you go blind or something, this being your first time and all. I wouldn't want to be responsible for that."

The silent tension of the moment was broken by the sound of someone coming around the building. "Quick, lets get out of here," Horace said, "hurry follow me." They raced around the edge of the building just as the scoutmaster rounded the front corner in search of the two stray scouts. They managed to subtly return to the main part of the gym without being noticed.

"Where have you two been," asked Steve's dad. "Oh, we had to go to the bathroom, dad. I think Horace is getting diarrhea," Steve answered. It was the best lie he could think of at the time, but his father bought it with no further questions. "C'mon, lets get home," his father said, "you know mom will worry if we're not home on time."

Another sharp gust of winter wind brought Steve back to reality. Now I remember why I can't use the compass, he thought, as he continued to walk back toward his tree stand. "Good old Horace," he said to himself, "I wonder if he will ever find some girl to marry? Oh well, he mumbled, can't worry about Horace right now. I've got more important things to worry about, like finding that tree stand. I know it's around here somewhere. The important thing is to stay calm."

As the bolt slid back, it pulled a shining new cartridge into the open chamber of the high-powered rifle. The sleek lead bullet moved effortlessly into the breech. A strong steady hand deliberately eased the bolt forward cradling the lethal projectile in preparation for its eventful journey. A glint of sunlight reflected momentarily from the cold blue steel of the rifle, as an unknown thumb moved quietly to release the safety. All is ready. The cross hairs of the Weaver 3X9 power scope fell deftly on its mark. Just above and slightly behind the shoulder. Hold still, don't move, just one more step and.

The sound was first, loud; too loud; Followed by a sharp stab of pain. "Oh! My God, what's going on," Steve cried, as he looked at the large gaping hole in his right shoulder. "I've been shot! Some damn fool deer hunter has mistaken me for a deer." The high-powered bullet reacted much the same way in human flesh as it does in the deer. The smaller hole in the back of Steve's right shoulder was the entrance point. On its journey through his body, it managed to shatter his shoulder blade and remove much of the superior lobe of his right lung. At the same time it managed to mutilate most of the pectoral muscles of his chest.

"It's funny the thoughts that go through your mind when you are facing death. How long does it take to die? What will it be like in death? Will it hurt? I'll never see Sheila or Jennifer again. Darkness. Why is it so dark? I can't see anything. Am I already dead? I can't be, there is too much pain. Steve lay on a bed of leaves, his blood slowly beginning to pool around him. I must open my eyes, he thought, I'm not dead yet. Seconds, minutes, hours or even days, he had no way of knowing just how long he had laid there before he was able to open his eyes. Its hard to tell the time when you are waiting to die. I'm not dead yet though, he thought, as he struggled to open one eye. Trees, sky, its getting dark, but at least I'm not dead.

"Who are you?" Steve saw the silhouette of a man against the setting sun. "Who are you? Did you shoot me? Please help me, I'm dieing." Steve screamed to the dark image but got no response. This is it, he thought, I'm going to die here in the woods and never get to say goodbye to my family. " Why did you do this you son-of." As Steve closed his eyes he noticed the boots of the tall dark shadow. That's unusual, he thought, why would I notice this man's boots, when I'm about to die? The image of those boots blazed into the retina of his eyes as they closed and everything went black.

CHAPTER 4

The last rays of the winter sunlight were dieing behind the hill, as Tom finally managed to load the deer into the back of the pickup. "Need some help?" The sudden voice caused Tom to jump out of his skin and turn around to see a man walking up the hill. It appeared to be a wildlife officer judging from his green coat and badge. "I asked if you need some help?" the officer asked, as he leaned against the tailgate of the pickup. "No, no thanks," Tom replied, "I just got him loaded. Isn't he a beauty?" "Sure is," said the officer, "by the way, my name is Dave Black, I'm the wildlife officer for this area." "Good to meet you," Tom said, "You caught me by surprise." "Dave grinned, "Sorry about that. Can I see your license?" Again Tom was caught by surprise, but answered, "Oh sure thing," as he reached for his wallet.

"Are you hunting alone," Dave asked? "No, I'm not, as a matter of fact." Tom answered. I was just about to go out looking for my friend Steve Mason. He should have been here by now. I can't imagine what has happened to him."

"Well, Mr. Gregg, your license and tag seem to be in order. Come on and I'll help you look for your friend. He sure doesn't need to spend the night our here," Officer Black said. "Which way did he go? Tom replied, "he went toward that pine thicket, but that has been hours ago. I sure hope he hasn't wondered off and gotten himself lost. He's not exactly what I'd call an outdoorsman. As a matter of fact, this is the first time he has ever been deer hunting, and the only reason he came this time is because I begged him to come along."

"The woods can be tricky, especially the first time," Dave said. "I remember the first time I got lost in these woods. I got turned around and soon every tree looked just like the last one. I must have wandered around out there for two or three hours before my dad finally found me. The funny thing about it was, that I was not more than two hundred yards from the truck. I'd been walking in a circle the whole time."

"Yeah, that's what I've heard happens," said Tom. "It's been said that people travel in a circle until they die. Well, I can't let that happen to Steve. Come on lets go find him."

Tom and Dave walked together through the woods in the direction of the pine thicket. "Lets separate about a hundred feet, "said Dave, "we'll keep in shouting distance in case you see something." "Sounds good to me," Tom answered. They walked through the pines and into the hardwoods beyond but saw nothing. "Lets go back and get help," said Dave, "It's almost seven o'clock. We'll have to get some more people to continue the search in the morning." "I can't believe this," Tom groaned, "I told him to stay close to the truck and not wander off. Like I said, this is his first time hunting, and I'm the one who talked him into coming. I can't leave him out here all night; he'll freeze to death." "Too late to worry about that now," said Dave, "we're not going to do any good out here tonight. We'll come back first thing in the morning with enough men to do the job. Don't worry, we'll find him. Do you think he has enough sense to find a warm place to shelter for the night?"

"I don't know," Tom replied, "I just pray to God he covers up with leaves or something."

It's about time you got home, Sheila thought to herself as she watched the headlights of the truck pull into the drive. "He makes me so mad," she mumbled to herself, "always thinking of himself, never thinking of what I want or need, or what I would like to do. Well big fellow, you can find your own dinner tonight. I had it all ready, but you didn't show up on time so good luck with a can of beans."

Her thoughts were interrupted by the sound of the front door bell. Why is he ringing the bell, she thought, as she reached for the doorknob. "Tom! What are you doing here? Where is Steve?" she asked, as she looked past Tom and into the darkness beyond. "Sheila," Tom said, as he looked sorrowfully into her anxious eyes. Lets go inside, we have to talk." "Why, what's wrong? Where is Steve? Something has happen to him hasn't it? I know something is wrong, please tell me," Shelia began to sob. "Okay," Tom said, "just calm down. It isn't all that bad."

Tom tried to explain what had happened. "I don't know why he left the area where the tree stand was. I told him to stay put unless he shot a deer and had to trail it. I did hear one shot from his direction. I don't know if he shot a deer or if he was trying to signal me. My guess is that he shot at a deer; then tried to follow it. He must have lost his sense of direction and is now lost somewhere in the woods. But don't worry, Dave Black, with the Wildlife Agency, says that we'll gather enough men in the morning to search the woods until we find him. Besides, Steve is a big guy he can take care of himself. I'm sure he'll find a safe and warm place to spend the night, and we will find him first thing in the morning. Why, we'll all be laughing about this tomorrow over lunch. Now, let me fix you something to calm your nerves."

"Thanks," Sheila said, "I sure could use something right about now."

"Where is Jennifer?" Tom asked. "Oh, she's already in bed, and I'm not going to wake her," she answered.

"No," said Tom, "let her sleep. There is not need to worry her with this tonight. Besides, he'll probably be home before she even wakes up anyway." Tom handed Sheila the scotch and water, as he sat beside her on the couch. "Here, this will help calm you down," he said, as he patted her gently on the shoulder. Sheila turned to him and asked. "Have you been home yet?"

"No, not yet," Tom answered, "I came over here as soon as I got back. I know you would be worried."

"But what about Judy. Won't she be worried about you? You'd better give her a call to let her know where you are. I'm sure she is frantic."

"Yeah, you're right," Tom said, "hand me the phone, and I'll give her a ring. I'll be home soon as I can." He hung the phone up then took Sheila by the hand and said. "There, that takes care of Judy, now how about you? Need another drink?"

"No thanks," she answered, "I'm fine now. Thanks for coming by. You'd better be getting home now, but I really do appreciate your concern for Steve."

"Yeah, I guess you're right," Tom said, "I'll check back with you in the morning and let you know what we find. Don't worry! Everything will be all right. If there is anything you need, don't hesitate to call." Tom leaned over and gave Sheila a kiss on the cheek before leaving. "Thanks Tom," Sheila said, "I'll see you tomorrow." Tom closed the door behind him and stepped off the front porch. He watched through the living room window as Sheila walked back down the hall toward her bedroom. Steve sure is a lucky son-of-a-gun, he thought. Shelia is one good looking lady.

Tom had known Steve and Sheila for most of their married life and had always admired Sheila's beauty. Her blonde hair and five feet four inch well maintained figure had always appealed to Tom's covetous nature. Not a brick out of place there, he thought.

His mind wandered back to that day at the lake. It was a hot Saturday afternoon, and he and Judy were there with Steve and Sheila. This was before Jennifer was born, and Sheila looked even better, if that was possible. Steve had gone down to the water to take a dip, and Judy was gone to the restroom. Sheila was lying on her back absorbing the sun's rays. Tom sat admiring her firm young body, as her bathing suit top rose and fell with each breath. Tiny droplets of perspiration, glistening like diamonds in the summer sun, began to collect on her navel.

"You sure are getting dark," Tom said, "need some more oil?" "Yeah," said Sheila, "but I'm gonna roll over. Would you rub some on my back?" "Sure thing," he said, with a slight tremble in his voice. He opened the cap to the lotion bottle, and watched as Sheila rolled over. He held the bottle of Hawaiian Tropic Deep Tanning Oil in his hand and waited. "Untie the top for me, would you please?" Sheila asked. "I don't want any white lines on my tan."

Tom's fingers were trembling as he untied the knot that held her bathing suit top in place. He poured a thin line of the milky white oil down the center of her back and began to slowly run it into her already dark skin. His hands made small circles over her shoulders and down to the small of her back. His hands came painfully close to the edge of her bikini bottoms, but he kept his restraint. Just as he finished, he saw Judy approaching from the direction of the bathhouse.

"Thanks a bunch," Sheila said, " that feels much better."

"Sure, anytime." Tom replied with a raspy voice. He sat there for several seconds admiring her beauty. He knew he would never do anything that might jeopardize his friendship with Steve. For now, he thought, all she would be was eye candy.

"Tom, hey Tom, come here a minute. I've got something to show you." The sound of Steve's voice echoing off the water brought him back to reality, and just in time. Judy would have surely seen him catching a glimpse at Jennifer.

Tom turned from the picture window and walked back to the truck. Sure is one lucky fellow, that Steve. He climbed into his 1981 Chevy 4X4 pickup and started home; home to Judy, his slightly overweight, slightly graying, and slightly nagging wife. Ah home sweet home, he thought.

CHAPTER 5

Cold. Cold. Cold, when will I ever be warm again, Steve thought, as he lay bleeding in the bed of cold leaves. Wet! My lips are wet. It must be raining. Am I dead? Is this heaven or hell? No more water, I'll drown. Who's putting water on my lips?

For an instant Steve thought of the tall man silhouetted against the sky, then the water on his lips stirred the subconscious computer of his brain to search the random access memory for an event in time to correspond with the sensation of moisture bathing his lips.

The brain responded with the perfect image to correspond with the sensations. In a flash Steve was on the banks of the Little Turkey River in the hills of Middle Tennessee. He was leaning against one of the largest Tulip Poplar trees he had ever seen, with his Zebco 202 rod and reel held loosely in his left hand. The red and white plastic float danced happily on the water, as the current gently moved beneath it. This was one of those days then nothing could go wrong. He had told Sheila, that he would be gone all day, and he had every intention of keeping his promise.

The silence of the quiet afternoon moment was broken by the sound of a curious gray squirrel trying to determine just who, or what, had the nerve to invade his protected habitat. Steve sat quietly and watched as the small rodent inched his way closer and closer toward him. With movement so rapid and subtle, it was almost impossible for Steve to tell if he was alive or stuffed. Then the tiny gray visitor began to flick his tail and twitch his head from side to side so as to guarantee that he would not become lunch for some hungry hawk soaring overhead. The squirrel barked, as if telling Steve to leave his domain or else. Steve had to stifle a laugh to keep from frightening the amusing intruder.

With Steve's lack of motion, the squirrel became more adventurous and moved closer. He continued to bark occasionally and flick his tail, all without losing sight of what was going on around him. His curiosity brought him to within a few feet of Steve; he became motionless. Steve also froze and fixed his gaze on the furry rodent. It soon became a battle wills. Which of the two would break his stare first.

Suddenly, the squirrel broke and made a dash up the tree. Steve sat wondering momentarily, what might have caused the squirrel to bolt so quickly. But, his question was soon answered.

Splash! The red and white float was gone. The line on his Zebco 202 was as tight as a violin string. Good grief! What a fish, he thought, as he attempted to reel in his prize. From behind him, Steve could hear the squirrel barking once more. He had obviously found a safer place from which to watch the ensuing battle. The reel was bent so that Steve was afraid it might snap into. The taught line sliced through the water like a laser, as the fish on the end of the line fought for his life.

Steve's eyes widened, as he saw his adversary for the first time. The huge small mouth bass broke the water with a violent twist and danced across the surface with all the grace and finesse of a ballerina performing with the New York Ballet.

Steve was beginning to think he was going to lose the fight, but soon the valiant warrior began to tire. Minutes later, Steve leaned over the edge of the river bank and retrieved his prize, just as the big fish made one final attempt to free the hook from his mouth. The splash was so fast and strong, that it sprayed Steve's face with cool clear water. As the water washed over his face and onto his lips.....

"Pain! Oh, the pain. I can't stand it," Steve moaned. He was now in a state of semiconscious and only distantly aware of anything going on around him. "I can't stand any more pain," he cried, "I wish I would just go ahead and die. Please just let me die, just let me die so the pain will go away." The pain soon became unbearable and he was about to pass out, when he heard the voice.

"I'll do my best, but you'll have to cooperate."

"What? Who said that? Who's there?" Steve screamed, as he tried to open his eyes. "That's not important," said the unknown voice. "The question is, do you really want to die, or do you want to live?"

"God! Is that you God? Am I finally dead an on my way to heaven?" Steve asked these questions, but knew the answer had to be no, because of the intense pain that continued to rack his body.

"No, I'm not God." The voice again answered, "I am just a man like you, so it is a real possibility that you could die. Now do you really want to die or do you want me to help?" Steve opened his eyes only to gaze through pools of tears and sweat into the darkness that was broken by splinters of light coming from somewhere near the ground.

"Where are you," he asked, "Who are you? Come into the light so I can see you." "I'm right here," the voice said, "right beside you." Steve blinked his eyes in an attempt to clear some of the water away. "I don't see you anywhere," Steve said, as he looked upward in search of the owner of the voice. "Not up there, I'm down here beside this gaping hole in your shoulder." The voice answered. Steve turned his head to the side from which the voice and all the pain was coming. There in the shadows of a small oil lamp, stood a man not more that ten inches tall. The little man was dressed in leather britches and a fur coat that looked like it might have been made from rabbit. His shoes appeared to be leather also, stitched together with chords of leather.

He had a full but rather short beard that was only tinged with gray. His features were rough and weathered, as though life had dealt him some hard hands to play. Curls of brown and gray hair protruded from beneath the leather and fur cap that sat squarely on his head.

"Oh my God!" Steve said, "Now I'm seeing little gnomes in the woods that is going to save my life. This must be the final insanity just before death."

"A wise man believes half of what he sees, and none of what he hears," said the little man, "but sometimes the wisest man must learn to trust what he hears in his heart. I am no figment of your imagination. I am as real as the blood that is oozing from this mass of mutilated flesh that used to be your shoulder. I can help you, but you will have to trust me and do exactly as I say. Now, can you trust your heart and do as I ask?"

"This beats all I have ever seen," said Steve. "What else do I have to lose? It looks like I'm going to lose my life anyway. I might as well listen to my heart, because my head sure isn't thinking straight. I've got just one question. Who are you?" "My name is Sebastian," the little man answered," but that's not important right now. What is important is for me to get you home where I can begin to treat and repair your shoulder and chest. It is the only place where you might have a chance to live. Now, I'm going to have to prepare you to be transported, so be patient and trust me. You lie still, I'll be back in one moment."

Sebastian was gone in a flash, and Steve lay in the dampness, cold and shivering, convinced that he was slowly losing his mind before he lost his life. His mind began to play computer games once again. The multitude of different events that made up his life were stored somewhere on the hard disk in the back of his brain, and for some reason, this state of semiconscious was activating those memory recall circuits. He thought of the day Jennifer was born. He was fortunate to be in the delivery room to help in the birth process. The image of Jennifer covered with blood and the white pasty junk, was as real now as the day she was born. Man, did Sheila ever scream when Jennifer came out. It must have been like trying to pass a watermelon.

Further back in memory, Steve's brain finds his wedding day. Sheila was the most beautiful girl in the whole world, and he remembered how much he truly loved her. Art. His cousin Art was there. And boy was he drunk. He made such a fool of himself at reception. Man, was Sheila mad about that. As quickly as the memory image came it was replaced by another.

This time it was only a few weeks ago at the University of Tennessee Thompson Boling Arena for a Boston Celtics exhibition game with the Washington Bullets. C'mon Byrd, lets have a three pointer, Steve thought. Then that noisy loud fan sitting directly behind him kept yelling in his ear. I wish he would shut up, he thought, but the fan kept yelling louder. "Wake up, wake up."

Who was telling him to wake up? Then he heard the same voice. "Wake up, wake up. I can't help you if you don't wake up. Steve then began to realize that it was the little man talking to him. He struggled to open his eyes and saw Sebastian standing in front of him.

"Wake up," Sebastian said to him, "I have something for you. Here, drink this." He tugged on Steve's hear to turn his head and moved a leaf filled with a green liquid toward his mouth. "What is it?" Steve asked. "It looks like ground up grasshoppers." "It will probably taste even worse," said Sebastian, "but it's the only thing that stands between you and certain death."

Sebastian was right it did taste worse than ground up grasshoppers. "you might feel a bit different," Sebastian said. "It may hurt some, but don't worry. It won't last long, and besides you have no other choice." No sooner had he finished his forecast of things to come, than Steve began to feel a tingle in his arms and legs. He thought of the many times that his foot had fallen asleep and the millions of pins and needles that attack the foot as it is trying to wake up. It felt much like that, only worse. The tingle soon grew to a feverish intensity. It was replaced by pain; not severe at first, but pain. It wasn't as bad as the pain in his shoulder, but it was growing. Now the tingle was completely gone, and the mounting pain was making it's presence known.

He tried to turn over onto his side to ease the pain, but the effort only intensified the torture. His legs and arms were on fire and the blaze was making its way up his back and chest. Soon his entire being was ablaze, as the tiny nerve endings throughout his body were on fire. The pain rapidly became more that Steve could stand.

"Oh my God!" Steve screamed. "What have you done to me? The pain is more than I can stand. My arms and legs are on fire. My whole body is on fire. Please make it stop, please." Steve's body stiffened in a final effort to ease the pain, and he screamed at the top of his lungs, or what was left of them, as a final plea before passing out. The scream echoed through the silence of the nighttime forest. But, his screams found no other human ears. The shouts bounced off trees and rocks and soon fell into deafness, buried in the wet leaves of the forest floor.

As Steve slipped into the comfortable world of the unconscious brain, he heard the noise. It sounded like twigs breaking. Was someone coming through the woods? Had Tom heard his cries and come to rescue him? No, it wasn't twigs it was the bones of his arms and legs. The noise was coming from his own body, as his bones began to shatter and splinter into thousands of pieces. "What have you done to me?" Steve screamed. "You've killed me, thank God."

CHAPTER 6

Tom had just finished lacing his boots, as the sun was coming up over the ridge in front of his house. The first beams of morning sunlight broke through the window and danced across the floor. He pulled the curtains back and peeked out. It looks like we're going to have a good day to look for Steve, he thought, not a cloud in the sky. I wonder what the temperature was last night?

He walked into the den and flipped on the TV. Channel 20 always had the temperature and weather report, and there it was. Twenty-three degrees, not too bad, he thought. The wind wasn't blowing to hard, so the wind chill shouldn't be a factor in the search. The forecast appeared on the screen next. (High today in the low 30's with increasing cloudiness. Winter storm warning in affect for tonight and early tomorrow, with snow accumulations of up to six inches. High tomorrow only in the 20's. The extended outlook has the highs in the upper 20's to lower 30's.)

"Well, I'd better get started. It's almost six o'clock, and Dave will be waiting for me," Tom said to himself, as he finished dressing. He made sure he had his insulated hunting suit on before stepping outside to face the cold morning. He inhaled deeply, as the crisp morning air filled his lungs. "Crap," he mumbled to himself, "I wish I had started the truck and let it warm up." He climbed in the cab and turned the key. The big Chevy engine roared to life. It'll probably be warm by the time I get there, he thought.

Dave and the other wildlife officers were already waiting at the edge of the woods, where they had agreed to meet. "Been waiting long?" Tom asked. "Nope," said Dave. "We've only been here about five minutes haven't even had time to get cold." "Don't worry," said Tom, "you'll have plenty of time for that before this day is over. Well how are we going to do this?" "Okay," Dave began, "here's the way we'll work it. Tom, you and I will try to follow the trail that you saw Steve take yesterday. Dennis and Bob will go around the north end of the woods, and James and Greg can go around the south end. You've all got walkie-talkies so lets keep in contact. When we get to the backside of the woods, we'll meet and make another sweep through the center. He's got to be in there somewhere."

"What if he went past the pine thicket on the back side?" Tom asked. "That next stand of timber extends for nearly fifteen miles. If he wandered off into those woods, he could be lost forever. We could hunt until the cows come home and never find him."

"Lets just pray that he had enough sense to stay in the first stand of woods." Dave said, as he slung the pack containing food water and a first aidc kit across his back. "Lets go." Tom and Dave walked for nearly a mile in the general direction in which Tom had seen Steve walk the day before.

"See anything?" Tom yelled. "Nope," replied Dave, "not a sign. It doesn't look like anyone has been in these woods for a long time. I don't even see a fresh foot print broken limb or turned leaf. Are you sure they came this way?" "Of course I'm sure," Tom said, with a hint of anger in his voice. "But I don't know which way he went after he got in here. That's the problem now. Check with the other guys and see if they've had any luck."

"Dennis, come in Dennis. This is Dave. Have you had any luck? Over."

"Not a thing Dave, not even a sign that anyone has ever been hunting in these woods. Are you sure he came this way? Over." "Yeah, I'm sure, just keep looking and we'll see you on the backside. Over and out."

"James, come in James. This is Dave. Have you had any luck? Over." "Nothing to speak of," James answered, "just a couple of rubs and one scrape, but no sigh of any human that might be hot on the trail. Over." "Okay," replied Dave, "keep up the search. Yell if you find anything that looks promising. Over and out."

Another mile of walking brought Tom and Dave to the back edge of the woods, with nothing to show for their efforts but a little shortness of breath. "It'll take Dennis and James a while longer to circle around and meet us here," said Dave, "we'll have a few minutes to catch our breath. Why did you leave him out here by himself in the first place Tom, you know that Steve knew nothing about the woods."

"I know." said Tom. "But I figured that he could surely stay within shouting distance of me. I guess I just never thought about him wondering off in the wrong direction. I wouldn't have had this happen for anything. Steve and I have been friends for too many years. I won't quit looking until I find him."

"Here comes James." Dave said. "I sure hope he has some good news." "Sorry fellows." James said. "We didn't see anything that even remotely resembled human tracks. Maybe Dennis and Bob will turn up something. Here they come now." "Well, how about it." Asked Dave. "Any luck?" "Nothing solid." Said Bob. "We did find a blood trail and some foot prints, but they headed in the direction of the briar thicket. We can go back and follow them if you think it's worth a look."

"No, never mind." Said Tom. "That's my trail. That's the deer I killed yesterday. I had to trail him into that thicket and drag him out, so I know Steve wasn't in that area." "Well, lets close up the space between us and make another sweep back through the middle." Said

Dave. "This time lets separate about a hundred yards and keep in shouting distance. We can cover more territory that way."

The six men began their walk back through the woods in the direction from which they had started the search. About a half mile into the woods, James screamed. "Hey Dave, come here. I've found something." Everyone converged on the spot where James was standing. "What did you find?" asked Tom. "Look at this." Said James, as he held up a spent rifle cartridge." "What caliber rifle was Steve using?" Asked Dave. "I loaned him my 243. He doesn't even own a gun of his own." Tom said. "What caliber is that shell casing?" "It's a 30-06." Said Dave. "This didn't come from Steve's gun. This could have been left by someone last week or last month." "Sorry!" said James. "I was just hoping I had something." "Lets spread out and continue our search." Dave said. "We're burning daylight."

"Steve! Steve! Can you hear me? Answer me Steve. This is Dave Black." No answer came. After several hours of walking and searching, with little success, Dave sat down to rest. It was getting close to lunchtime and he was beginning to get hungry. First, he had to take care of the problem of a full bladder. He stood beside a huge old red maple tree and relieved the pressure. "Man, that feels better. I just can't think with a full bladder." Tom muttered, as he looked for a place to sit down. Looking around, he noticed the scrape. On the backside of the maple tree was one of the largest scrapes he had ever seen. Good grief, he thought, that buck must have been a monster. I'd better take a closer look around here, I might want to come back here and look for that big fellow myself.

As Dave began to search the ground around the red maple for signs of deer tracks, he caught a glint of sunlight reflecting off something on the crest of the ridge. He ran up the hill to where he thought he saw the reflection. There, leaning against a young hickory tree was an Apache port-a-stand and a Remington 243 hunting rifle. Dave called on the walkie-talkie immediately. "James, Bob, Tom, everyone, come in this is Dave. I've found his tree stand and the rifle, but there is no sign of Steve. Get over here as quick as you can. I am Southeast from where we split up and about five hundred yards up the hill. Now hurry."

"That's my tree stand alright and my rifle too." Said Tom. "But where did Steve go from here?" "Why would he walk off without his gun?" Dennis asked. "The only thing I can figure," said Dave, "Is that he was probably looking for firewood and got lost, but what happened to him after that is anyone's guess." "Well." Tom said. "I'm going to take this stand and rifle back to the truck. Then I'll start searching back toward you guys, and we'll meet near the center of the woods. I expect we'll find him curled up under a log or in a pile of leaves half frozen and maybe unconscious, so keep yelling for him.

The six men continued the search for most of the afternoon. It was nearly three o'clock when Bob got lucky, or so he thought. He stumbled and nearly fell into an open pit that led into a cave. "Steve. Steve. Answer me Steve, it's Bob Grishom with the wildlife service. Are you in there?" Not a sound came from the empty cavern. Even his words were lost in the imposing darkness of the abyss. Bob reached for his walkie-talkie and began to speak. "Dave. Dave. This is Bob. I've found a cave. I've called for Steve several times, but I'm not getting an answer. I still think it's worth checking out. I'm in the Northern quadrant about a half-mile from where we found the tree stand. Get here as quick as can. Did you copy that?"

Tom and Dave arrived at the cave about the same time. Dave took his backpack from his shoulder and tossed it to the ground. "Have you got a flashlight in there?" Tom asked. "Sure." Said Dave. "Here, but be careful. Tie this rope around your waist just in case." Tom slid slowly and carefully into the small opening. It was no larger than a manhole cover. The sides were smooth and worn, indicating that something had been using the entrance on a regular basis. Tom slid on his back for about five feet, before finally settling on a large rock. The flashlight revealed a large room but no sign of Steve. "I'm afraid we've reached another dead end." Tom shouted. "There's no sign that anything human has ever been in this cave. I think it's probably foxes or coyotes that have been using it. Pull me out, we're wasting time."

A light snow began to fall, as Tom emerged from the tiny opening. "Oh great." He said. "This is all we need. If this snow keeps up, it will bury any hopes of finding Steve's trail." "Lets go." Said Dave. "We've still got about an hour of daylight. Lets keep looking."

In the forest the last thirty minutes of daylight is totally different from any other time of the day. The eyes do not see what they think they see. Strange shadows begin to come alive, and creatures that live during no other time, nor in any other place, begin to stir. The forest comes alive with ominous sounds and a strange silence fills the air with deafening quiet.

Tom was less than five hundred yards from the edge of the forest, when his eyes began to deceive him. The light was so dim, that he was barely able to distinguish trees from shadows cast by the fading light. He turned his head so quickly that a pain, as sharp as a dagger, sliced through the back of his neck. Ouch! I hate it when that happens, he thought, but paid little attention to the pain. The reason for his sudden movement had his true attention. I could swear I saw something move over behind that tree, he thought to himself, but I don't know what it was. He decided to investigate further by sneaking behind the tree and surprising whatever was there. Just as Tom took his first step something small and extremely fast streaked from behind the large tree and disappeared into the haze of the dusky forest floor. "I know I saw something." He said. "But I have no idea what it was. It moved too fast for a raccoon or possum." Tom shook his head and rubbed his eyes in disbelief. He continued walking, but became more and more uneasy about what he had just seen. He was sure of it now, whatever it was that raced through the trees in front of him, was definitely running on two legs. A chill ran down his back. "That's it." He muttered to himself. "I've had enough of these woods for one day. I'm out of here.

CHAPTER 7

Apple pie! I'll bet Sheila is baking an apple pie right now, Steve thought. Man! That sure smells good, apple pie is my favorite. I'd better get up and see if she needs any help. The reality of pain is a stimulant that has a profound affect on the brain. The pain in his shoulder and chest was still there, and that pain vividly reminded Steve that he was not at home waiting for Sheila's apple pie, but somewhere in the woods in a pile of leaves freezing and bleeding to death. Wait a minute, he thought. I'm not cold. As a matter of fact, it's rather warm and comfortable in here. The strangeness of his environment prompted him to open his eyes and survey his surroundings.

His eyes were still blurred from the sleep, but he could see that there was light. It wasn't the fading light of the setting winter sun, nor even the glow of moonlight on the forest floor. This was an artificial light, maybe an oil lamp or even a soft electric bulb. He blinked his eyes several times to remove the sleep. As his vision cleared, Steve was amazed to find himself lying on a soft bed of clean sheets and warm blankets.

His surrounding appeared to be a small room in what was most surely a cave. The walls were stone, as was the ceiling and the floor was dirt. The dim light was coming from a small opening that led into another room. It wasn't visible from where Steve was lying, but it was obvious that it was a much larger room. It also sounded as if there were several people in the outer room. The noise and commotion was loud enough for Steve to hear, and there were voices mixed in with the noise. He tried to raise his head to get a better look, but his injury and loss of blood caused a swirling dizziness to overcome him and he had to lie back down.

Where am I, he thought, and how did I ever get in here? The pain was the most memorable part of the past several hours. He remembered the pain in his shoulder and chest. It was unbearable. He remembered the pain, but there was something else. A little man, was that a dream, or was there really a little man in the woods? Sebastian! Was he real? Was he part of the hallucination caused by the pain? He must have been a dream. There is no way a ten-inch man could have managed to get me down here in this cave. It would be impossible. What if someone else found me? What if this is some type of satan worshiping cult? Maybe they are out there getting ready to sacrifice me in the name of something ungodly?

Steve's thoughts were halted by the sound of footsteps approaching from the opening. He lay back down and closed his eyes. Maybe they won't kill me if they think I'm still unconscious. Someone came into the room and walked to the side of Steve's bed. He knew someone was there, but his frightened imagination would not allow him to open his eyes. I can hear him breathing, he thought. I'll wait until they start to leave then open my eyes. Suddenly, the person in the room was no longer a distant sound but a real person. It was obvious, as the intruder began to move and pull at his mutilated shoulder. The pain exploded in his shoulder like a stick of dynamite. It was so loud and sudden that it was impossible to keep from screaming. Soon it became more than he could bear. He opened his eyes. There, bent over Steve's shoulder was Sebastian, as big as life and oh so real.

"Ouch! That hurts." Steve screamed. "Where did you come from? How die you get in here? Wait a minute. You're not ten inches tall, you're as big as I am. How did you do that? What's going on here?" "Slow down." Sebastian responded calmly and gently. "I'll answer your questions, but one at a time please. First of all you are in my home. This is where I live, and this is the safest place for you. Second, I'm not six feet tall like you. I am still only ten inches tall. The truth is, and this may be hard for you to believe, but you are the same size as me."

"What?" Steve asked. "What do you mean? I can't be the same size as you. I mean, I can see we are the same size, but I'm six feet tall. Now what are you talking about?" "Well my friend," Sebastian began. "I am afraid that you are now only ten inches tall, and you are now resting comfortably in my home deep underground. And just how do you suppose I got you down here? I obviously couldn't carry a six foot man. But, if I had left you out there in the cold forest, you would have been dead by now. So, I decided to bring you down here and tend to your wounds. Do you remember the green liquid I had you drink just before you passed out?" "Yeah!" Steve said. "It tasted like crap, and I thought I was going to die from the pain. My body began to ache like it was on fire. So what happened to me?"

"That liquid is a special concoction of several plants that grow in the forest. Those plants mixed together in the proper proportions produce a chemical reaction in the body that causes the molecules to shrink. It removes most of the empty air space between the atoms and increases the density of the molecule resulting in a smaller you. It is very painful the first time, but the person usually passes out before it becomes unbearable, and that is exactly what you did. Once the transformation was complete, I was able to move you down here to my humble abode."

"I and some of my companions then returned to the spot where you had been shot and disposed of the blood and tissue that you had left behind. Now you are ten inches tall and resting comfortably in my spare bedroom. Your shoulder has already stopped bleeding, and it appears as though you are going to live. That, however, you owe to the efforts of my dear wife Isabel. She is the resident physician here in 'Spelonia'. She worked for several hours on you sewing pieces of your body back together. You will most likely have the opportunity to thank her very soon. But, for now, are you hungry?"

"Oh my God!" Steve exploded. "I can't be ten inches tall. This is impossible. I must be having a bad dream. That's it, I'll wake up soon and everything will be back to normal." "I'm afraid not." Sebastian replied. "This is no dream. You do remember being shot, don't you?"

"Sure I remember being shot. How could I forget that?" Steve said, with a certain air of resentment. "I also remember lying on the ground bleeding and being very cold. Then there was this little elf….." "You'd better rest for a while." Sebastian said. "Lay back and take it easy, while I get you something to eat. You need to build up your strength, as well as your blood supply. You know you lost a lot of blood out there in the woods. I'll be right back."

Sebastian turned and walked quietly from the room. Steve lay back on the bed and tried to sort out all that had just transpired. This is impossible, he thought, no one could be changed from a six foot grown man to a ten-inch elf. Wait a minute. What am I saying? No one can even be ten inches tall in the first place. He must be lying to me. That whole story is just impossible. Besides, my clothes would never fit. Hey, wait a minute, where are my clothes? I know they didn't shrink. Steve raised his head to look at the rest of his body. He quickly became dizzy and his body shook with pain, but he managed to raise the covers and look beneath them. There among the down filled mattress and the soft flannel blankets was Steve, dressed in a warm soft cotton nightshirt. There was no sign of his hunting suit, his boots, or his hat. Now what? He thought. That didn't prove anything. I guess I'll just have to figure this out a little at a time.

Sebastian returned carrying a small bowl of steaming liquid. "Here drink this," he said. "It will help you get your strength back." "I'm not so sure about this," Steve replied. "The last time you asked me to drink one of your concoctions, it looked like grasshopper guts and tasted even worse. Believe me it was no gourmet delight." "Trust me," Sebastian laughed. "This will taste much better, besides my wife made this, not me."

"It sounds like this Isabel is quite a woman, but it is just hard for me to imagine someone only ten inches tall being married, and living a normal life." "It may seem odd," Sebastian agreed. "But you must understand, we were not always Spelons. She was my wife long before, and she will be my wife forever."

"I understand," Steve said. "When do I get to meet her?" "Soon," said Sebastian. "I would expect that she will probably want to come in tomorrow and check you wounds. She is very thorough and will no doubt want to make sure you are healing properly. Then, when you're feeling stronger, you will be able to meet everyone."

"Everyone!" Steve exclaimed. "What do you mean everyone? You mean there are more here than you and your wife?" "Oh my goodness yes," Sebastian laughed. "There are many more here than just Isabel and I. But, you'll have sufficient time to make the acquaintance of everyone very soon. But for now, eat your soup and rest." Sebastian lowered the spoonful of hot soup to Steve's lips. "Be careful," he said. "It is still very hot." Steve sipped some of the soup into his mouth, without knowing what to expect. Delicious, he thought, this is delicious. "Give me some more," Steve said. "That's the best soup I've ever tasted." Steve ate several more bites, before finally asking. "By the way, what kind of soup is this anyway, it's delicious." "That is one of Isabel's most favorite recipes," he answered. "Its called bat wing soup, but I think she uses more than just the wings. Isn't it wonderful? She is a marvelous little cook, if I do say so myself. You should see what she can do with cave crickets and cave moss. Ummm."

The tiny valve at the base of Steve's esophagus began to relax, as the onboard computer in his brain began creating a visual image of several bats floating in a cauldron of hot frothy soup. The resulting image began to play games with his stomach. The normally relaxed muscles of his stomach began to constrict, and he had to fight the urge to relieve his stomach of its contents. His mind was filled with images of tiny little bat wings in the boiling water. Quick, he thought, think of something else. Steve fought with his brain in search of a more pleasant topic.

He thought about Sheila and Jennifer. "I'll bet my wife and daughter are worried to death about me," he said. "How long have I been here anyway?" "You have been sleeping for two days. You have slept ever since I brought you here," said Sebastian. "This is the third day since you were injured." "I have to let them know that I'm okay," Steve replied. "Is there any way for me to get a message to them?" "Soon," Sebastian replied. "When it is safe, we will deliver a message." "Safe?" Steve asked. "What do you mean safe?" "Snow storm," said Sebastian. "There has been a terrible blizzard. It must have dumped 8 to 10 inches of snow out there, and it is very difficult and dangerous to travel under those conditions. Don't worry about that now, he reassured Steve. It's time for you to rest. Get some sleep, and we will talk later." Steve closed his eyes as Sebastian stepped quietly from the room. Sleep came rapidly for Steve. He was still very weak and all but totally exhausted. Sleep soon came and with the sleep came the dream.

CHAPTER 8

The snow began to fall hard and fast by the time Tom and the others returned home. The snowfall was fierce all night and dumped more than 8 inches of clean white snow on the small rural middle Tennessee community of North Ridge. It was one of those wet snows that stuck to everything, the kind that makes a perfect snowman. The power lines were dress in a clean white coat, as were the trees and shrubs. The limbs of the small white pine trees drooped sadly in an effort to relieve themselves of their excess weight.

Tom returned home in time for dinner. Judy had prepared a delicious meal of hamburger steak with rice and gravy. The aroma of gravy filled the room as Tom walked into the house. "Um that smells good," he said. "What's for dinner?" "Your favorite," Judy replied. "Hamburger steak and gravy. Now come on in and eat while it is hot." "I'll have to eat quickly and leave," Tom said. "We had no luck at all today. We didn't find even the slightest clue as to what might have happened to poor Steve. I've got to go over to see Sheila right after dinner. I'm sure she is worried to death." "Do you want me to go with you?" Judy asked. "I'll be ready as soon as I finish the dishes." "That's okay," Tom said. " I really don't have time to wait. Just wait here incase Dave Black calls. I won't be gone long."

Tom shoveled his dinner down much faster than he normally did, and Judy could see that he was in a hurry to leave. I'll be back in a little while," he said, as he walked toward the front door. He was throwing his coat over his shoulder and grabbing for the door handle at the same time. A quick glance over his shoulder made Judy even more suspicious. The door slammed shut behind him.

He fired the big Chevy engine to life and drove the few short miles to Steve's house, paying little attention to the speed limit or to the new fallen snow covering the roads. He was in a hurry. He needed to get to Sheila. She didn't need to be along right now, and it was his job to be there for her. The large flakes of snow flew past his truck window as the headlights caused them to shine like stars. It was as though he were in a space ship traveling at the speed of light, watching all the stars go rushing by. His mind, however, was on more important things than stars and snowflakes. He had to get to Sheila.

Sheila came to the door looking very tired and nervous. She was wearing her housecoat and house shoes. It was obvious that she had done nothing all day except wait by the phone for some news of what happened to Steve. "Tom, oh Tom, am I glad to see you," she said. "Please tell me you have some good news. At least let me know what has happened to him. I have been a nervous wreck all day." "Well Sheila," Tom began. "I'm afraid I don't have any good news. Lets go sit down on the sofa and talk." He led her around the coffee table and sat beside her on the sofa. "We found the tree stand and his rifle, but there was no sign of Steve. There was no sign that anything bad has happened, that's the problem. There is just no sign of anything at all. It looked to ma as if he wandered off in the wrong direction. He might have been looking for the truck or firewood and just lost his bearings. I suspect that he is probably held up in a cave somewhere waiting out the storm. Don't get all upset just yet, I'm sure we'll find him just as soon as the storm is over. Can I get you something to drink?"

"No thanks," Sheila replied. "I'm too upset to eat or drink. Tom, what will I do if something has happened to Steve? How can I go on without him? And what about Jennifer? He means everything to her. She'll just die." "Sheila! Stop worrying. You're making this worse than it is. Trust me, we'll find Steve just as soon as we can. Have a little faith in him too he's not a stupid man. He has enough sense to find shelter and wait out the storm. He'll be fine." Tom said, as he slid next to her and eased his arm around her shoulder. He drew her closer and placed his other arm around her back in an attempt to console her. Sheila began to sob on Tom's shoulder. "I'm so afraid," she sobbed. "What would I ever do with out him?" "Now, now," Tom comforted. "I told you not to worry. Tom pressed her even tighter against his chest. He could feel her warmth against him, as she continued to cry on his shoulder. He thought to himself how good she smelled. It was a mixture of perfume and her natural body essences. The aroma permeated his nostrils and caused him to imagine what it would be like to hold her under different circumstances. What would it be like to inhale her sweetness, while lying beside her? What would it feel like to have her hold him in return. The visions of a love embrace danced through his head, as he held her close. They were totally unaware of the eyes at the window.

"Thanks again for being such a big help." Sheila said, as she moved away from Tom, but continued to hold his hands. She gazed into his eyes and said. "I know you must have lots of things to do, so don't worry about me. I'll be fine."

"Hey, I don't mind a bit. It is my pleasure to comfort a beautiful lady when she is in distress. After all, what are friends for?"

"You're a real sweetheart." Sheila said. "Maybe I will take that drink after all. She started toward the kitchen to get the drinks, when she suddenly froze in her steps. She turned and looked at Tom. "What is it?" Tom asked. "Did you hear a noise? I heard something outside." Sheila said. "I didn't hear a thing." Tom said. But, I'll take a look if it will make you feel better." He walked to the window and moved the curtains back. The blackness of night and the snow on the ground was all that Tom could see. The eyes had long since gone. "I don't see a thing from here, but I'll check outside to be sure. You wait here."

Tom opened the front door and stepped outside. The darkness enveloped him like a blanket. The night was cold and wet. The clouds had begun to break up and stars were peeking through. The moon had also made an appearance and cast an eerie light on the new fallen show. The light from the moon was enough for Tom to see the yard clearly. "There's nothing out here," he said. "I'll check around back to make sure." He stepped off the front porch and eased his way around the edge of the house. The juniper bush grabbed at his clothes, as he squeezed between it and the corner of the house. Man, I hate those bushes, he thought, as he continued the search.

The back yard was darker than the front. The shadows from the trees and house created several black zones where anything could be hiding. The darkness made every object resemble something else. The large barrel looked like a table and the tricycle looked like a fox. The trash can, or whatever it was, beside the steps looked like a man trying to hide. Convinced that there was nothing in back, Tom continued his search around the house. Stepping onto the front porch once again, he said. "Not a thing out there. I told you there was nothing to be afraid of. Lets go back inside." Tom and Sheila balked back into the house, convinced that Tom's search had been thorough. They walked back into the livingroom to finish their drink.

Two large powerful hands held firmly to the windowsill once again, and the cold dark eyes gazed through the curtains, watching Tom and Sheila sitting together on the couch.

"It's after ten o'clock, "Sheila said. "You'd better be getting home. I am sure Judy will be worried about you. I really appreciate you coming by. It really is nice to know that Steve has such good friends." "Don't mention it." Tom said, as he leaned over to give her a hug. He held her softly in his arms and gave her an affectionate kiss on the cheek. I'd better let go, he thought. If I hold her any longer, I won be able to leave. "Good night." He said. "I'll see you sometime tomorrow."

"Good night, and thanks again." Sheila said. "You are such a help." Tom waved goodbye, as he climbed into the big Chevy and headed for home. The hands were gone from the windowsill, as were the eyes. All that was left were the tracks in the snow. Large tracks left by a pair of boots, the same boots that haunted the dreams of Steve Mason as he lay miles away deep underground. Tom arrived home to find Judy already in bed. Good, he thought, I won't have to explain why I'm so late. Tom tiptoed into the bedroom and began to undress. Judy was a light sleeper, and Tom knew she would wake with the slightest noise.

"Getting home a little late aren't we?" Judy asked. Tom jumped. "Oh!" He said. "I didn't mean to wake you. Yeah, Sheila was frightened. She thought she heard someone outside the house, and I had to search the place before she felt safe."   "My goodness, aren't you the helpful one." She growled. "How in the world did she ever make it before you came along?"

"For goodness sakes." Tom said.   "She has a husband who happens to be my best friend, that happens to be lost in the woods because of me. I'm just trying to be a friend. It's nothing more than Steve would do for you, if something happened to me. She is scared to death that Steve will never come back. She's afraid he's lost forever. All she needed was a little comfort and assurance that everything was being done to find Steve."

"Just make sure that assurance is all that you give her." Judy snapped then rolled over to go to sleep. Tom lay down and closed his eyes. Sleep came quickly and so did the dreams. Tonight he dreamed of Sheila, beautiful Sheila.

CHAPTER 9

Steve had picked up the last stick of wood. This should be enough to build a fire he thought, now to find my way back to the tree stand. Lets see, which way did I come from? Steve stood silently in the middle of the forest. The huge oak, maple, hickory and poplar trees stood towering above him as he turned in slow circles searching for the right direction. He turned faster, and the trees began to spin about him. Slowly at first, then faster and faster until he became dizzy. It was that same dizzy feeling that you get when you spin around on a swing as a child. The earth is spinning around you, and there is nothing you can do to stop it. He began to scream. "Stop." Stop. This can't be happening to me. Not again!"

Boom! The noise was so loud and so sudden, that it made everything stand still. What in the world was that, he thought. It sounded like someone shot at a deer.

Pain! Now the pain became real, as Steve looked down to see his right shoulder and chest explode into a bloody volcanic eruption of muscle, bone, and body tissue. Oh my God! He screamed. "I've been shot," and fell to the ground. As he lay in the bed of leaves now covered with his own blood, he thought, or more exactly, he knew he was going to die. The sun was filtering through the naked trees in broken shafts of light. It bathed his face with glowing evening rays and blinded his vision. After an eternity, he opened his eyes to see the silhouette of a man against the sun sprinkled canopy of the forest. "Who are you? Who are you?" Steve screamed. "Did you shoot me? Why? Why would you do this?" Steve turned his head to the side. It was the side where his shoulder and chest used to be, but now he saw a tangled mess of blood and tissue. Beyond his shattered shoulder the man stood. Steve could not see his face for the daggers of light slicing through the limbs and dancing across his eyes, but just before he lost consciousness, he saw the boots.

Aaaaaah! Steve screamed, as he awoke in the cave. It was the same safe warm cave and the same warm bed where he had fallen asleep. Slowly he began to remember the cave and the man, Sebastian. Pieces of memory began to fit together like a puzzle, and soon he remembered. Tiny beads of sweat began to collect on his forehead and make their way into the corner of his eye. His hair was wet with perspiration, and his bedclothes were soaked. Slowly, his rapid breathing began to subside and return to normal. His heart began to slow and find a happy normal rate. The pounding in his head began to ebb, as he raised his hand to his face and wipe the sweat from his eyes. Sebastian came racing into the room, when he heard the screaming. "What's the problem my friend? You look as if you just saw a ghost." He said, as he reached for a towel and began to wipe the sweat from Steve's face. The towel was damp, and its coolness help bring Steve back to reality.

As his breathing returned to normal, he looked helplessly at Sebastian and said. "It was a dream, a terrible dream. I was back in the woods, and I heard the shot and felt the pain. I saw the blood and looked at the bits of meat and tissue that was hanging from the shredded remains of my hunting suit. It was horrible, but it was very real. In fact, it was so real, that I could see the man standing above me. I can't see his face. The sunlight is in my eyes. All I can remember is his silhouette against the bright sky. He had to be the one that shot me, but why. I can't remember much more about the dream, but I know that I have to find this man and settle the score."

"In due time." Sebastian replied, with a gentle calmness that was his nature. "The answer will come when you are ready for it. How are you feeling after your short nap?"

"Some better" Steve replied, but I'm still very tired, and its hard to sleep with the pain in my shoulder. Do you have anything to help ease the pain? I really need to get some rest, but I need the rest without the dreams."

"Give me a second." Sebastian said. "I'll check with Isabel. She is the physician in the community. If there is something to ease the pain, she will know about it." Sebastian left in search of his wife and the relief Steve so desperately needed.

While waiting for Sebastian to return, Steve began to think about his beautiful wife and daughter waiting for him at home. God, how he missed his girls, especially Jennifer, she was the joy of his life. He could see her long blonde curls as they cascaded about her shoulders. Her deep blue eyes were as bright and alive as the morning sun. She brought such joy to his life. And then there was Sheila. She was the most beautiful girl in their graduating class. All of the other guys envied Steve, because Sheila wore his class ring. She looked like Cinderella at their senior prom, as they danced around the gymnasium floor. It was so obvious that they were deeply in love. They married two years after high school, while they were both sophomores in college. Sheila dropped out soon after the wedding to help finance Steve's education. He graduated three years later, while working part-time at Ramco Industries. His degree was in business management, which qualified him for his immediate position as Associate Manager of Quality. Sheila had planned to go back to school and finish her degree in elementary education, but shortly after Steve's graduation, she became pregnant. After Jennifer was born, she could not stand the thought of leaving her with a babysitter while going back to school. She hoped someday to be able to finish her studies.

The last year of their marriage had experienced some shaky moments. They argued more during the past year than ever before.

The arguments were not serious, but it was as though they were getting on each other's nerves. But, in spite of the disagreements, he knew he loved her more than ever, and was sure she still loved him.

Steve was just becoming content with these thoughts, when Sebastian walked quietly into the room. "Don't you ever make any noise when you walk from one place to another." Steve asked. "I never hear you coming or going."

"When you're only ten and a half inches tall, my friend, it is imperative to your very existence to move quickly and quietly. Normally man has no natural predators, because he stands six feet tall. But, when you are the size of a large rabbit, the forest takes on an entirely different personality. It becomes a very threatening place. We teach the importance of this type movement to our children when they are very young. It is vital to our existence outside, in the terrestrial world, and it carries over into the normal life we live here in our subterranean community."

"Yea!" Steve said. "I've gotta talk to you about this community of yours, but now I really need something for pain. I need some sleep." "As I told you previously," Sebastian replied. "Isabel is the best cook, the best wife, and the best physician in the whole community. She wants to see you and examine your shoulder while you are awake. I think I hear her coming now."

Both men turned and waited for Isabel to round the doorway. She was slightly shorter than Sebastian, and a little on the heavy side. Her salt and pepper hair was pulled back into a bun behind her head. "Mr. Steve Mason, I would like for you to meet my lovely wife, Isabel." Sebastian said, with a grin that spread from ear to ear. It was quite obvious that he loved and prided Isabel above all else.

"It is a pleasure to meet you, Isabel." Steve replied. "I've heard so much about you, and it has all been good."

"Thank you, Mr. Mason." She said. "I am pleased to meet you too. Or should I say it's a pleasure to see you while you are conscious."

They all laughed. "If I might disturb you for a moment, I would like to see how you are healing. The herbs and medication that I used works very well, but I like to keep an eye on the progress." "Sure," Steve answered, "but I sure could use something for pain. It's getting pretty hard to handle right now."

"I have something here that will ease the pain, but I want to wait until I have finished the exam. This herb works really fast, and you will probably be asleep before I have time to re-bandage the wound." "Now that sounds like my kind of herb," Steve said with a slight laugh. Sebastian chuckled. He rolled over onto his side and allowed Isabel to examine his damages shoulder.

"Oh my goodness," she said with a smile. "I do such nice work. Everything is healing nicely. I suspect you will be up and around in another day or so."

"What did you do to me anyway," Steve asked. "Well, there was quite a lot of damage done to you," Isabel explained, "but fortunately, most of the damage was to the muscle and soft tissue. Only a small piece of the lung was damaged, but a small amount of witch hazel mixed in the proper proportions with some juice from the cedar tree makes the tissue shrink and close off the open area. It sealed itself within hours, and the lung is working fine. The rest of the shoulder will just take time to heal and regain your strength. Many of the herbs I have given you will speed up the process.

"I know you had a lot of sewing to do back there," Steve said, "but what did you use to sew me up? I know you don't have sutures, or do you?"

"Spider web," Isabel replied without so much as a smile. "Spider web!" Steve exclaimed. "You've got to be joking."

"Oh no, I'm quite serious," she replied. "Spider web is a very strong material, and it is totally natural. So after the body heals, the silk web will break down and your body will absorb what is left. And besides, silk web is very strong. It is even stronger than steel cable."

"That's awesome," Steve said, with a look of astonishment on his face. "But now how about something for pain. "Here, drink this. It will ease the pain and allow you to get some needed sleep." "What is it?" Steve asked. "I hope it tastes better than that stuff your husband gave me in the woods."

"I have absolutely no idea how it tastes," she answered. "I have never found myself in such physical condition that warranted the use of this particular concoction. But, trust me, it will do exactly what I have told you it will do, so drink up."

Steve drank the entire contents of the cup. It was a liquid with a faint orange and yellow tint. The odor was familiar, but he couldn't place it at first. He knew he had smelled it before, but where? It wasn't bubblegum flavor it was more of a mint, maybe pepto-bismol, but not exactly. Then he remembered. When Jennifer was about three years old, she had contracted a severe case of the Asian flu. It lasted for several days, and the doctor prescribed some form of penicillin. It was a pink liquid that smelled and tasted exactly like the remedy he had just consumed. Where in the world would she get penicillin out here he wondered, but really didn't care, as long as it let him sleep and ease the pain. He had no more finished his thoughts, than his brain began to fade in and out. The room became distant, sounds became faded and fuzzy, and his entire body began to float on a cloud. The cloud was floating only inches above the bed. As the cloud rose, the pain fell away. Soon it was gone completely, and Steve was floating in a sea of tranquility. He could see Sebastian standing ten miles away in the opposite corner of the room. Why was he so far away? He couldn't remember the room being so large. He was talking, but his words were not words. He could see Sebastian's mouth moving very slowly, but only low rumbles, that made absolutely no sense to Steve's brain, were coming out. Soon Sebastian began to fade. He became blurred and far away until everything turned to black. Steve slept.

CHAPTER 10

Horace Farley sat behind the huge desk in his office at the Ramco Corp. staring blankly at the ever-blinking cursor on the screen of his AutoCad computer. He looked very pensive, as if searching for a way to outsmart his electronic adversary. "Screw this," he blurted out loud. "I've had all this crap I can take for one day." His hands moved mechanically to the keyboard and began to type in the appropriate letters and symbols, which would command the computer to store the work he had thus far completed. The machine, being intelligent only to the point of the commands entered into it, completed the assigned task, and signified its completion with the appearance of the ubiquitous flashing cursor.

Horace stood and stretched, as he looked at the large oak clock on the wall. Ten minutes after five, and here I am working late again, he thought. Oh well, that's why I get paid the big bucks. He chuckled under his breath. He was secure in his position as product engineer with the Ramco Corporation. He had been working there for over five years and was well thought of by the management. No one questioned Horace as to why he had never married. Everyone just thought that the right girl had not come along, but the truth lay in Horace's shyness.

He became quite flushed in the presence of any female, and bright red if one ever spoke to him. He didn't know why he was so bashful, because he really did like girls. It was just that he didn't know how to act in their presence. You would think that someone in his late twenties would have overcome that shyness by now, but not Horace.

He shut off the computer and grabbed his coat from the coat tree, which stood near his office door. His secretary, Ruby, was the only girl in the entire plant, that he could talk to without becoming the warning light atop a radio tower. Of course, the fact that Ruby was fifty-eight years old, gray, wrinkled, and slightly on the heavy side might have had something to do with it. She was more like his mother than anything else.

"I'm gone Ruby, see you in the morning," he mumbled, as he breezed past her desk. "Good night Mr. Farley," Ruby happily answered. "I'll see you in the morning. Have a good evening." He's such a nice man, she thought, and he works so hard at his job. He never bothers anyone or has anything bad to say about anybody. Yep, he is a nice young man. He will make some lucky lady a wonderful husband someday. I just can't imagine why he has never married. Oh well, that's his business and not mine, she thought, as she began to tidy up her desk for the evening. Maybe I should introduce him to my niece Wanda. She is such a lovely girl and so domestic. Hum! I just might do that.

Horace left the building and got into his 1978 Datsun B210 station wagon. He knew it wasn't the classiest car in the world, but it was very practical. It got 32 miles per gallon and still didn't use much oil. It was totally paid for and maintenance was relative inexpensive. So what if it didn't impress the girls. He didn't have any girls to impress anyway. The tiny four-cylinder engine groaned out its discontent, as he turned the ignition and it fired to life. The odometer registered 186,000 miles and still turning. If I ever find the right girl, he thought, then I'll buy a nice new car. I'll get one of those fancy sport cars. That should impress the ladies. A thin trail of blue smoke floated from the exhaust, as Horace rounded the end of the parking lot and sped out into the flow of traffic.

What to have for dinner, he thought, since it's only me. I guess it really doesn't matter. As he drove away from the North Ridge Industrial Park toward town, his stomach began to tighten. Tonight, he had to go out tonight. He had sat home last night, and it made him very nervous. I have to get out tonight, he thought, as he pulled the Datsun into the parking lot of the Pizza Inn. Pizza sounds good, he mumbled to himself, besides they have the buffet tonight, and I'm really hungry. He pushed the large glass and metal doors of the Pizza Inn open and stepped inside. A quick glance around the room assured him that he did not recognize anyone. He slowly approached the cash register. Directly behind it stood the most attractive blonde girl he had ever seen in his entire life. She was about five feet four inches tall and must have been in her early twenties.

Her eyes were large round and a beautiful deep blue. They reminded him of the color of the Caribbean ocean that you see in travel magazines. Her hair cascaded over shoulders in long rivulets of golden spun silk. Her beauty caused a hard knot to form in the pit of his Stomach.

Where did she come from, he wondered, he had eaten here hundreds of times and never saw anything as beautiful as her. Small beads of sweat began to seep from the pores of his forehead. His shirt collar became tight, and his voice began to fade. I've got to order, or I'll starve to death, he thought. Courage, you can do it. Just walk right up there and tell her you'll have the buffet. That's all you have to say. You don't even have to look at her for goodness sake, just speak. The droplets of sweat began to flow down his forehead and into his eyes. He wiped his face with the sleeve of his coat, and walked boldly up to the register.

"Good evening sir," the lovely blonde said with the softest most seductive voice Horace had ever heard. "May I help you?" "I'll have the fubay," Horace said, and smiled. "I beg your pardon," she asked. "Did you mean buffet?"

"Oh! Crap," he mumbled under his breath. I did it again. I made a complete fool out of myself. Now how do I get out of this without wetting myself and die of embarrassment? "Yes please." He said, as he looked at the floor.

"That's quite alright," she said with a smile. "Sometimes I get my tongue twisted also. Don't worry about it. What would you like to drink?"

"Coke." He said.

"Large or Small?"

"Large."

"That will be four seventy-five." She said, with a smile. Horace handed her a five-dollar bill and continued to look at the floor. "What's your name?" She asked, as she handed Horace his quarter change. An invisible hand, large and powerful, grabbed Horace around the throat just as he was about to give the young lady his name. All that came out was a squeak that sounded more like a bad case of asthma, than a name. She looked at him somewhat confused as he cleared his throat. Then, with a rough cough, he said rather loudly, "Horace." "Hi Horace, I'm Cindy." The lovely blonde answered. Her words floated through the air like feathers in a breeze. Her voice was that of angels singing in the clouds. He had never heard anything so lovely. He wanted to say thank you, but he knew it would be a fruitless effort. He simply smiled and walked to a table and sat down. It took Horace several minutes before he was calm enough to return to the buffet table. He was still nervous as he sat down with his plateful of pizza.

He kept his eyes on Cindy all during his meal. When she would raise her head and glance at him, he would quickly look away and hope she had not seen him looking. He finished his meal and rose from the table. He stood for a brief moment to enjoy her beauty. His eyes followed her, as he walked between the tables toward the door. He even glanced back over his shoulder, while walking to the car. She was the one. Tonight, he would get to know her better tonight. She was definitely the one for this night. The cloud of blue smoke remained briefly after the Datsun B210 had left the parking lot of Pizza Inn.

It was shortly after seven o'clock, as Horace drove into the parking lot of his condo. It was a modest two bedroom apartment, that had recently been remodeled, but it suited his needs. As he opened the door and walked in, his thoughts were on Cindy. During his shower, his thoughts were on Cindy. As he dressed for the evening, his thoughts were on Cindy. He knew the Pizza Inn closed at ten o'clock, so he left his condo shortly after nine-thirty.

The return trip to Pizza Inn was relatively uneventful. He had but one thing on his mind, and that was Cindy. He parked in the back of the parking lot, so as not to draw attention to the Datsun. The location was perfect. He could still see Cindy clearly with the binoculars. It was the next best thing to being there.

At twenty minutes after ten, Cindy walked from the building to her car. She was driving an old Camaro, and had parked near the side of the building. He watched as her lights came on and the car backed out of the parking space. He waited until she pulled out of the lot, before starting his B210 and pulling out after her. He stayed several cars behind her, not wanting her to think that she was being followed.

Cindy lived in a small house near the community college campus. She must be a student, he thought, as he turned the engine off and watched her go into the house. She fumbled momentarily with her keys, before opening the door and stepping inside. A moment later the front porch light went off.

The house was off by itself and surrounded by trees and shrubs. This is perfect, he thought. Tonight is going to be a good night. He reached up and removed the bulb from the dome light in his car, then opened the door. Two army combat boots came to rest firmly on the wet pavement. With a slight grunt, Horace emerged from the small foreign import and stretched his back. The camouflage fatigues made him almost invisible in the darkness.

He moved swiftly and quietly across the street and into the yard. The shrubs and trees provided excellent cover. He slipped to the edge of the house and eased catlike to the window he thought might be the bedroom. As he raised his head slowly above the windowsill, Cindy came into full view. She was standing at the edge of the bed, just about to remove her Pizza Inn uniform. I made it just in time, he thought. This is perfect.

His gaze was fixed on her body, as she removed her blouse first and then her skirt. She stood briefly in her bra and panties before reaching for the bathrobe. She slid gracefully into the robe and walked to the mirror. She picked up a large hair brush and ran it through her long flowing blonde mane with ease. The very sight of her brushing her hair was almost more than Horace could stand. His imagination was running rampant. He could see himself brushing her hair for her and stroking it gently as she sighed. He could see himself putting his arms around her and kissing her on the neck, while whispering, "I love you" in her soft ear.

She laid the brush down and left the room. She must be going to the bathroom, he thought. I need to find the bathroom window. He slipped around the back of the house and peered into the kitchen window. She was not there, and this convinced him that it was time for her shower. He crept quietly around the side of the house and saw a window that was slightly smaller than the rest. That has to be it, he thought. All bathroom windows are smaller than the others. The ground level at the backside of the house sloped considerably more than the bedroom side, making the bathroom window slightly above his line of vision. I've got to find something I can stand on, he thought, and began to look around. Then he remembered seeing a garbage can at the very back of the house. He wasted no time in scurrying around the house and fetching the can.

He turned it upside down and climbed onto the shaky support. There she was in front of the mirror still in her robe, with her face covered with white cream. She was just starting to wash the cream off her face, when Horace heard a car. The front of the house was bathed in light, as the car passed by. Was it going to stop here? If it pulled into the front of the house, the lights might shine directly on him. He hurriedly jumped down from the trashcan and hid behind it. Seconds later the car disappeared around the curve and out of sight. "Whew!" Close calls like that made his heart rate soar, but he enjoyed it.

He climbed back onto his perch and peered over the edge of the window. His heart sank, his vision has now been obscured by the curtain that Cindy had drawn. She had obviously closed the curtains while the car was passing by. All Horace could see was her silhouette against the bright light of the bathroom. He could see her image as she removed her robe and underclothes. He heard the sound of the shower, as the water began to splash inside the tub. In an instant she was gone behind the shower curtain and her beauty existed only in his imagination. Filled with dejection, he climbed down from the can and quietly made his way back to the cat. No one noticed him. No one ever noticed Horace. He drove faster than normal back to his condo. He had to get back and relax. He was very upset and tense. She sure was beautiful, he thought. She was even as beautiful as Sheila.

CHAPTER 11

There is something different today, thought Steve. There is something drastically different about this morning. He hated that feeling, the one where you know something is different or wrong, but you just can quite figure it out. I'll think of it in a minute." He said to himself just as Sebastian walked into the room.

"Think of what," he asked, with a grin that spread from one side of his whisker covered face to the other. "Oh nothing." Steve replied. "There's just something different about this morning, and I can't place my finger on it. Not or worry, I'll figure it out soon.

"Well," said Sebastian, "how are we feeling this morning? You slept for almost thirty-six hours. You must have been really tired. It's quite obvious that your body needed the rest."

"That's it." Steve shouted. "That's what is different about this morning. The pain is gone, or at least most of it is gone. I feel so much better. As a matter of fact, I'm really hungry."

"Well bully for you." Sebastian said with a smile. "I told you my Isabel was the best doctor in the world. Her concoctions are some of the finest medicine ever made. I'm really not surprised that you feel so much better. Do you feel up to a little walk? Maybe we can go get a little food?" "You know." Steve replied. "I believe I am strong enough to take a walk. Heaven knows that I'm hungry enough."

Steve sat up in the bed and swung his feet to the floor. "Wait! Hold your houses." Sebastian said, with a start. "Lets take this a little at a time. Here let me help you sit up. I want to make sure you don't get dizzy or pass out on me before you stand up." He slid his large hand behind Steve's head and helped him to the sitting position. Steve cradled his injured arm in his lap and opened his eyes. The room tilted to one side, bobbed and weaved a time or two before finally settling down into its normal position.

"There, that's better." Steve said, with a sense of confidence. "I think I can make it now." "Wonderful!" Sebastian exclaimed. "Just wait here for one minute, and I'll get someone to help us. We need someone on each side of you while you try to walk." With that, he disappeared through the opening in the rock wall. He was gone no more than a minute or so, when he returned with the help. Standing there beside him was the most beautiful girl Steve had ever seen. Her hair was as black as midnight, and her eyes were deep blue, as deep and blue as the Caribbean. She must have been in her early twenties, and her appearance was enough to spark a desire in Steve that he had not felt in many years.

"Who is this?" Steve asked. "This is my daughter, Gabrielle." Sebastian proudly answered, with his shoulders held back and his chest protruding. "She is my eldest daughter, and a joy to have. I am a fortunate man. "Oh Papa!" She giggled and bowed her head in a blush. "Come child, let us help this poor man to his feet and allow him to take a short walk. A walk that will allow him to join the rest of our happy community for a hearty breakfast."

Sebastian held securely to Steve on his injured side, while Gabrielle placed his good arm around her shoulder to give him support. Steve could smell her hair, as she placed her arm around his waist. She smelled so clean and fresh. She was without a doubt the most beautiful creature he had ever seen, either above ground or below.

They walked slowly through the opening of Steve's room and out into a large well lighted central room of the cave. There in the room busily moving about were forty or fifty more people just like Sebastian and Gabrielle. "Who are these people?" Steve asked. "These are the remaining members of our community." Sebastian answered. "There are a hundred and sixty two of us in all. Come, let us sit at the table and we can talk while we eat."

As they sat down at the table, Isabel appeared with two bowls of what appeared to be oatmeal. "Good morning Isabel." Steve said, with a smile. "How are you today?" "I'm doing just wonderfully." She answered, in that gentle motherly tone and the endearing smile that made her face glow. She had a smell about her that reminded Steve of something from his above ground past. His grandmother always smelled the same way. It was a mixture of cookies or bread, or pie. It was always something right out of the oven, and Isabel was no different. Her look and her smell meant that you had to love her.

"How is my favorite patient?" she asked. "Oh I'm much better. The pain is almost completely gone, and I'm about to starve to death, if that's a good sign." "Oh, it is a good sign." She agreed. "So here enjoy your breakfast. I hope you like the porridge. I wasn't sure how you prepared yours, so I sweetened it to my own taste. Hope you like it."

"Porridge?" Steve exclaimed. "You mean there really is something called porridge. I thought that it was something found only in the Mother Goose stories. But, I'm sure that if you prepared it, it will be perfect." Isabel laughed and answered. "Oh, I don't know if I make it as good as Mother Goose, but this is the way I've made it for many years. Now try it and let me know what you think.

Steve brought the spoonful hesitantly to his lips. His taste buds waited in joyful expectation for the unknown flavor, with which they were about to be treated. The texture on his tongue was similar to that of oatmeal, but had a much more grainy flavor. It was slightly sweet, and a little salty, but it was without a doubt delicious.

"This is awesome!" Steve shouted with enthusiasm. "It's better than oatmeal or grits. It's even better than cream of wheat. What is it made from? No! Wait! Don't answer that question. I'm not sure I want to know." They all laughed.

He finished the entire bowl, then turned to Sebastian and said. "Tell me about your community. This is the most amazing thing I have ever seen. Where did you come from? How did you come to live down here, or better yet, why do you choose to live down here?

"That's a good question." Sebastian began. "This community, this small city, if you will, is known as Spelonia. We, its inhabitants, are known as Spelons. We have lived here for the past two hundred years. Not me personally, mind you, but the community. We arrived here on a boat from England, much like your ancestors, except that our ancestors arrived unnoticed and unannounced. Our settlers traveled for months before finding this cavern system in which to build this city. We live here in perfect harmony, and we have all we need to live a delightfully happy life. We have found that we do not need all the extra things that can be found on the topside. We are safe warm and well fed, as you can tell from my waistline." "But what about your size?" Steve asked. "Why are you only ten inches tall?" "Ten and a half." Sebastian answered, with a smile. "That's an entirely different story. The first Spelon came into existence several hundred years ago in England. It began quite by accident. Fortunately, it was an accident that saved the life of one man and brought about the existence of this whole community. It began with a man by the name of John Wesley Danford, lord and landowner of the Danford Estate. The Estate was near Dover, south of London. It seems that Mr. Danford had a definite affinity for the ladies, and he was constantly surrounded by the most beautiful women of that area. There was one lady, however, that proved to be his downfall, and the demise of his entire estate.

One day Mr. Danford met a lovely young lady by the name of Anne Boeylin. He immediately fell hopelessly in love with her, but it was somewhat of a one sided affair. History now shows that she had fallen prey to the clutches of the King of England. I'm sure you have heard of him. They called him Henry the VIII. Nevertheless, Mr.

Danford was determined to have the hand or any other part of Miss Boeylin in matrimony.

The King soon discovered the existence of Mr. Danford and his attempts to steal his precious Anne. Henry promptly ordered the head of Mr. Danford to be delivered to him on a platter. Mr. Danford was forced flee for his life. He stole away from his home in the middle of the night and hid out in the large wooded area south of his estate. After several days of hiding, he became quite hungry. He found several plants that he knew were edible and some that he was not so sure of.

One evening, in search of some variety in his diet, he created a concoction of several different plants. It formed somewhat of a thick frothy drink. It was green in color and had a distinctive aroma, but he was hungry and wasted no time in consuming the entire portion. The reaction was much the same as you experienced out there in the forest, before I brought you down here.

"You mean it made him small?" Steve asked.

"I'm afraid so." Sebastian answered. "But the advantages to being that size were many. He soon found a small cave, in which he could live and keep warm. Due to his small size, he was able to survive on substantially less food, and his energy level was tremendously elevated. Needless to say, it changed his life forever.

I can't explain to you how the concoction works or even why it works. All we know is that it has been handed down from generation to generation for the past two hundred years, and it still works today.

But, to continue the story, he lived in this cave for several months, until he was sure the king had abandoned the quest for his head. The only problem now was the fact that he was only ten inches tall. It seems that Mr. Danford's attraction for the ladies soon became the driving force in his life. But, again, being only ten inches tall presented a problem.

He set about in search of a remedy for his situation. Once again, he mixed the same concoction of the same plants and held it in his hands. He gazed intently at the green liquid and pondered his options. If he drank more, would it make him even smaller, or would it reverse the process? As expected, his ultimate decision revolved around the women. He decided that a life without women was not a life worth living. He drank the potion in one long swallow. Once again, the pain was unbearable. It was so intense, that he passed out and fell to the ground. He awoke several hours later, aching and naked. He was almost six feet tall, and the clothes that had covered his ten inch body were but mere rags around his wrists and ankles.

He wasted no time in returning to his estate. His heart sank, when he found his beautiful home and property in ruin. It seems as though the king had taken his estate into his own kingdom, because the owner was presumed lost or dead. He immediately began searching for his slaves and farm hands, that he now presumed to be homeless also. He gathered all these peoples together and told them of his new discovery. He convinced them that they could start a new life below the ground in the safety of the caves. He also convinced his second love, a lovely young lady by the name of Elizabeth, to return with him to his land of Spelonia. He assured them that in this new land there were no slaves or masters, only Spelons. Everyone was the same and all worked for the good of the community.

Elizabeth and the others agreed, and the beginning community is reported to have consisted of about twenty people. The community was very successful and thrived for many years under the leadership of Mr. Dansford. On one occasion, it became necessary for Mr. Dansford to return to the natural world. It is not certain as to the reason for this fateful journey, but never the less, he created a new concoction and drank it. When he regained consciousness, he was his normal size. The nature of his business required that he be gone for several days, before returning to the cave. After drink the concoction for the fourth time, he began to shake and twist in agony. The pain was so horrible that he passed out. He never regained consciousness.

His body was laid to rest in an unmarked location deep in the forest near the cave. It was from this event, and his untimely death, that a person can only consume the concoction a total of three times. On the fourth consumption, death is swift and final. To make a long story short, the community flourished and grew in numbers for several years. It is reported that, at one time there were as many as five hundred Spelons living in caves all over England. In the late eighteen hundreds, a brave group of Spelons stowed away aboard a ship coming to America. This small band of travelers was the founders of this American community. So that, my friend, brings us to where we are today. Any questions?"

"Wow!" Steve said in astonishment. "That is the most amazing story I have ever heard. But, aside from the fact that you consume less food and have a high energy level, are there any other advantages to being a Spelon?"

"I'll be honest with you." Sebastian answered. "I wasn't going to tell you just yet, but since you seem so concerned, I will. How old do you guess me to be?" "Oh, I'd say somewhere in your early fifties." Steve said, with some certainty.

"Not a bad guess, but I'll be one hundred and five years old on my next birthday and still going strong. "No way!" Steve exclaimed. "You mean because you are a Spelon, you can live to be over a hundred years old?"

"More like two hundred." Sebastian answered. "I'm still a young man." "What about your wife and daughter? How old are they?"

"Isabel is eighty-four, but if you say I told you so, I'll beat you to within an inch of your life. Gabrielle is only a child of twenty-four. So yes, my friend, there are some very good advantages to being a Spelon."

Steve laid his head in his hands and closed his eyes, as the room began to spin about him. "What's the matter?" Sebastian asked. "Are you alright?" "Yeah." Steve answered. "Just a little dizzy. I think I'd better go lay back down. This has been quite a bit for one day."

"To be sure." Sebastian agreed. "Come Gabrielle, help me get him back to bed." Once again, Steve was entranced by the beauty of Gabrielle and held to her shoulder as she helped him back toward the bed. In spite of his dizziness, he enjoyed her embrace and her fresh clean scent once again made its way to his nose. He savored the aroma. He had barely laid his head on the pillow before he sank into a deep and fitful rest.

CHAPTER 12

Mud flew from the large deeply grooved wheels of the Chevy 4X4 State vehicle, as Dave Black brought it to a stop at the edge of the woods. As best he could remember it was close to the spot, where Steve had disappeared. Dennis Weatherby, another wildlife officer, picked up one of the walkee talkee units and slammed the door of the truck. "Which way do you want to go today?" He asked. "I'll swear we've been over every inch of this patch of woods in the past five days, and I'm telling you, he ain't out here. There hasn't been any signs of him either dead or alive."

"He has to be out here somewhere." Dave exclaimed. "A person just doesn't disappear, especially if he is dead. I'm going to walk along this ridge to the east. Why don't you follow the trail leading into the pine thicket. I'm sure we've missed something. Use the walkee talkee if you find anything."

"But I walked that path yesterday with two National Guardsmen." Dennis complained. "We went through that area with a fine tooth comb and came up empty. Plus, there were twenty-five other guardsmen roaming through over the back side of the ridge and came up empty handed."

"I don't care how many men combed this area yesterday." Dave shouted. "We're going to go through it again today. Now get moving."

Dennis walked down the path in the direction of the same pine thicket he had searched the day before. I just can't imagine why Dave is so bent on finding this fellow. For all I know he used this as a way of getting away from his wife. The guy probably has another woman in another state waiting for him right now. They're probably shacked up in some hotel room in Kentucky laughing their butts off, while we're out here freezing ours off.

Dennis stopped at the edge of the pine thicket, not more than three hundred yards from the truck, and sat down. The heck with Dave Black, he thought. Let him look for himself, if he's so all fired set on being the hero besides its naptime. Dennis leaned back against the stump of a huge chestnut tree. The stump must have been six feet in diameter. It's a doggone shame that the darn blight from Europe killed every one of these American Chestnut trees. They were the most valuable trees in the woods too. Yep! It's a dang shame.

He closed his eyes and let the warm sun find its way through the tangled web of limbs and branches high above his head. It bathed his face in shadowed warmth and brought sleep on quickly. Its funny, he thought, just before he fell asleep, how you can feel so warm on such a cold winter day just by getting out of the wind and letting the sun work its magic. Sure feels good. He settled back against the stump, crossed his arms, and began to snore. Dennis was totally unaware of the small figures moving quickly and quietly through the forest. He never saw the Spelon standing at his feet and gazing into his face. What a curious looking fellow, the Spelon thought.

Dave Black walked back and forth across the area where he thought Steve should have been. Not a sign of him. Not a trace anywhere. Where could he have gone, he wondered. A man just doesn't vanish into thin air. I'd better check with Dennis. Maybe he has had better luck today.

"Dennis! Come in Dennis. This is Dave Black. Dennis, do you have a copy? Can you hear me?" The voice was far away at first, as in a dream, but more realistic. Dennis wasn't dreaming, but he thought he heard someone calling his name. He opened his eyes, and the sunlight quickly forced them shut. He had to cover his eyes with his hand to protect them from the dazzling sun. The bright sunlight quickly brought him back to reality. Then he realized that the walkee talkee was the culprit that had so rudely brought him out of his restful slumber.

As he reached for it, something caught the corner of his eye. He noticed a movement off to his right, just below the edge of the hill. He couldn't tell what it was, it moved much too quickly, but it was low to the ground and moving very fast. What the heck was that, was the first thought to splash across his brain. "Yeah, go ahead Dave, this is Dennis. What do you want?"

"Have you seen anything yet?" Dave asked. "Any sign of him?"

"Nope." Dennis replied. "Not a sign of anything human, but I did see something move just below the break of the ridge. Let me take a look and I'll shout back at you. Just hold on."

Dennis eased down over the edge of the hill to the spot where he had seen something race by. Must have been a rabbit, he thought, but I'll swear it looked like something running on two legs. Beats the heck out of me." He grabbed the walkee talkee and pressed his thumb against the talk button. "Dave, this is Dennis. I didn't find anything over the ridge. I'm heading \ back to the truck. I'll meet you there. I'm over and out."

It was nearly dark before Dave returned to the truck. Dennis was in the front sear nearly asleep, as he opened the door. "Wake up you lazy thing." Dave shouted. "You sure are a big help. I'd been better off bring my bird dog along on this trip." "Suits me." Dennis laughed. "Tomorrow you bring your dog, and I'll stay at the office and answer the phone. Never can tell, maybe this fellow will call the office to let everyone know he made it home." "Well, you can bet I'll be back tomorrow." Dave said. "I'll be back every day until I find some clue as to what happened to Steve Mason. Dave climbed behind the wheel of the state truck and fired up the engine. The wheels threw dirt and leaves as he hit the gas. Several sets of tiny eyes watched the truck and its occupants, as it disappeared into the dusky forest haze.

69

CHAPTER 13

Steve stood motionless in the hall outside the bathroom door. It was his bathroom. He knew the door well. The tiny scuff mark beside the doorknob happened the night Jennifer was born. He was in a hurry to get Sheila to the hospital, and he rammed the door with the overnight bag. It was his bathroom, it was his house, and he could hear the shower running. He kn3w Sheila was taking a shower and would be out soon. He waited. He would surprise here, when she came out. The water stopped. It wouldn't be long now, soon the door would open and he would see the surprise in her face. She would run to him and throw her arms around him.

Slowly the door opened, and Sheila stood there with a towel wrapped around her body. He smiled and held out his arms, but she walked right past him toward the bedroom. She walked as if she had never seen him, as if he weren't even there. She disappeared into the bedroom and closed the door. Steve stood there for a moment frozen in fear.

Why didn't she stop? Why didn't she see me? He had to find out. As he neared the door, his body froze. His heart jumped into his throat, and his hands began to tremble. Was that voices he heard coming from the bedroom? Steve's chest began to tighten and his breathing became labored, when he realized that it was a man's voice he heard coming from the bedroom. A man in the bedroom with his wife, that couldn't be happening. His hand was trembling, as he reached for the doorknob. He had to know what was happening in his own house. The door opened slightly, and Steve peered inside. There stood Sheila beside the bed, with a towel still around her body. She was partially hidden behind the man. He stood there with his back to Steve, his face hidden from view.

Slowly the man loosened the towel from beneath Sheila's arms, and let it drop to the floor. She stood there naked and unashamed. He slipped his arm around her waist and pulled her to him. Their lips met with a soft touch. Steve's heart was pounding so loudly in his chest that he thought it was going to explode. He had to find out who this man was and stop it. He pushed the door open and stepped into the room. Just as Steve was about to reach for the man's shoulder and spin him around, he noticed something unusual. The man was naked also, except for his boots. His boots. His boots! Those same boots! "Who are you?" He screamed.

"Wake up. Wake up. It's me, Sebastian. Wake up Steve. You've been dreaming, and why must you keep yelling something about those boots?" The haze of sleep began to ebb from Steve's eyes, and the realization of where he was began to sink in. A slight stab of pain passed through his shoulder, as he raised himself up and sat on the edge of the bed. "What boots?" Steve asked. "What are you talking about?" "I have no idea." Sebastian answered. "The only words passing from your lips were something about boots those horrible boots. I was hoping you could enlighten me as to the meaning of your statements."

"I don't know." Said Steve. "The dream is just a blur. I know it had something to do with Sheila, and there seems like someone else was with her. It just doesn't make any sense to me. It's so confusing. "In due time my good friend." Sebastian said, with an easy comforting tone. All these things will be answered in due time. After all you've been healing for only a few days. You are still a very sick man. You can't expect to be back to full force in such a short time, even with the help of Isabel's cooking and nursing."

"How much longer, Sebastian, before I'm able to return to the top side? I've got to get back home. There are things going on that I can't explain. I've got to find out who shot me and why. I've done absolutely nothing to anyone. I have no enemies that would want me dead. It just doesn't make any sense at all. Each day I sit here the trail gets colder and colder. Wait a minute! What if the creep that shot me has gone after Sheila? She could be in danger. He could be trying to kill her too. Sebastian! I've got to get home quickly. My family might be in danger. I need to be there to protect them. If anyone hurts Sheila, so help me I will destroy him with my bare hands.

"Easy now my friend." Sebastian said, with a calming voice. "I know you are concerned for the safety of your family. You are a good man, and you must be an excellent husband and father. It is right that you are afraid for their safety, but I must remind you that you are still very weak. If you tried to return to normal size now in your condition, the strain of the transformation would surely kill you. So, I'm afraid that the best you can do for your family is to remain here and get well as soon as possible. When the time is right you will be able to return, and you will have plenty of help in finding the person responsible for this horrible act.

But for now, lets see if I might be able to ease your troubled mind. If you can tell me where your home is located, and the best and fastest route to follow, we may be able to help." Help! How are you going to help?" Steve asked. "What are you going to do? How can you help?"

"Well, I can't help at all if you keep interrupting me." Sebastian replied with a stern voice. "So keep quiet and let me explain. My brother, Daniel, and several other men of our group have been discussing your situation. We have come to the conclusion that it is necessary for someone to venture into the city for the purpose of investigating the safety and well being of your family. We also need to look for clues that might help explain why you were shot in the first place. Daniel and another man by the name of Otis have been chosen to make the trip.

With your permission, they will travel to your house to check on your family. How does that sound to you?"

"That sounds great." Steve answered enthusiastically. "But, it's several miles to my house. How do you plan on getting there?" "They will leave tomorrow evening at dusk. We Spelons most often travel at night for safety and security sake. It is not that we are afraid of any full size man, but if our presence and whereabouts were made known, I'm afraid our blissful way of life would come to an untimely end. We therefore travel at night, whenever possible, or very quickly if traveling by day.

"Like I said, its over eight miles to town. How are you ever going to get there? Steve asked, with a puzzled expression on his face. It will take you two or three days to get to town." Sebastian stood up from the bed and brushed his thick beard with his hand. He walked to the foot of the bed and stood with his back to Steve. Steve heard a very low chuckle from the man's robust chest. "Just let us worry about how we are to get there." Sebastian said, with a chuckle. "We have our ways of moving about the forest. Let me just say that there are methods of transportation available to us that humans of normal size can only dream about. Why, who knows, we might just decide to take an American Eagle." "American Eagle?" Steve asked, and scratched his head. "How are you going to get an airplane here in the middle of the forest? Are you sure you feel all right. You're talking crazier than me now."

"Excuse me, may I come in?" Steve was startled by the sound of a strange voice coming from the doorway. "Oh! Daniel. I'm glad you could come." Said Sebastian. "This is our guest, Mr. Steve Mason. Steve, this is my brother, Daniel."

"Glad to meet you Daniel." Steve said, as he extended his good arm.

" The pleasure is mine." Daniel replied. "I'm the handsome brother in the family, in case he failed to tell you that." Sebastian chuckled, and Steve grinned, after realizing the family joke. "I've heard a great deal about you. I'm glad that I finally get to meet you."

"Come." Sebastian said. "Lets sit down and talk. By the way where is Otis? I thought he was going to come with you." "He was, but there was a problem with the biomass generator, and Otis is the best engineer in the place. If something goes wrong, he's the first one we call."

"What the heck is a biomass generator?" Steve asked. "Is that some type of septic tank system?" "Septic Tank!" Daniel replied, with a hearty laugh. Sebastian too found the statement funny and joined in the chuckle. "Heavens no my friend, our biomass generator is the energy source for our community. It's a system we have designed to convert the forest biomass into electrical energy. You remember when you made electricity with a potato in Science class? Well, its something similar to that."

"We'll explain all that to you when you are better able to travel." Sebastian said. "But, now on to more important things. We must design a map for Daniel and Otis to follow. Remember, it must be the safest and most expeditious route." "No problem." Said Steve, as he took the pencil and began to sketch a map highlighting the route to his home. Overhead footsteps continued to walk; footsteps of someone fervently searching for something.

CHAPTER 14

Sheila had just finished cleaning the breakfast dishes, when the doorbell rang. "I'll get it, Mommy." Said Jennifer. "Don't worry. I'll answer the door. "Oh no you don't, young lady." Sheila scolded her. "I'll get the door. You know never to open the door to anyone. That's a job for Mommy and ….Daddy." Sheila's voice cracked, as she realized what she had said. Jennifer didn't say a word. She either didn't hear or chose to ignore it. She walked to the door and peeked through the peephole. She didn't recognize the face, but the uniform was obviously that of the Sheriff's office. She opened the door slightly, but kept the safety chain hooked just to be sure.

"May I help you?" She asked. "Mrs. Mason. I'm Clayton Mills, ma'am, the Sheriff here in Jackson County. I'd like to ask you a few questions, if you have a minute."

"Oh yes, of course sheriff. Please come in." Sheila said, as she removed the chain from the door and motioned the officer in. "Please tell me that you have some good news about Steve."

"I'm afraid I can't give you any good news right now, Mrs. Mason. There is still no sign of your husband, nor any clues as to what might have happened to him. All that has been found is the gun and tree stand he was using. I'm afraid that doesn't leave us much to go on. That's where I was hoping you might be able to help. Did Steve have any arguments or disagreements with anyone lately?" "Heavens no!"

Sheila answered with a note of resentment in her voice. "Steve was a friend to everyone. He always helped whenever anyone was in need of anything. He was liked by everyone in this community.

"How about his friend Tom?" The sheriff inquired. "I believe Tom was his hunting partner. How well did they get along? Would he have had any reason to…..?" "Stop right there! Sheila exclaimed. "Tom is a dear friend and a sweet person. He and Steve have been best friends for as many years as I can remember. There's no way Tom would have ever done anything to harm Steve. Besides, he would have no reason to. For heaven's sake, Tom spent several days out there in the woods looking for Steve. Absolutely not the thought of something like that is completely out of the question."

"I see." Sheriff Mills said. "But, you do understand that I have to ask these questions. I must cover all the possible leads, and that includes his closest and best friends. I'm just trying to do my job and find your husband."

"I understand." Sheila answered in a sympathetic tone. "I really do appreciate your work, and I am glad you came by, but I really have nothing to tell you. There is nothing that I know that would be of any help. All I know is that my daughter and I are about to go insane with worry. I just want Steve back home and my family back together." The sheriff nodded his head, as he rose from the couch. He closed the cover of his notepad and placed it in his shirt pocket. "Thanks for your time ma'am. I'll be on my way. I'll let you know if I get any more and better information."

Sheila closed the door behind Sheriff Mills and leaned against it. Her eyes began to burn, as the tears fill to overflow. Oh Steve, she thought, where are you, and when will you ever be home? Faith. I have to have faith. I know that he will find his way back. If he were dead, they would have found him by now. I have to believe that he will come back to me.

Having reassured herself that he would return, the tears slowly began to dry. She realized that she had so much to do that day, and the first was to finish the dishes and do some shopping. A quick shower and some clean clothes, and I'll feel much better, she thought.

"Jennifer! How would you like to go visit Grandma for a couple of hours, while mommy does some shopping?

"Oh boy!" Jennifer shouted. "I'll go get my coat and hat. Do you want me to call Grandma and let her know I'm coming?" "Sure thing, Sweetie. You call Grandma, while I take a quick shower and get some clothes on. Tell her we'll be by in about forty-five minutes."

Sheila walked out of the bedroom as Jennifer was hanging up the phone. "Grandma said it would be great if I came and stayed with her, so lets go mommy, lets go." Jennifer shouted, while bouncing up and down on the couch.

"Just a minute, little girl." Sheila answered. "I have to set the trash out on the back steps before we leave, and there is a load of clothes in the washer that needs to be put in the dryer. Let me take care of this and we will be on our merry way.

Sheila opened the back door in the kitchen, which opens onto a small porch with steps leading into the back yard. She set the bag of trash on the edge of the porch and took a deep breath of the clean winter air. She turned and started back into the house, when she noticed the snow at the corner of the house. It looked as if it had been walked through. It really looked like a set of footprints. She moved across the porch and looked closer at the prints. They were most definitely footprints, and large ones. A tightness began to form in her chest, as fear quickly seized her. Who would be outside her house? Could it be a peeping tom? Cold chills ran down her neck and arms. They were both from the chill in the air and the fear in her heart.

She turned and started back into the house, when Tom Gregg crossed her mind. "Tom!" She shrieked. "Tom came around the house the other night to check on the noise. That's it. Those are Tom's prints." With a sigh of relief and a satisfied mind, she walked back to where Jennifer was waiting to leave.

The morning air was cold, much colder than the normal November Tennessee temperatures. Sheila wondered if Steve had been out in the cold weather with no protection for four days. It would be almost impossible for anyone to survive temperatures below freezing for any length of time. With each passing thought, Sheila became more and more award of the very real possibility that Steve would never survive, and that she may never see him again.

As she slid her fingers under the door handle of the Oldsmobile and pulled up, nothing happened. The ice had frozen the door shut. She pulled and pulled, with no success. She started to yell for Steve to come and help her open the door, but instead, began to cry. "What's wrong, Mommy. Why are you crying?" Little Jennifer asked. "Mommy, is something wrong? Are you hurt?"

"Oh no, honey. Mommy's fine. It's just the cold air making my eyes tear up, and I broke a nail trying to open this stupid door. But I'm all right, don't worry. Stand back while I try to open it again." She made a fist with her small hand and began to pound on the edge of the door. Her efforts were futile, until she made a sudden and swift move with her hip that slammed into the side of the door. She heard the ice break and a smile crept across her face. "There, that should do it." She said. "Now let's try." Once again she slid her fingers under the handle and pulled. Nothing happened. "Pull harder." Jennifer shouted her encouragement. "You can do it Mommy. Pull harder." With another hard bump of her hip, the door came loose. The broken ice crystals sparkled like diamonds in the bright morning sunlight, as they floated to the frozen ground.

"Quick, hop in." She said, as she motioned for Jennifer to get into the front seat. "Buckle up, and I'll see if I can get this thing started and warm us up a little." The four-cylinder 2.5liter engine groaned its discontent, before bursting to life. "Ah, we'll be warm soon." Sheila said. "Now lets get going to Grandma's house.

The streets were covered with a layer of snow, from the storm that blanked the entire area only two nights before. I wonder if Steve is buried under the snow, she thought. He might even be frozen and not be found until the snow melts. "Stop it!" She screamed. "I have to stop think like this." "Stop what?" Jennifer asked. Shelia blinked her eyes and slowly shook her head, as she looked down into the innocent eyes of her beautiful young daughter. "Oh nothing." She said softly. "Nothing at all." She thought how much Jennifer looked like her father. "Watch out Mommy, look out for that car!" Jennifer screamed. Sheila was jolted back into reality by Jennifer's screams, just in time to see that she had crossed the line into the path of an oncoming car. She hit her breaks and the car began to slide. Oh no, she thought. What do I do now?

She remembered that Steve had told her to always pump her breaks on snow or ice, and never lock them up. She released her foot from the pedal and began to pump the brake. She was able too ease the nose of the Olds back into the proper lane. The car brushed by without incident, but the driver felt it necessary to register his protest of her mistake by blasting the horn as he passed. What a jerk, she thought. He didn't have honk the horn. I know I made a mistake. Suddenly, it was funny, and she began to laugh. She was scared and shaking all over, but she laughed anyway. Sheila eased the car to a stop on the side of the road and continued to laugh.

"Are you alright?" Jennifer asked. "Why are you laughing?" "Yes, I'm fine." Sheila chuckled. I'm just laughing at myself for getting upset with that horn tooter." Jennifer laughed too at the idea of a horn tooter. "I guess I'd better pay closer attention to what I'm doing. Lets get to Grandma's house." She looked into the rear view mirror, as she started to pull back onto the highway, but had to wait for three vehicles to pass. An old pickup driven by a farmer with a red hat on his head, and several bails of hay in the back, was the first to pass. The second car to pass was a bright yellow Cadillac driven by a little blue haired lady with a death grip the wheel. The last vehicle was a large dark green 4-wheel drive blazer of some kind. She didn't pay attention to the driver, but did notice how large the tires were, as the passed by her window. "That's the kind of tires I need." She told Jennifer. "That would keep me from sliding off the road."

Before she could ring the doorbell of Mrs. Mason's house, the door opened and Harriet Mason's bright blue eyes and wrinkled face peeped around the door. "Hi you two." She said, with obvious joy in her voice. "How are my two girls?" "Hi Grandma." Jennifer squealed, as she rushed into the open arms of her grandmother. "We're both just fine." Sheila answered. "How about you? How are you doing?"

"Just a little tired. I haven't been sleeping much these last couple of days. But I'll be okay. How about you? How are you holding up?" "Not much sleep here either." She answered. "I keep waiting for the phone to ring, waiting for some good news."

"It will come." Grandma said. "You've just got to have enough faith." She smiled, as she gave Sheila a hug. A tear began to form in the corner of Sheila's eye, as she hugged her mother-in-law. She loved Harriet very much, almost as much as she loved her own mother. "I know." Sheila said. 'It's just hard some times to keep the faith, but I haven't given up. Thanks for watching Jennifer while I do some shopping. I haven't been out of the house since Steve left, and we're about out of supplies."

"I understand. Don't worry about Jennifer and I. We'll be just fine." Harriet said, as she placed a gentle loving hand on Sheila's shoulder. "I think we'll eat a bite of lunch and probably make some cookies. How does that sound?"

"Oh boy!" Jennifer shouted. "Bye Mommy. See you later."

Sheila hugged her daughter and said. "I'll be back in a couple of hours. You behave and mind Grandma." She turned and started toward the door. Harriet followed, as Sheila stepped off the front step and walked toward her car. "Be careful." She said, as she closed the front door." Mrs. Mason Stood momentarily in front of the curtained window and watched Sheila drive off. "Now how about some lunch and then some cookies?"

The sun was warm through the windshield of her car, as she turned the corner into the parking lot of the local Wal-Mart. This was her favorite store. She could always get anything she needed right here. And what luck, she thought, a parking space right up front. I knew this was going to be a good day. She eased the Olds into the space and shut off the engine. She hadn't noticed the big green state blazer parked in the next row. As she got out of her car and locked the door, she heard someone call her name.

"Sheila. Sheila Mason. Wait up a minute." Sheila turned to see who was calling her name, and noticed a man in a light brown uniform walking toward her.

"Are you Sheila Mason?" He asked.

"Who wants to know? She answered.

"Oh, I'm sorry." He said. "Please forgive me. I'm Dave Black, with the Wildlife Resources Agency. I've been working with the local authorities in the search for your husband."

"Oh, I see." Sheila said. "Do you have some news? Have you found anything?" "Well no, not yet." Dave answered, but we're still looking, and we won't give up until we find you husband."

"I appreciate that." Sheila said, with a forced smile. "Was there something else you wanted?"

"Uh, er, no, no." Dave mumbled. "I just wanted to see you and see how you were doing. If there is anything that you need or anything that I can do please call me. You can reach me at the TWRA office. I'm also listed in the book. "Thanks again." Sheila said, "I'll be fine. I have several good friends and family members that are helping, but I appreciate your offer. I really do need to be going. I've got a lot of shopping to do."

"Sure thing." Dave said. "I didn't mean to hold you up. Just wanted to check on you. I'll be seeing you."

Sheila smiled and turned to leave. As she walked through the double doors of the Wal-Mart store, she glanced back over her shoulder and noticed Dave Black still standing by her car watching her.

"Mighty good looking lady." Dave mumbled under his breath, as he watched her walk toward the store. "That Steve Mason sure was a lucky man to have a lady like that waiting for him every night when he gets home. If he ever does come home again."

CHAPTER 15

The alarm clock burst to life with a constant buzz. The LED display showed 6:00 a.m., as the large hand of Horace Farley came down with a force to shut off the incessant buzzing. He opened his eyes and gazed at the clock. It can't be six o'clock already, he thought. I just laid down a few minutes ago. It was actually several hours ago that he had laid down, after he had finished watching the young Pizza Inn girl prepare for bed. He had returned home to an empty house, and empty shower, and an empty bed. He had lain in bed for several hours thinking of Cindy. He fantasized about actually asking her for a date.

In his mind it would be a perfect date. He would be Mr. Cool, pick her up in his classy car, go to an elegant restaurant, perhaps some dancing, cap the evening off at the movies, then return to her house for a night of passion. It really could be like that, he thought. I know I can do it. I really could be like that. I could be that cool. Today! Today is the day. I'll ask her for a date this evening. I'll go by Pizza Inn right after work this evening and ask her out. I won't stutter or jumble my words. I'll be as cool and calm as 007. She'll be glad to go out with me. After all, I'm not a bad looking guy, and I can clean up kind of nice. Yeah, that's what I'll do today. Today is the day I, Horace Farley, come out of my shell and become the man I am supposed to be. These were the thoughts that filled the mind of Horace, as he showered and dressed for work. Better dress sharp, he thought, I want to make a good impression this evening, when I ask her out. Pressed slacks, oxford shirt, red tie, dark sport coat, not bad, he thought, not bad at all.

As Horace stepped out of his apartment and onto the ice covered sidewalk, the brisk winter air hit him directly in the face. He took a deep breath and felt the chill run down his back. Man, its cold, he thought, should have worn my heavy overcoat. As his weight came down on the ice covered concrete, the leather soles of his shoes failed to make solid contact, and his feet began to slide. His left arm made a large loop in an effort to stop the fall and landed sharply on the hood of the Datsun station wagon. A sharp pain traveled up his arm and into his shoulder. His right arm swung behind him and his right hand came to rest on the sidewalk, barely preventing him from landing flat of his back.

"Good grief!" He mumbled under his breath. "I hope this is no indication of what the day is going to be like." He regained his footing, but held firmly to the roof of the wagon, as he opened the door and eased inside.

I sure hope she starts, he thought. It was pretty cold last night, and I know she doesn't like the cold weather. Come on baby start for daddy. He turned the key in the ignition, and listened for the motor to complain. But, after only a couple of turns, the engine roared to life and all four cylinders began their work. "Atta girl!" He said happily. "I knew you wouldn't let me down." As he eased the gearshift into reverse and backed out of the parking space, he realized that he had not scraped the windshield. The frosty night air had left a thick layer of ice on the glass. He put the car in neutral, pulled the parking break, and got out. After retrieving the scraper from under the seat, he began to remove the coating from his windshield.

Finally back in the car and back on his way, a small cloud of blue smoke again trailed from the exhaust of the wagon, as he drove out of the parking lot and on the street.

Horace parked his car in the lot outside the huge Ramco Corp. building and walked inside. "Good morning Mr. Farley." Ruby said, with a smile and a musical note in her voice. "How are you this morning?"

"Oh I'm great. This is going to be a great day; I can just feel it. Why, I might even make it through the day without getting irate with this dumb computer. Now what do you think about that?"

"Why, I think that is a marvelous plan." Ruby said, with an obvious look of surprise on her face. "I'm really glad to see you in such a good mood this morning. I'm sure it is going to be a great day. See you later."

Horace grinned, as he walked past her desk and down the hallway to his office. He flipped on the light switch and stared briefly at the computer. His spirits fell slightly as he remembered the technical problem that had plagued him until after five o'clock the day before. The problem was still there, only his attitude was different. I'll beat you today, he thought, as he removed his coat and hung it on the rack. You're not going to ruin my day. Nothing is going to ruin my day.

Horace walked the short distance to the office lounge for a cup of coffee. As he entered the room, his heart leaped into his throat. Standing there beside the coffee pot was Valerie Beacon from accounting. Horace had always thought she was beautiful, but he could never quite sum up the courage necessary to carry on a conversation.

Valerie was very attractive. She has about 25 years old, with strawberry blonde hair and green eyes. She always wore red lipstick on her very thick and luscious lips. When she spoke, Horace could not take his eyes off her lips. He could only think about what it would be like to actually kiss them.

But today was different. Today, he was going to take control. Today he would not crack. He was confident that he could speak to anyone. After all, she was only a girl, nothing special. She was not any more important or better than he or Ruby.

Valerie turned, when she heard someone enter the room and saw Horace standing there in the doorway. "Good morning Horace." She said with a smile that stretched across those beautiful red luscious lips. It was a smile that caused her face to light up and display a set of sparkling white teeth. "You certainly are dressed sharply this morning. What's the occasion?"

"No occasion." Horace replied, with only a slight quiver in his voice. He began to feel the temperature increase in his forehead. He knew that the color of his face would start to change at any time and reveal the insecurity he was trying so desperately to hide. "I just thought I would dress up a little for a change. Nothing wrong with that is there?"

"Heavens no! Valerie exclaimed. "Not at all. As a matter of fact, I think you look very nice. You should dress up more often. It makes you a quite handsome man. Can I pour you a cup of coffee?"

"Sure." He said, and held out his cup to be filled. As she poured the coffee, he began to look at her lips and his hand began to shake. "Better hold still." She warned. "I wouldn't want to burn you." Horace suddenly realized what she had said and pulled his cup away. The coffee poured over his hand and onto the floor. The hot coffee caused him to drop his cup. It fell from his hand and splashed on the front of his trousers. The cup came to rest on the floor after leaving the last few drops of its precious liquid on his nicely shined shoes. He was beginning to lose control and knew it.

"Ouch! Dang that's hot." He yelled, as he started slinging the hot liquid from his hands. "Oh I'm sorry! Valerie exclaimed. "I didn't mean to pour it on you. Are you alright?" "Yeah, I'm okay." Horace mumbled. "I've got to go. I'll see you around Valerie." He turned and quickly raced from the room without looking back. He walked directly toward the men's room hoping not to meet anyone along the way.

With water and paper towels, he was able to clean his slacks without leaving any stains, but it did leave a rather obvious large wet spot on the front of his trousers. If I can only make it back to my desk, he thought, I can work there until this dries. Everything was going so well, he thought. Why did I have to loose it at the last minute? Well, at least I was able to speak to her with jumbling my words and making a complete fool of myself. That was a step in the right direction.

Throughout the entire day, Horace Farley thought of nothing but Cindy, the beautiful blonde Pizza Inn girl. This afternoon, he would summon all the reserve courage he had within his very being in order to succeed. He was sure he had it under control. He could pull this off without a hitch. He was convinced that if he maintained his cool and kept his composure, that she would certainly agree to a date with him. He was ready.

He was even able to solve the technical problem with the Autocad program, another indication that this day belonged to him. Nothing could go wrong. The little incident with Valerie was just a brief setback, but it would not affect what was to take place that evening at Pizza Inn.

As the large oak clock on the wall approached five, he became anxious. There was a knot in the pit of his stomach. His palms began to sweat at the thought of what he was planning to do. He had all the confidence of a matador facing the raging bull, but that didn't keep fear from creeping into his stomach and letting loose the butterflies.

Horace flipped the switch on the computer and cut the power. He threw his coat over his shoulder and strode from the office down the corridor, with a rare display of poise and confidence. He passed in front of Ruby's desk and caught her eyeing him as he passed. "Have a good evening Ruby." He said, as he walked confidently past her.

"Leaving a little early this evening aren't you sir." Ruby said, with a distinct note of optimism in her voice. "You're usually the last one to leave this place. Is there somewhere special we're going tonight?"

"Lets just say I've got a date this evening." He smiled.

"Oh! That's wonderful." She replied. "Who is the lucky girl? Do I know her? Is she from around here? Oh my goodness, listen to me. I shouldn't be asking such questions. It really is none of my business. You just go on and have a good evening."

"That's perfectly alright." Horace replied. "Lets just say that she is my little pizza girl. A broad grin eased across his face, and the joyful anticipation shone through. With that, he turned and walked toward the door. He never looked back, as he walked from the building and made his way through the remaining snow to his car. The familiar puff of blue smoke left its mark in the still winter are, as the B210 wagon disappeared from the parking lot and into the evening traffic.

Ruby watched as Horace walked out the double doors of the Ramco building. He was walking differently, she thought, sort of like he had a purpose. She had no idea just what purpose was on Horace's mind.

By five-fifteen in the evening of that cold November day, the sun had all but completely sunk from sight. Only the dim glow of the last remaining beams of orange purple and red sunlight now shone above the ridge of trees that shadowed highway 111. The headlights of the station wagon strained forward to break through the haze of dusk and brighten the way that led to the Pizza Inn.

Horace rehearsed his introduction and subsequent conversation over and over in his mind. He knew exactly what he was going to say. Confidence, he thought. I have to exude and air of confidence in everything I do and say. She will never be able to resist me. This is going to be my night. He could see the Pizza Inn sign less than half a mile ahead. His vision was momentarily obscured, when the bright lights of the car behind flashed into his eyes. "Turn off those bright lights you jerk!" he exclaimed. He was about to turn around and deliver an unmistakable hand gesture, when the blue lights began to revolve. Oh no! He thought, not the police. What have I done now?

He slowly tapped the brakes and eased the Datsun onto the shoulder of the highway and waited. He was looking at his watch, when he heard the loud rap on the window. "Would you please roll down your window sir?" The officer asked. Horace's hands were trembling ever so slightly, as he grasped the window crank and began to roll it down.

"Yes sir officer, was I doing something wrong?" Horace asked, with a hint of worry in his voice. "I didn't think I was speeding."

"May I see your driver's license?" The officer asked, with a face as hard as flint. "Sure!" Horace agreed. "Sure thing, just a second. Here you go. He was all thumbs; trying to extract the license from its hiding place in his wallet. The officer let the beam of his flashlight shine on the license, and asked. "Did you know that you have a tail light that is out on your car, Mr. Farley?"

"What? Oh no sir. I didn't realize I had a light out. You see, sir, I live alone, and no one else to let me know things like that. I guess if I had a wife or girlfriend, they could let me know those things. But, when its only you, you have to figure things out for yourself. Horace soon realized that he was rambling on and on and not making very much sense. He decided to shut up and let the Officer talk.

"When can you get this taken care of?" The officer asked.

"I'll get it repaired tomorrow." He assured the policeman. I know the car isn't much to look at, but it is mine, and it's paid for. I know that's no excuse for letting things like that go, but like I was saying.

"Tomorrow will be fine." The officer interrupted. "Just get it fixed. Have a safe evening Mr. Farley." With that, the officer turned and walked back to his patrol car. Horace sat there and listened to his useless words echo in his brain. Why couldn't I just sit here and keep my mouth shut? Why did I have to ramble on and on uselessly? He had just rolled up the window and leave, when another loud rap on the glass. It startled him, and he jumped dropping his wallet. Horace looked out the window only to see the officer still standing there. He rolled the window down and said. "Yes sir. Is there something else?" "Don't forget your seatbelt." The officer said, and was gone.

"Oh my seat belt." Horace muttered, looking down for the safety strap. "I always wear my belt officer. It just slipped my mind this evening. You see, I've had a lot on my mind lately, but I'll do it right now." He turned back to the window to tell the officer thank you, but noticed that he was already gone. After taking a deep breath, he eased the car back into the flow of traffic and left the puff of blue smoke behind.

The parking lot of the Pizza Inn was almost full. Horace eased his car down the second row looking for an empty space. Where did all these people come from, he wondered. Any other night this place would be almost empty. He hit his brakes as the lights of a Dodge minivan came on and started to back out.

"Finally!" He exclaimed. "Now let destiny take its course." He pulled the Datsun into the space and shut off the engine. Horace sat staring out the window. Staring at nothing. The knuckles of both hands began to grow white, as his grip on the steering wheel increased. His grip started to ease as tiny drops of sweat began to form between his palms and the wheel. I can't loose it now, he thought. I've come this far. I've got to see it through.

He forced his hands from the wheel and opened the door. The cold night air was a refreshing blast to his shaky nervous system. He stepped out of the car and shut the door behind him. Standing with his right hand on the hood of the Datsun and staring at the flashing Pizza Inn sigh, he looked like a mountain climber contemplating the Matahorn. Standing here looking for an excuse is what the old Horace would do, he thought, but not me, not tonight. "Here I go." He said, as he stepped briskly toward the restaurant door.

When he walked inside the restaurant, he was bathed in the warm air of the room and the aromatic fragrance of the pizza cooking in the oven. He closed the door behind him and moved into the line. There she was, standing behind the cash register. Her blonde hair was pulled back into a ponytail, revealing the soft curve of her neck and the small gold earring hanging gently from her lobe. She was beautiful. How could he ever go through with this? She was so beautiful, and he was just Horace. The line began to move forward and Cindy came closer. His palms began to sweat, and he could feel the tightness in his throat, with every inch the line moved. He waited, knowing that soon she would make eye contact with him. How would he handle that? Would he look fearlessly into her beautiful blue eyes and give his order? Only time would tell.

She raised her eyes from the register and glanced down the line of customers. A brief smile crossed her lips, as her eyes met his. He was sure he saw a smile. It was unmistakable. She had smiled at him. She must remember him. How could she forget him, he had made such a fool of himself only twenty-four hours earlier. Just three more people, and he would be face to face with her and face to face with his own destiny.

He rehearsed his lines in his mind. I'll order the buffet first then ask how she is doing this evening. She will say fine, and I'll say I got it right tonight. She will look at me somewhat puzzled then all I will say is fubay. She will definitely remember then. The look of recognition will cross her face, and I will then introduce myself and say. "Hi, I'm Horace Farley. Remember me?" Then she will tell me her name and.....

"Hi. I see you're back again tonight. Are you going to have the fubay again?" Cindy asked with a smile. Her bright cheerful question caught Horace completely off guard. All he could do was to stare, first at her, then down at the floor. His head began to spin, and he was certain that he would pass out, but he didn't. His inner power came forward, and he began to speak. It wasn't exactly as he had rehearsed, but close. "Yes." He said. "The fubay will be fine. He laughed. A beautiful set of straight white teeth shown from her smile that came across her face.

'Nice of you to remember." He said. "Hi, I'm Horace Farley. He extended his hand across the register. Cindy shook it briefly and said. "Nice to meet you, Horace. Will that be a large coke also?"

"Yes, coke is fine."

"Great! That will be four seventy-five again."

Horace handed her a five-dollar bill, and was preparing himself to ask if she would like to go out, as she held her hand out. "Here's your change." She said. "Enjoy your meal." Before Horace could utter another word, she was already turning her attention to the next person in line. She gave the gray haired little old lady the same sweet smile that she had just given him. It was just a front, he thought, as he picked up his tray and made his way through the crowded dining area in search of a table, a table for one. He found a spot near the front partition. From here he was able to see the cash register and Cindy. He sat there for several minutes just staring at her. That same smile appeared every time someone new came down the line, they got the same smile. It was like it was painted on her face. She put it on when she came to work, and took it off when she left. It was a customer smile. It wasn't real. It wasn't me she was smiling at; it was my five dollars.

"Screw her and screw the pizza." He mumbled under his breath. His words were only loud enough for the young couple sitting behind him to hear. The young teenage boy with straight brown hair that brushed his shoulders, turned around to see who was complaining about the pizza.

"What are you looking at kid?" Horace said with a growl. "Mind you own business." He left his plate and drink sitting on the table and stormed out of the restaurant without looking back.

The glass in the door of the small wagon rattled, as he slammed the door. His right foot began pumping the gas, as he turned the key in the ignition. "C'mon! He moaned. "C'mon start you piece of crap." A large cloud of blue-black smoke bellowed from the tailpipe of the Datsun, and the engine coughed and sputtered its way to life. A faint squeal sounded from the tires, as Horace popped the clutch and sped away into the night.

He pulled the car into the space in front of the liquor store, slammed the door and got out. He stormed inside, swinging the door open wildly as he entered. Horace knew exactly what he wanted and where to get it. His hand came to rest firmly around the neck of the bottle of Jack Daniels sippin whiskey. Old number seven, he thought. That'll be my mistress for tonight. "You never get an argument from old number seven, he mumbled under his breath. "You won't get a fake smile from her either."

"Will that be all sir?" The clerk asked, while placing the precious bottle into the brown paper bag. "Yeah, that's all." Horace answered.

Horace looked at the clerk. He was an older man with several days growth of whiskers on his chin and a stub of a cigar held tightly in his yellow teeth. "That'll be eight seventy-five." The old man uttered with a raspy voice. It was a voice obviously abused by years of sucking in cigar smoke and downing shots of Jack in the black.

Horace handed him a ten-dollar bill and started to walk away. He was thinking of Cindy. All he could see was her face and her phony smile. It was the same smile she gave everyone. "Here's your change pal." The old clerk said. The sound of his rough voice startled Horace, causing him to turn quickly. "Keep it." He said. "I don't need it where I'm going," and kept on walking. He threw the bottle onto the passenger seat, climbed in and closed the door. The unmistakable crack made by the seal, as it breaks open the bottle of seven years old Tennessee whiskey filled the interior of the station wagon.

Horace brought the bottle to his lips and took a long deep drink. His lips curled back over his teeth, and he exhaled from deep within his chest, a sigh of pleasure. "Ahhh! Now that's just what I needed." He muttered, and quickly pulled another huge swallow before sealing the bottle and starting the car.

A full fourth of the bottle was gone by the time Horace pulled into the parking space of his condo. While walking up the steps to his front door and placing the key in the lock, he was still thinking of Cindy. He was thinking of Cindy, when he fell across the bed, with his bottle of Jack tucked safely under his arm.

What a worthless tease, he thought. I know what would wipe that artificial smile off her face. A night of good rough passion would definitely make her see me differently. That would put a real smile on her face, and maybe I should be the guy to do just that. His mind began to fill with thoughts of love and pleasure and Cindy. He thought of what it would be like to hold her and kiss her; to smell her sweet perfume and savor the fragrance of her hair. He had to let her know how he felt. He had to let her know he loved her.

Horace sat upright in the bed with a start. He stared blankly at the mirror attached to the large oak dresser. "Wait a minute." He said. "Maybe I could wait for her at her home tonight at her home and love her there. It would have to be in a way that she could not reject me. But what if she turns me away and laughs at me. I can't take that. I could stand any more rejection. I've got to show her my love, but it has to be on my terms. I don't need any arguments or resistance from her. The question is, how can I keep her from rejecting me.

The wheels and cogs in Horace's brain began to spin in an attempt to crank out some worthwhile idea and a solution to his problem. His subconscious mind kicked in, and he was instantly standing in his high school biology class. The teacher, Mr. Kent, was about to put the cat to sleep. "How are you going to get the cat to sleep?" one of the students asked.

"I'm going to use chloroform." Mr. Kent explained. It's clean safe, and it doesn't have that horrible odor that comes with ether. Since I have the cat in the class cage, all I have to do is to open the door and drop this ball of cotton soaked with chloroform into the cage. It will only take a few minutes and Sylvester here will be sound asleep. We can then open the abdomen and view the viscera."

"Chloroform! That's what I'll use." Horace said out loud, startling himself. "All I need is a little chloroform. I'll wait until she has gone to bed. I'll sneak into her room, give her a little sniff of chloroform, and boom she is out like a light. Then I'll be able to show her just how much I really love her, and how so very gently I can be. But, where do I get the chloroform? The only logical place would be the high school lab. I'm sure Mr. Kent still keeps some in his desk drawer just for emergencies. All I have to do is go in and get it. Its that simple."

Horace went to this closet and removed his camouflage hunting suit. This is perfect, he thought. Its warm and it will keep me well hidden. He quickly dressed in his army fatigues and hunting boots. He slid the hunting suit on and was out the door.

The school was only minutes away, and it was always easy to get inside the school. Students learned hot to break in sometime around the third grade. He parked the car behind the fence near the football field and scaled the fence from there. He had to cross a small edge of the schoolyard before he got to the window of the furnace room. That window was always unlocked. As a matter of fact, he didn't think that the window could be locked. He thought the latch was broken, and no one ever thought of replacing it. As usual, the glass slid up with ease, and Horace climbed inside.

The building was dark and quiet. It was starkly different from the noise and clatter that echoed from the halls during the school day. It was an eerie silence. He quietly made his way down the long corridor to the science wing. The lab was the last room on the right. It was right across the hall from the girl's bathroom. Horace could still smell the odor of smoke permeating from the restroom, where no smoking was allowed. Ha, he thought. That was a joke. He was sure that even some teachers went in there just to smoke and blame it on the kids.

The lab door was locked. He would have to pick it, but that would be no trouble, since all the doors opened toward the hallway, they were simple to open. He slid the knife between the door and the latch, made a few quick moves and the door opened with ease. Yep, this was definitely going to be his night.

He opened the door and quietly slipped inside. The odor of the lab had not changed in the several years since he had studied biology. The odor of formulin and stale dried specimens filled his nostrils. Some things never change, he thought. I could pick this smell out of a line up almost anywhere. Most of the time, even Mr. Kent smelled this way, though no one ever told him.

He opened the cabinet door beside Mr. Kent's desk and found several bottles. HCl, KOH, NaOH, H2SO4, denatured alcohol, and aha! There it is, the prize he was looking for. Horace grabbed the bottle labeled Chloroform from the shelf and held it firmly. Good old Mr. Kent, he thought. Good thing he is so reliable. Its nice to know that there are some things in this world that are dependable and Mr. Kent was definitely one of those. He checked the cap on the bottle to be sure it was tightly closed, and then hid it safely away in one of the many pockets of his hunting suit. The trip out of the building was just as easy as the one coming. In a matter of minutes, he was nestled safely in the front seat of the B210 wagon with his prize held firmly in his hand. He took a zip-lock bag out of his pocket. Folded neatly in the bag, was a washcloth that he had taken from his bathroom. He poured a generous amount of the chloroform into the bag. He massaged the bag making sure that the cloth was completely wet, then zipped the bag shut and put it back into his pocket.

He looked at his watch. It was nine forty-five. Cindy would be getting off work at ten o'clock. She will be home by quarter after. He had plenty of time. He drove slowly and safely. The last thing he needed now was for that nosy cop to pull him over again and smell the Jack on his breath and the chloroform in his pocket. He could never explain that away.

He parked the car less than a block from Cindy's house. He managed to pull behind a van that was along the side of the road. It had 'Ace Uniform Rental' printed on the back doors, and someone had written, "wash me" in the dirt and grime that coated the back doors. Nice touch, he thought. Had to be some wise guy kid. He glanced back at his watch and saw that he had only about a ten-minute wait. He reclined the back of his seat and relaxed to wait for Cindy. He turned the bottle of Jack up for another shot of courage, then laid his head back against the seat and closed his eyes. He thought about Cindy. Only one other person had ever caused this much arousal in him, but she was married. He knew he couldn't have the married lady; she was already taken. Cindy was pretty, but not quite as beautiful as Sheila Mason.

Sheila was the most beautiful person he had ever seen. He had wanted her from the first time he had laid eyes on her at school. But, as it turned out, she was married to Steve, and Steve was his friend. He knew he couldn't have Sheila until they got a divorce, or until Steve was dead, and nobody knows when Steve might die.

Headlights came from behind the curve and caused shadows to dance across the dash of the Datsun. Horace had to slide down in the seat, so he was completely out of sight. The car passed and Horace raised up only enough to see over the edge of the wheel. It was Cindy. She pulled her car into the driveway and turned off the engine. The headlights went off, and he heard the door open. She stepped out of the car carrying something in her left hand. It was a big box. It was a pizza box. She had brought home a pizza for supper. Horace suddenly remembered that he had left the restaurant without eating. He was definitely getting a little hungry. But first, he must satisfy a completely different appetite.

Cindy stood briefly on the front steps of the house, fumbling with her keys. Finally the door opened and she disappeared inside. He would wait a few minutes. He was in no hurry. He knew she had to change clothes, probably shower and eat some pizza. He had plenty of time.

He thought about leaving the car and waiting outside the house, but after careful consideration, decided not to take any unnecessary risks. He could see the house clearly from where he was sitting.

The light in the bedroom came on. She must be changing clothes, he thought. She's probably getting ready to take a shower. He would wait until all the lights were out before making his move. The steering wheel of the Datsun became wet with the perspiration from his hands. It was one thing to peep through a window, while she undressed, but to actually go into her room. Well, this was going to be traveling in uncharted waters.

He looked at his watch. It was quarter after eleven. Only the bedroom lamp was on. That meant she must be reading or watching TV. Horace decided that it was necessary to explore the outside of the house to find the best entrance. He removed the bulb from the dome light overhead then opened the door. The cool November night air felt good against his sweaty skin. His black hunting boot sat firmly on the pavement, as he quietly closed the car door. He walked casually along the edge of the street until he came to the corner of Cindy's yard. A quick glance over his shoulder to be sure no one was looking, and a dash for cover.

He stayed close to the house buried beneath the shadows cast by the house and trees. The previous night's excursion was helpful in finding his way to the bedroom window. The window to Cindy's room was close enough to the ground for Horace to see inside. The blinds were drawn, but there were sufficient cracks to provide a somewhat limited view of her room. Only the night lamp beside her bed was on. She lay on her side, with her back to the window. Her head rested on two large pillows. She had a book in her left hand, and what looked like an oreo cookie in the other. She reminded him of a painting he had once seen. She seemed so quiet and so inviting. It was as though she were waiting for him to come.

The hem of her nightgown came just to the ridge of her hips. He could see the edge of her panties as it curved around her buttocks and disappeared between her legs. She held the cookie in her lips, while she used her right hand to turn the page in the book. She took a small bite of the cookie and removed the rest from her lips. Her right hand, now holding the cookie, came to rest on her hip, and she continued to read. He watched. He drank in her beauty, becoming so entranced by her presence, that he became unaware of where he was, or what was going on around him. He did not hear the footsteps as they approached from around the house. He was blind to everything but Cindy. The footsteps came closer without making a sound.

Suddenly, with a sound as loud as a cannon, the small dog broke the silence of the night and sent a wave of horror surging through Horace's entire body. He could feel the heat rise in his body as his adrenal gland shot a huge dose of adrenaline into his blood stream. He turned from the window and leaned against the house. He grabbed his chest in an effort to slow the runaway beating of his heart. Bark. Bark. The small black dog with curly hair and one white spot on its head continued to make its presence known. Horace was faced with a moment of indecision. If he made a grab for the dog and missed, it might cause such a commotion, that the entire neighborhood would be awakened. Or, he could stand quietly and perfectly still and hope that it would soon tire of him and just leave. He opted for the latter and crouched below the window in an effort to conceal himself behind a small shrub.

Bark. Bark. The mutt continued to harass him. After what seemed an eternity of barking, he heard the back door of the house open, and Cindy's voice echoed through the night. "Bosco! Bosco! You go home right now." Bosco was obviously familiar with Cindy's voice, for no sooner had she finished her command, than bosco made a mad dash through the yard toward the neighbor's house.

He heard the back door close with a loose thud. He waited for the sound of the lock button being pushed, or the deadbolt being turned. Neither sound was heard. Maybe it's a twist lock, he thought. Or, maybe it was locked before she shut the door. I'll try there first.

He hid behind the shrub until the light in the bedroom was out. Horace waited. After what seemed an eternity, he glanced at his watch. It was five after twelve. She must be asleep by now, he thought. Besides, I've got to get up for work tomorrow. He quickly ran through his mind how things were going to play out. He would crawl quickly and quietly into her room. Once he was beside her bed, he would remove the cloth soaked with chloroform from the sealed sandwich bag. He would place it lightly over her nose and mouth, not enough to wake you, but enough to be sure she inhaled it all. Once she was definitely unconscious, he would love her.

Confident all would go according to plan, he crept around the house. He climbed the four steps to the small square concrete platform that was the back porch. With his body pressed flat against the building, he grasped the handle of the storm door. It was unlocked. He opened it slowly, only about ten inches. He held it open with his right foot, while he grasped the doorknob with a slightly shaking hand. He turned the knob slowly waiting for the resistance of the lock to bar his way, but no resistance came.

The knob turned freely in his hand, and the door opened effortlessly. He pushed the door open slowly listening for any squeals that might live in the old hinges. But, fortunately, none lived in these hinges. The door opened deftly and Horace was inside. He did not shut the door completely. He left it slightly ajar, in case he had to leave in a hurry.

He had seen the kitchen with the lights on from the outside, so he knew where the table was and how to avoid it. The unmistakable aroma of pizza suddenly caught his attention. A quick glance at the tale, and he spotted the source of the fragrant smell. The remains of Cindy's dinner sat undisturbed on the table. As appetizing as the pizza looked, and as hungry as he was, Horace had more important urges to fulfill.

He made his way safely past the table and into the hallway. The light from the streetlamp shown through the front window and lighted the hallway enough for him to see where he was going. The door to Cindy's room was only partially closed. He stood beside her door and peered inside. She was asleep on her side, with her face fully exposed. She was perfect. He removed the plastic sandwich bag from the deep pocket of his hunting sit and lowered himself to his hands and knees. With the bag held in his teeth, he began the longest crawl of his entire life.

The bed, on which she lay, looked miles away. It would take all night to reach her. Small beads of sweat began to appear on his forehead as he made his way toward his prize. He covered the immense distance in only a few short steps. Her face was only inches from his. He could see her nostrils flare slightly with each breath of air. He could see her shoulders rise and fall with each breath.

He opened the bag and removed the chloroform soaked cloth. The faint odor of chloroform rose to meet his nose and eyes. He held the cloth less than an inch from her nose. She breathed. Each breath sent her already sleeping brain into a deeper level of unconsciousness. Deeper. Deeper. If Horace had known when to remove the cloth, she might have been able to wake up the next morning.

After several minutes, he removed the cloth. Now came the test. He had to make sure that she was completely out. He took the edge of the blanket and began to tickle her nose. If she is only sleeping, she will surely move to stop the tickling, but if she is unconscious…. Cindy lay like a corpse against the continued tickling of her invader. She could not move even if she had wanted to. The brain cells necessary for movement had already begun to die.

"Perfect." Horace said to himself. "She's out." He brushed her forehead with his hand and felt the cool smooth skin before it gave rise to a thick head of beautiful blonde hair. He leaned over and kissed her on the cheek. She was so beautiful, he thought, and she was all his. Tonight he would show her just how much he loved her. He was sure, that even though she was asleep, she would still know that he had been here to share his love with her. He stood over her and removed his hunting suit. He reached with his left hand to ease back the blanket that covered her and noticed that his hands were no longer shaking. He was calm and at ease. He was at peace. The soft blanked floated off her shoulders and down to her hips.

Horace was amazed at how beautiful she was, and she was his. She was his to do with as he wished. He had fully planned to love her tonight, even while she slept the silent sleep. But, now, as he gazed down at her silent beauty, he realized that he only needed her beside him. Without a word or another thought, Horace lay down beside Cindy on the bed and cradled her head under his arm. Her head fell against his shoulder, and he kissed her forehead. His fingers combed through her hair like a mother soothing an anxious child. He held her and loved her. That night he gave his heart to her. But, Cindy's ability to ever love again had vanished with the chloroform that clouded her brain. She simply forgot to breathe. Horace slept.

CHAPTER 16

The orange winter sun cast long shadows across the forest floor, as Daniel and Otis were preparing for their long journey. There was still a small amount of snow covering the ground in places where the sun had managed to warm for only a brief time. The sun had come out on the sixth day after the shooting, and the temperature had climbed up into the low 50"s. The leaves that covered the forest floor were wet and soft from the melted snow.

Steve and Sebastian stood silently watching, as Daniel and Otis prepared for their expedition. They were both wearing leather and fur. The combination of colors was such that it created a perfect camouflage. Each carried a small pouch filled with a container of water and a small amount of food.

"I still don't see how they are going to get from here to town in such a short time." Steve questioned. "You've still got eight miles or more to cover. I don't see any horses. They can't drive a car. I've got to see this." "Well my friend, it's time for you to see just how we Spelons travel over great distances in a short time." Sebastian said, with a slight chuckle. "We must call the local airlines."

"Airlines!" Steve exclaimed. "I still don't get it."

"Then stand back and watch." Otis walked to the small mound that stood at the edge of the clearing and began to whistle. It was a loud sharp clear sound. For a brief moment, Steve thought he recognized the sound. "What is he trying to do?" Steve asked. "Who is he whistling for?"

"Quiet!" Sebastian whispered. "We must be quiet for the call."

After only a few short calls, all four men heard the answer echo through the woods like a siren through the streets of New York City. It was an unmistakable sound. Steve recognized it instantly, even though he was not an avid outdoorsman. The sound came closer and louder, until the shadow crossed over the ground at Steve's feet. His eyes widened at the sight of the shadow, and quickly he turned his gaze toward the sky.

There! Coming to rest on a mighty oak limb, some forty feet above their heads, was a huge red tail hawk. The brown black and white feathers blended together in perfect harmony, produced a pattern characteristic only to the red tail. As he fanned his huge tail, the distinguishing rusty brown feathers of the undertail came into view. It was magnificent. All four men stood motionless and speechless for several seconds. The sight of such a majestic creature perched on the wooden throne above his private domain is a pleasure to be savored, a sight experienced by few. Though Steve was a newcomer to the forest, he was obviously moved to the experience and moved not a muscle. After what seemed an eternity, Otis motioned toward the ground with his right hand. He made two slow arching motions across the sky and pointed toward the ground beside his feet.

The silence of the moment was broken by the chilling cry of the hawk, as it quit its perch and began a decent to the point where Otis was directing. It made two large circles overhead, and with a force that moved the air about their heads, came to rest with the grace of a ballerina.

Steve was frightened. It was one thing to see a large hawk in a tree or flying overhead, especially when you were six feet tall, but to stand and stare eye to eye with one was a different story. The talons of its feet looked like the curved blades of the ancient warriors, and its curved beak was large enough to remove Steve's head with one blow. He took a couple of steps backward, and Sebastian chuckled.

"Fear not my friend. You are perfectly safe. 'Raptor' is a friend. He will not harm you, while you are with us."

"Well, I'll make darn sure that I stay close by your side." Steve nervously replied. "Now just what do you plan to do with that beautiful creature?"

"As I said, he is our friend. You see, when you spend your entire life in the forest, as we do, you develop a relationship with all creatures. After all, we are all sharing the same habitat."

We are viewed by the animals, as creatures similar to them. Because of our size, we offer no real threat to them. Consequently, we have developed a mutual relationship with all forest inhabitants. We help all the animals whenever we can, and they in turn help us as needed. This magnificent beast enjoys flying, and he also enjoys carrying someone on his back. So tonight, Daniel and Otis will be his passengers. Otis is able to communicate with him by his whistle sounds, and he will guide him to where he wants to go. That would be your house. If all goes well, they should return by morning with some good news about your wife and daughter.

The large bird spread its wings and lowered its body to the ground. Otis was first to climb aboard. He nestled himself just in front of the wings and astride its neck. Daniel climbed on behind Otis, as though he were mounting a Tennessee walking horse. A keen whistle from Otis, and the bird began to move its massive wings. The air began to whirl, as though a small tornado were approaching. In the blink of an eye, the large raptor was off the ground and gaining altitude. Soon it was soaring overhead with the two passengers firmly astride its massive neck. Steve saw Daniel glance back over his shoulder and wave, as they flew beyond the tree canopy and out of sight.

"Come!" Sebastian said. "Lets get back inside. I have many things to show you about our community. Your strength is returning rapidly, and I think it's time I answer some of your questions." Sebastian's rough calloused hand came to rest on Steve's shoulder, as they walked toward the opening to the cave system that was their home.

CHAPTER 17

"That will be $35.50." The girl at the cash register said, with a smile that was obviously issued simultaneously with her nametag. The nametag, which hung somewhat off perpendicular and just below her left shoulder, was covered with smiley face stickers and the name "Jackie" was written with large blue magic marker.

Sheila returned a half-hearted smile, as she opened her checkbook and began to fill in the blanks. It came naturally to sign her name as Mrs. Steve Mason, but seeing his name on the check made her hands began to tremble. She finished her signature and handed the check to Jackie. Sheila noticed that Jackie was taking quite a long time looking at the check. Jackie's eyes came up from the check and looked at Sheila.

"Is your husband the one that has been missing for several days?" Jackie asked, with a somewhat fearful look on her face.

"Yes." Sheila answered, in a quiet voice. "That's my husband, but I expect him home any day now."

"Oh, I'm sure he will. We all hope so." Jackie stammered, with obvious embarrassment and sympathy. "I'm sure he's going to be just fine." Her attention returned to the check, as she finished making the necessary entries in the register. "Here is your receipt Mrs. Mason. I sure hope everything turns out okay." "Thank you." Shelia said. "I appreciate your concern. I'm sure everything will be fine." She pushed the cart carrying the plastic bags of groceries to the car and placed them in the back floorboard. As she set the last bag on the floor, and was about to shut the door, a cold chill came over her. She was frozen with fear, an unexplained fear. It was a fear that comes with knowing that you are being watched. She could feel the presence of unseen eyes watching her every move.

For a moment she was too gripped by fear to ever turn around and confirm her fears. She remained frozen. A deep breath brought her back to reality. This is ridiculous, she thought, why would anyone be watching me? She closed the door to the Olds and turned around. The small Geo Metro beside her was empty, as were most other cars parked nearby. The only other person in sight was an old man about sixty-five. He was unloading his cart of groceries into his pick-up truck. A long look around the parking lot revealed nothing suspicious.

She opened the car door and sat behind the wheel. With both hands firmly grasping the wheel, she took a deep breath and glanced into the rear view mirror. Nothing! She turned the ignition and put the car in reverse and backed out of the parking space.

The afternoon winter sun reflected briefly off the glass lens of the binoculars that were pressed firmly against the dark eyes watching Sheila's every move. Eyes that devoured her, loved her, and wanted her for their own.

Sheila glanced at her watch, as she eased the car into the driveway of Grandma Mason's house. Placing the gearshift into the park position, she noticed the face of her daughter peeking out from behind the living room curtains. She sat for a brief moment looking into the face of her beautiful

Little girl. If only she could see her father again, she thought, she loves him so much. She knew she had to keep the faith. Better put a smile on my face, she thought, as she walked up the steps to the opened front door.

"Mommy, Mommy, we made cookies!" Little Jennifer shouted with joy. She came running in from the kitchen with her arms outstretched. Sheila met her half way and scooped her up into her embrace. The excitement overflowed as she said. "We made cookies, and I got to take them out of the pan. I tasted one while it was still hot and gooey. That's the best way to eat a chocolate chip cookie. Did you know that mommy? They're always best when they come right out of the oven. You want a cookie? We have plenty left. I'll go get you one, okay?" Jennifer left the room in a skip, her long pigtails bouncing off her shoulders.

"How has she been this afternoon?" Sheila asked. "Fine." Mrs. Mason answered. "She only mentioned her father once all afternoon." Sheila walked into the living room and sank into the large overstuffed couch, that she and Steve had bought his mother on Mothers Day the previous year. Mrs. Mason continued, "She die mention how much her daddy liked chocolate chip cookies too. Have you heard anything else, any good news?"

"No, not a thing. I met the wildlife officer that's been working on the case, and he has nothing new to offer, but he assures me that they are doing everything possible. All we can do is sit and wait, hope, and pray."

"I'm sure you're right." Mrs. Mason said, with a soothing and consoling tone in her voice. "I'm good at doing all three."

Harriet Mason had been doing a lot of waiting and praying since her husband had passed away the previous winter. Luke Mason had been cutting wood all morning in the grove of trees just behind the house. He had accumulated quite a stack of wood, more than a rick.

With a might swing, he buried the axe in the splitting block and quit for lunch. He had felt good all morning, but after eating a bowl of soup and a sandwich for lunch, he decided to lie on the couch for a short rest. He turned on the television and lay down on the couch. Erica walked across the set of All My Children. He never awoke from his nap.

Mrs. Mason found him dead on the couch an hour later. Since then, she has been praying and waiting all the time. The loss of her husband was very hard for her to deal with. Steve and Sheila were there for her through it all, and she relied on them for everything. Now, a year later, she has developed a sense of independence and began to manage very well by herself.

The brief silence was shattered by the sound of Jennifer barging into the room waving a large chocolate chip cookie over her head. It was still soft and beginning to bend at the middle. Sheila noticed the cookie folding over and touching Jennifer's small fingers. "Here Mommy quick, get it. It's going to break." She shouted with obvious concern for the welfare of the cookie. The delicious morsel fell into the outstretched hands of her mother just before it broke loose. "Thank you, sweetie." Sheila said. "This is the best cookie I have ever tasted." "See Grandma. I told you these were the best cookies in the whole world." They all laughed.

Sheila rose from the couch, and said. "Well, I suppose we had better be going. Get your coat Jen, we've got to get home." "Mommy, can I stay the night with Grandma, huh? Can I please?" Jen asked, with a whine that was irresistible. "No." Sheila answered. "We've imposed on Grandma enough for one day. You had better come with me."

"Oh no, let her stay." Harriet said, with obvious love and affection. "She is a joy for me to have around. It gets lonesome around here sometimes, and Jennifer is a pleasant break from the silence. She will be fine. I have extra clothes here for her, and besides, I might need her to help cook come supper." Why don't you stay the night also? There's plenty of room."

"No, I'm afraid I can't." Sheila answered. "I've got so much to do at the house. Are you sure she won't be a bother?" "Absolutely not." Harriet answered. "We'll have a great time." Sheila scratched her head and thought about the situation. "You know, she said, I've got a car load of groceries to put away and some cleaning to do. Come to think of it, I might be able to get more done if Jen did stay with you. She looked at Jennifer. You had better be on your best behavior young lady."

"I will mommy, I promise."

Harriet smiled and said. "She will be a perfect angel. She always is for me. You go on and take care of your business, and we will take care of ours.

If you come back tomorrow about noon, I'll have a nice lunch ready for you. How does that sound?"

"That sounds wonderful." Sheila said with enthusiasm. "Thank you Grandma, thank you so much." She gave Mrs. Mason a hug and a kiss on the cheek, then picked up her daughter and hugged her also. She looked into the face of her little girl and told her she would be back tomorrow. "You and Grandma can cook dinner for me tomorrow. How about that?" "Okay, Mommy. Bye. I love you." Jennifer wiggled out of her mother's arms and made a dash toward the bedroom, where her toys and videos were kept.

Sheila gave Mrs. Mason another quick hug, then turned and opened the door. "I'll see you tomorrow." She said. "Bye Jen. Mommy's leaving." There was no response from the bedroom. Sheila pulled the door closed behind her. The late evening air was cold against her face and neck. She pulled the top of her coat tight against her throat. She thought about Jennifer, while she walked to the car, opened the door and sat down inside. She glanced through the windshield, as she was backing out of the drive and saw Jennifer peeking out of the front window and waving. Once the car was out into the street, she waved and honked her horn at her little girl. She would have certainly waived longer, if she had known that she would never see her daughter again.

CHAPTER 18

The creatures of the night bring the forest to life, long after the diurnal inhabitants have sought restful slumber. The brown bat sends out her sonar signal in search of unsuspecting insects. She dives and climbs and turns in total silence consuming great numbers of mosquito moths and gnats.

The owl scans the forest floor with eyes capable of capturing the last remaining ray of sunlight, sunlight too faint for the eyes of man. And, when the light is gone, the ears of the owl pick up the sound of a shrew scurrying across the soft bed of leaves that litter the forest floor. The whip-poor-will begins to sing her song, as though she were the herald of the night.

Steve's eyes strained to capture what light remained in the thick forest, as he and Sebastian made their way back to the cave. Only the silhouette of the trees could be seen against the sky, as they inched their way through the timbers. A large barn owl sounded his ominous 'hoo, hoo-hoo'. For the first time since he was a small child, Steve was becoming reacquainted with the forest. Fortunately for both men, Sebastian knew exactly where he was going, and Steve was more than happy to rely on his knowledge of the forest.

Walking in the forest is an awkward, if not cumbersome experience for a man of normal height, but to travel in the dark forest when you are only ten inches tall, is a different ballgame. An average size limb becomes a log, and a small gully suddenly appears as the Grand Canyon. Steve was doing exceptionally well for a newcomer to the ten-inch world, not to mention the fact that his shoulder was not yet completely healed. But, to watch Sebastian maneuver over around and through the tangles of undergrowth, was artistic.

He was a man of age even for a Spelon, but he moved with the grace of a gazelle. It was obvious that he could have traveled much faster, had he not had to wait for Steve to catch up.

"How much further?" Steve asked, while pausing to catch his breath. "It seems like we've been walking for miles."

"Just up the hill and into the awaiting valley." Sebastian's voice was calm and tireless. It was as though he hadn't even started walking. "We should be there in another fifteen minutes."

"Thank God!" Steve puffed. "I just hope I can make it up the hill. I won't have any trouble going down into the waiting valley. That part should be a piece of cake. Speaking of cake, I wonder what your lovely lady has prepared for dinner tonight. I'm getting a bit hungry. How about you?

"Now that you mention it, I think I did hear my stomach sound out its demand for a tiny morsel." Sebastian answered, with a broad grin that crept from one side of his bearded face to the other. "We'd better get going. It's almost six o'clock now, and if I know my Isabel, she will have dinner sitting on the table promptly at six. I promise you, my boy, she will accept no excuses if we are late. So my good friend, unless you wish to suffer the wrath of the high-tempered Isabel, you'll get up this hill and in a hurry."

Steve laughed and started up the hill, following behind the surefooted steps of his new friend and mentor. They reached the cave opening minutes later, and Sebastian moved back a small shrub to reveal the narrow opening into their home. 'After you, my good man." He said, and gestured for Steve to enter before him. Once inside, they were able to make their way around a narrow passage and into a larger room. From the larger vestibule, Steve could see the light coming from beyond the next bend.

"How are you able to keep this system so well hidden?" He asked. "I know these woods are hunted extensively. Someone has to discover the opening sooner or later."

"Well, we've had some close moments." He answered. "But, remember the opening is really rather small. It is much too small for the average size man to enter. The shrubs are rather large and conceal the opening quite adequately. But, if all else fails, and it has once or twice, and we find an intruder who is determined to excavate our opening, we bring in the secret weapon.

"Secret weapon!" Steve asked. "What secret weapon?"

'I told you that we enjoy making friends with the animals that inhabit the forest. Remember?"

"Sure, I remember."

"Well, there is this cantankerous old woodchuck that occupies a burrow a short distance from here, and he has, at the appropriate time, scurried out of the underground network through our opening. The outside intruder, seeing the woodchuck, makes a mad dash for the forest. They are quick to assume that the woodchuck is the only one living in this underground condo. So you see, we are very safe down here, and its quite comfortable too. Come lets eat."

They rounded the corner and made their way down the steps into the large grand room of the cave network. There were thirty or forty men and women milling about performing various tasks. One man, by the name of Leif, with a graying beard and a shiny bald head, was bending over a large round pipe, that appeared to be a conduit system of some sort. Obviously a heating and cooling repairman, Steve thought, even in the cave you can't get away from it.

A lovely woman with graying hair and a plump round face walked up to Steve and Sebastian. She was a small woman, not more than eight inches tall. Dang, Steve thought, this is something, only two weeks ago I was thinking of people who are five or six feet tall. Now, I am looking at this lady and thinking of her as normal height. That's scary. Maybe I'm becoming a Spelon. That might not be too bad, he pondered. It sure is a lot simpler lifestyle down here. You don't have to worry about taxes, insurance, house payments, or any of that stuff. Humm! Could be something to think about.

"Good evening, Rose." Said Sebastian. "How are you this fine evening?" "Oh I'm just wonderful." Rose replied. "But you won't be if you don't get yourself home, and I mean soon. Isabel has been looking for you. I think she has your dinner ready, and you know how she hates to wait."

"Oh my Yes I do. Fear not, we are on our way."

They walked through the central room politely speaking to most of the people and climbed the stairs leading to the corridor that was their home. Steve led the way up the stairs. As he sat his foot down at the top of the stairs and raised his head, his gaze fell upon the face of Sebastian's daughter, Gabrielle. For a brief moment, all Steve was able to do was stare at her. He was certain that she was the most beautiful creature he had ever seen. The eyes, the hair, the complexion, was perfect, everything about her was perfect.

"Good evening sir." She said. Her soft gentle voice floated through the cave air as though it had wings of its own. "I certainly hope you are hungry. Mama has prepared a delicious meal and has been waiting for some time. And, as father well knows, the colder the food gets, the hotter her temper gets."

"Oh flapstacks!" Sebastian said, with his loud and dominating voice. "I'm not afraid of your mother. Besides she's all talk." An obvious note of humor was drifting between the two, as though an old familiar joke was once again being shared. The smile on the lips of

Gabrielle told Steve, that she know quite well who was in charge of this family, at least when it came to the household items.

"How is your shoulder?" She asked Steve, as they walked side by side toward the dining area. "Much better." He answered. "I think I'll be as good as new in a few days." It was hard for Steve to concentrate on the conversation, while looking into the face of Gabrielle. There was a special magic about the deep dark blue liquid pools that were her eyes. Her long black hair fell over her shoulders and curved below her neck to frame her chin. It was the face any artist in the world would dream of painting. Had Mona Lisa been this beautiful, DeVinci would have married her.

For a brief moment Steve's imagination took control. What would it be like to spend his life in a cave, especially if he were married to Gabrielle? A loud cough from Sebastian brought him back to reality, just as Gabrielle placed her hand on his right arm and pointed toward the dining table. "Here we are." She said. "Have a seat, and we will serve dinner right away."

Sebastian sat at the head of the table, with Isabel on the right and Gabriel on his left. Steve took his place at the foot of the table facing his host. After a brief prayer, Sebastian said. "Lets enjoy this delicious meal that my lovely wife has worked so hard to prepare."

"I'm afraid I can't take all the credit." Isabel chimed in. "Gabrielle helped prepare most of it. She is becoming quite the little cook Papa." "You'd better not take too much there, Steve." Sebastian said. "You don't want to become Ill."

"Papa!" Gabrielle exclaimed. "That's not funny. I am a good cook. Just taste it and you will see."

Steve joined Sebastian in a hearty laugh, as his knife sliced effortlessly through the delicious looking cut of meat waiting on his plate. He didn't recognize the meat from its looks, but it appeared to be chicken. He sliced off a thin piece and tasted it. His taste buds were pleasantly awakened to the familiar flavor of garlic and herbs, but the meat was still a mystery.

"I give up." He said. "This is delicious. I'm guessing this is chicken, or maybe even rabbit, but at this point, I really don't care. If it tastes this good, I'll eat it."

"Isabel answered with a smile. "Its venison its been cooking in a special sauce. That's what gives it that unique flavor."

"Venison!" Steve said in surprise. "So that is what I was hunting when I got shot. Well, it is certainly worth the hunt, but not worth being shot for." Gabrielle laughed, as she quickly picked up her cloth napkin and held it over her mouth in an effort to hide her smile. Once again Steve caught himself staring into her deep blue eyes.

"Needless to say, a deer lasts us quite a long time." Sebastian said. "When you are our size, food goes a long way. As a matter of fact, that deer that we are having this evening was killed in September. It was a yearling doe. That's another reason for the flavor. The young does are the absolute best for eating. Their bodies are tender and the meat flavor is not tainted by the presence of the testosterone and adrenaline that the bucks will always have." Steve asked. "How have you kept it fresh for almost three months? I know its cool down here, but the meat would have gone bad by now."

"You must think we live in the eighteenth century." Sebastian answered. We are highly civilized and well organized. Our technology is state of the art. We have a cooling system in one of the rooms that is designed to keep foods, especially meats, at a constant 33 degrees. At that temperature it is just above freezing and will stay fresh for several months. Besides, even though we are only ten inches tall, some of us have rather large appetites. And, when one person brings in meat, we all benefit from it.

This deer was killed by a young teenager. It was his first kill, I believe. The entire colony has been feeding on it for over two months now, and there is still plenty left. So eat up, my boy, and enjoy your meal. Steve ate and ate without realizing how hungry he was. It was obvious that he was getting stronger, as his appetite was definitely returning.

He laid his silverware in his plate and pushed himself away from the table. "Oh, that was wonderful." He said. "I can't remember when I have eaten as well or as much. I must go for a walk to help it settle."

"Good idea." Sebastian agreed. "Gabrielle, why don't you show our friend around the community and introduce him to some of our friends." A stirring of excitement began to grown in the pit of his stomach, at the thought of sharing the evening in the company of the lovely Gabrielle. "That sounds like a great idea." Steve agreed. "I hope I'm not imposing." "I'll be my pleasure." Said Gabrielle. "There are many people that have been asking about you. They are all curious and anxious to meet you. Shall we go?" She rose from her chair and held out her hand. Steve took her hand into his and held it softly. The skin was as smooth as ivory and as soft as silk. He noticed her fingernail polish. He wondered where they might get nail polish out here in the middle of the forest, but he knew better than to ask. It was obvious that this was not your ordinary group of cave dwellers.

"We'll return shortly." She said, with a glance back over her shoulder. He held her hand as though her were afraid to let go, afraid that he might loose sight of her. He realized that he could look at her forever. She led him out of the dining area and into the adjoining hallway. They passed two girls about the age of Gabrielle in the hall, and Steve saw them giggling. "That's Megan and Hannah." Gabrielle said. They are two of my best friends. They smiled and hurried away. Steve chuckled.

"I wanted to ask your father about the man I saw working on some kind of ductwork system earlier." Steve said. "But, it slipped my mind. What was that pipe he was working on?" "That was either our fresh air supply duct, or the heating system. It depends on which line and where it was located." She replied. "Come with me, and I'll show you how they work."

They walked through the main room, nodding and speaking briefly to the people that were still working. The number of people working and milling around had diminished considerably. Must be home eating, he thought. Steve knew that it was dark outside, and it is supposed to be dark inside the cave, but this room was so well lit, it was unbelievable.

"I have another question." He said. "Where does the electricity come from? Are you robbing a line nearby or what?" "Heavens no!" Gabrielle exclaimed, with a little giggle. "We generate our own electricity. I'm not for sure exactly how it works, but I know it has something to do with the decomposition of the forest biomass. It produces some kind of gas, and the gas is then burned to produce heat and steam. I know there is a turbine involved in the system somewhere, but again, I can't explain all that technical stuff. I don't know for sure. You'll have to get Otis to explain that to you. He is the resident electrical engineer. All I know is that when I turn on the switch, the lights come on, and that makes me happy." Steve shook his head. "This is unbelievable. I am truly amazed.

"Well, there is still a lot more to see." Gabrielle said, still holding onto his hand. "Follow me." She led the way up another set of steps and into a small corridor. "This tunnel leads to our fresh air port system. As you know cave air tends to be a bit damp and stale. This system solves that problem by ventilating the cave system with fresh air and piping out the stale." "Your right." Steve acknowledged. Come to think of it, it doesn't smell like a cave in here. It smells fresh."

Gabrielle squeezed his hand slightly and said. "Here we are. Watch your step, its a little steep going down here." She stepped down into a small room containing some sort of fan system. She waited at the bottom of the narrow steps, as Steve finished his climb. He was much too interested in the fan system, and failed to notice the final small step. Before he could react, he fell forward. He tried to grab the archway with his right arm, and the pain shot through his shoulder like a knife. He let out a groan and fell into the waiting arms of Gabrielle.

She stumbles backwards before catching her footing and preventing Steve from hitting the floor.

"Are you alright?" She asked. The tone of her voice was that of concern, but she was obviously shaken. "Did you hurt your shoulder?" As Steve regained his footing, he realized that he was resting in the arms of Gabrielle. He had come to rest with his right foot and left knee firmly on the ground. His left hand was on Gabrielle's right shoulder, and his right hand was resting on her hip. He raised his head, which had landed against her chest, and looked up.

Suddenly he was thirsty, thirsty for those liquid blue eyes. He could drink of her beauty for eternity. He had heard her ask him a question, but he was unable to answer. They simply gazed at each other. One by one, his senses began to return. His sense of smell came to life and he suddenly became fully aware of her clean fresh scent. It was not of perfume, or of things artificial. It was just clean and inviting. It was an odor that had no description, only that it was pleasant, and he could have inhaled her forever.

The sense of touch returned with delight, and he was aware that he was holding onto her and she to him. He slowly rose to his feet, but refused to release his hold on her. For what seemed an eternity, they stood gazing into each other's eyes. Finally, she said. "Are you okay? Did you hurt yourself?"

The sound of her voice brought him back to sudden reality. It was a reality to which Steve was not yet ready to return. "Oh!" He said. "Yes. I'm fine. I guess I'm just a little clumsy. That narrow step caught me by surprise. I hope I didn't hurt you." "No. No. She answered. "I'm just fine. Maybe we'd better get back. It is getting late, and I know you must be getting tired." "Right." Steve said, as they stood there looking deep into each other's eyes. No words were spoken, but much was said. He took her hand, and they turned and left. The long walk back to the house was mostly silent.

CHAPTER 19

The engine speed of the Olds increased slightly as Sheila placed the gearshift in park. A second later the four cylinder engine was silent, as she turned off the ignition. She sat for a moment in the quiet darkness of the car. Only the occasional pop and crack of the engine cooling rapidly in the winter night air broke the silence. The porch light over the door was on, and the lamp in the living room had automatically come on. I sure am glad Steve installed that timer on the light switch, she thought, there's nothing worse than coming home to a dark house. It's even worse when you have to come home alone.

She had sat longer in the car than she had meant to, and her eyes had become accustomed to the darkness, causing her to squint for a brief moment, when the dome light came on. She stepped out of the car and onto the pavement. The warm sun, that had bathed the area in warm mid-winter relief, had melted most of the snow from the drive, and the night air managed to dry up what little remained. At least she didn't have to worry about slipping on the ice, while carrying the grocery bags inside. She looked at the bags in the back seat and decided that she would have to make two trips.

Needing one free hand to open the door, she was only able to carry three bags the first trip. Sheila pushed the door open with her foot and stepped into the warmth of the house. The light in the living room made her feel safe. She kicked the door shut and flipped the kitchen light on with her elbow. The bag containing the milk was growing heavy on her fingers, forcing her to hurry and set it on the table. She released the plastic bag and shook her hand in an attempt to relieve the cramp that was trying to make itself known. Where is Steve when you need him, she thought, he should be carrying in the rest of those bags. Can't think about that now. I've got to do it myself, at least until he returns.

She walked up the steps with the last load of groceries and started to open the door, when suddenly, she was seized by the same feeling that had given her such fear at Wal-Mart. She turned quickly and scanned the street. Nothing unusual caught her eye. The same old cars were parked in the same old places, and the same old shadows that were always there was all that she could see. I've got to stop this she mumbled to herself, this could drive a person insane. Once again she kicked the door shut behind her. This time there was no sunlight to reflect off the lens of the binoculars that watched her as she carried the last load inside.

Her arm began to ache from the weight of the bags just as she sat the last bag on the dining room table. "Ouch!" She said aloud, and rubbing her arm. "I'm getting out of shape. I'd better start working out again." She was still rubbing her arm, as she flipped the lights on in the dining room. Tonight would be a good night to listen to some oldies. The radio, which sat on the kitchen counter was always tuned to WRGK, the old time king of rock and roll. A quick flip of the switch and Diana Ross and the Supremes filled the room. The sweet sound of their harmony was soothing her raveled nerves and telling her to 'Stop in the Name of Love'. "Ah," she said. "That's more like it." She swayed to the music and kept perfect rhythm as the put the groceries away.

The music was loud, very loud. She didn't hear the door open. The doorknob turned slowly making very little noise. A strong powerful hand reached inside and grasped the inside knob firmly. The heavy wooden door eased open only enough for him to pass through.

The heavy boots left a temporary impression in the thick carpet. The impression would be long gone before anyone would ever see it. The hand shut the front door quietly, then, reached for the knob to the foyer closet. The closet door opened with out incident, and he was able to step inside and crouch down. The camouflage hunting suit he was wearing provided little help in concealing his form inside the closet. If someone were to open the door, they would certainly see him. The large powerful hand slid quietly to the side of his boot. Strapped to his leg was a large hunting knife. The thumb moved quickly, as it had done before, and a quiet snap released the shining steel blade from its sheath. He held the knife in his right hand, close to his chest. He held the knife just in case he might need it. With his left hand he checked the deep pocked of his combat fatigue. It contained the plastic bag, which he patted several times. "Got everything I need, he thought, soon she will be mine. He waited.

Sheila finished putting away the groceries, while Jerry Lee brightened her spirits with 'Great Balls of Fire'. She flipped the kitchen lights off and danced her way into the living room. She stopped suddenly and looked at the door. Had she forgotten to lock the front door? That doesn't seem like something she would do, but after all, she did have an armful of grocery bags. Oh well, she thought, and opened the door to take a quick look outside. All was quiet. She closed the door and locked it. The safety latch made a distinctive click, as it slid into place. She felt safe, not as safe as when Steve was home, but safe enough. And, she was getting braver.

The sudden chime from the grandfather clock standing in the corner of the living room echoed through the house, and caused Sheila to jump. The clock chimed nine times, the last note blended with the music of Roy Orbison singing 'Pretty Woman'. She glanced at her watch. "I've got time to take a shower and watch some television before I go to bed." She said to herself, as she turned the overhead lights in the living room off. The living room took on a dim romantic glow from the lamp over the TV. She stood for a moment remembering the many romantic evenings she had spent in here with Steve. They would snuggle on the couch and watch a movie.

If it were an unusually romantic or sexy movie, Steve would start to act out the part of the leading man. As the scene progressed, they would invariably end up on the floor for an intense night of passion. That's what she loved about Steve. He was such a spontaneous man and such a romantic. She didn't let the thought linger or try to embrace it. It only saddened her even more. Better to think about something else.

She turned and walked down the hall to the bathroom. The fluorescent light flickered, before coming to life and bathing the tile floor with that dull white light that she so hated. She flipped the switch on the wall heater and the coils began to crack and pop to life with a bright red glow. She shut the door and walked down the hall to the bedroom. The shades were already pulled, but Sheila was not satisfied. She had to check to be sure. Feeling confident that she was well hidden behind the shades, she began to undress. She removed her terrycloth bathrobe from the closet and slid it over her naked shoulders before returning to the bathroom. Sheila paused at the door to the bathroom. She thought she heard a noise coming from the living room, but changed her mind. I'm not going to start that stuff again, she thought, and stepped in the bathroom and shut the door. From the time that she and Steve had first married, neither of them ever locked the bathroom door. They were very open and relaxed, and it did not bother them to have someone in the room while they were bathing.

She turned the shower on to let the steam fill the room, then turned and looked at herself in the large mirror. She had definitely aged during the past few days. The dark circles that framed her eyes were certainly not there two weeks ago. And, there was no doubt, that if she searched hard enough, there would be some new gray hairs mixed in among the blonde.

The white terrycloth robe slid down her shoulders and into a pile on the floor. She stood there naked staring into the mirror, again thinking of Steve. A large tear began to burn her eye, as it filled to overflow. The sorrowful drop flowed gently down her cheek and hung for a brief moment on the curve of her chin. The tiny droplet clung to her skin in utter desperation, before letting go and falling to her breast. She lowered her head and began to cry. The hand towel beside the sink became the dam to stop the flood of tears. They flowed for less than a minute, before she could regain control. Every now and then, she thought, it helps to just let go and cry. She wiped the last of the tears from her now red eyes and once again looked at herself in the mirror. "Oh great." She said. "Now I not only have circles, but swollen red eyes to match. Might as well take a shower.

She slid the curtain back and stepped into the tub. The warm water immediately started working its magic on her tired and tense muscles. She turned her back to the stream and let the drops of relief cascade over her shoulders. She stood there for several minutes enjoying the moment. It was so relaxing that she felt she could go to sleep everything around her became distant—silent.

She did not hear the bathroom door open, nor did she see the eyes that peeked through the small crack. The curtain was translucent allowing the light to pass through, but her image appeared to be bathed in a cloud of mist. But, still the eyes watched, enjoying the vision that stood naked before him. Not how, he thought, he would wait. He waited.

After what seemed an eternity, Sheila turned the water off and slid the curtain back. She reached for the towel hanging on the rack beside the tub. The steam that filled the room had also clouded the mirror. She did not see that the door was slightly ajar, nor did she see the eyes that were devouring her naked beauty. She dried herself off and wiped the mirror. As she dropped the towel and turned to close the shower curtain, her back was toward the door. She did not see nor hear the door ease shut. By the time she finished dressing and ready to leave, the door was closed.

She flipped the light off, as she left and walked back into the living room. The large grandfather clock was only seconds away from chiming the half hour. She would have enough time to watch the last few minutes of Prime Time. She stopped by the kitchen first and poured a cup of hot chocolate, before sliding into the large recliner. It was Steve's favorite chair. The material even smelled like him, she thought, as she laid her head against the soft back.

Diane Sawyer was reporting about something dealing with drug trafficking in New England. After finishing about half of the hot chocolate, a sleepy haze started to creep over her, and drugs in New England was not interesting enough to keep her awake. She turned the TV off, before checking the front door once more. Locked tight, she mumbled to herself, maybe I can get a good night sleep. I sure am tired.

The small lamp beside her bed gave just enough light for her to find her way to the closet, where she hung her robe. She made here way to the bed and collapsed. With the light out, she was soon sound asleep. She heard nothing. The large black boots moved silently across the carpet, as they inched their way down the hall to where Sheila slept peacefully. He stood for a moment in the doorway to the bedroom. The street light outside funneled enough light through and around the blinds to softly light the room. He could see her lying quietly beneath the covers.

He slid his hand into the deep pocket of his camo suit and removed the Ziploc plastic bag. Quietly opening the bag, he removed the cloth. He placed the empty bag on the dresser and stepped quietly to the edge of the bed. She was so beautiful, he thought, and how she was to be his. The cloth came to rest just below her nose. After a couple of breaths, she turned her head and rolled over onto her side. He waited a few brief seconds then returned the cloth to her face. She breathed deep and long. After several seconds, he placed his hand against her neck and checked her pulse. "Perfect." He said, in a deep quiet voice. "Perfect."

When he was sure she was asleep, he slid the covers from her limp body. She was wearing a nightshirt that barely covered her hips. The soft curves of her legs were exposed. He twisted the rod on the blinds, and they opened allowing the full light from the street lamp to bathe the room. He had planned to take her with him back to his house, but after seeing her in this light, it was more than he could stand. Tonight she was his. He dropped to his knees beside the bed and held her face with his powerful hands. He softly kissed her on the forehead and on the cheek. He loved her, and this was the only way he could have her. Tonight she was his.

He pulled his vehicle into Sheila's driveway and left the motor running. The heater was on warming the interior. He had dressed her in her housecoat, put a winter coat on her shoulders, and wrapped her in a blanket. It was necessary to throw her over his shoulder to open the living room door, as well as the passenger door to his vehicle. With Sheila resting firmly and safely in the passenger seat, and the seatbelt around her, he returned to the house to tidy things up. He made the bed, turned out the lights, and closed the door. The cloth was used to wipe all the doorknobs to remove any trace of fingerprints. Locking the front door was a final measure. He was sure now, that everything was perfect. No one would ever know what happened to Sheila Mason. She would be his for as long as he wanted. Everything was perfect.

As he stepped off the front porch and started toward the car, his motion was halted by a frightening bark. He heard it first, coming from around the side of the house. It was a low deep growl, followed by four or five loud barks. As he moved closer to his vehicle, he could see the dog. A large black dog was standing at the corner of the house. It appeared to be barking at something near the ground. He was sure the dog was not after him. With another step toward the vehicle, the dog lost interest in whatever was beside the house and charged. He made a mad dash for the vehicle. His thumb missed the push button on the handle the first time, and he wasted valuable time. With a second effort, the button released the latch, and the door swung open, just as the dog opened its mouth. The moisture from the saliva glistened on the large canine teeth, as the mouth came closer to his leg. The huge mouth was about to clamp shut on his ankle, when a huge black combat boot came to rest firmly on the nose of the attacking beast.

The pain was instant and intense. It caught the dog by surprise and caused it to let out a loud cry. The dog sat back on its hind legs for a brief moment and shook its head. This gave the man in the combat boots just enough time to get inside the vehicle and slam the door. The dog was still sitting, as he drove away. He glanced back over his shoulder and said. "Now, everything is perfect."

The two pair of small eyes were only able to see a portion of what had just occurred. But, it was enough.

CHAPTER 20

The temperature of the air at an altitude of 250 feet is considerably less that that on the ground. That temperature compounded by the flight speed of a red tail hawk, produces a wind chill factor that might have given Otis and Daniel frostbite. Their clothing, however, was made of rabbit fur and duck down and proved to be more that adequate in maintaining their body heat. The natural body heat produced by the efforts of the huge bird beneath them added the necessary warmth they needed.

As they soared overhead, the lights from the city of North Ridge came into view. The schoolyard and football field were the most prominent visible landmarks. As the huge bird soared onward, the courthouse in the center of town came into view.

"There's the courthouse." Daniel said. "Which way from here?"

Otis looked at the map and answered. "We follow main street west out of town, then keep your eyes peeled for the K-mart store. We'll turn left on tenth-street. That should lead us out of town and into the subdivision, where the house is located.

As the powerful wings of the friendly raptor carried them along main-street, a large parking lot came into view. The enormous red "K" on the front of the building left no doubt as to where they were.

"Does that look like a K-Mart to you?" Daniel asked, with a smirk. "You're the college graduate." Otis replied with a chuckle. "I'm only the lowly plumber. You are the one with the flying skills. Now get this bird down there where we can see what's going on. Otis guided the bird closer to the ground. They were close enough to read the street signs.

"Tenth Street!" Otis exclaimed. "That's the one we're looking for.

"What's the name of the subdivision?" Daniel asked.

"Um, something about windmere or grassmere or some kind of mere." Otis chuckled. "But, it should be the first subdivision on this road."

In less that a mile, a blue and white sign with an arrow pointing to the entrance to Grassmere Park, came into view. "Looks like the right place." Otis said. "Here we go."

Daniel leaned forward into Otis's shoulder and said. "Okay, when the road forks, you need to bear to the right. That's the place up ahead. The second street to the right, and the last house on the right is our destination. There! There it is. Get lower. Wait! Who's that coming out of the house?"

"I don't know." Otis answered. "I don't know anyone in this subdivision, except Steve, and he's not here right now." "Circle around the house and land. We've got to get on the ground and find out what's going on." Daniel suggested.

The hawk landed softly in the short winter grass that blanketed the back yard. Otis commanded the bird to wait he obeyed. They moved swiftly to the back of the house and hid within the shadows. Otis led the way around the side of the house, with Daniel following close behind. The side of the house was very dark. The rays from the street lamp lit up barely half of the front yard and none of the side. They stood side by side, as they peered around the corner of the house.

Someone was carrying a large bundle. It appeared to be wrapped in a blanket. He carried it to the passenger side of the car and placed it inside. It was obviously a person. "Who do you suppose that is?" Otis asked. "Which one?" Daniel answered. "The one being carried, or the one doing the carrying?"

"This is no time for your feeble attempts at humor." Otis answered, with an obvious lack of amusement. "Do you suppose that's Steve's wife in the front of that car?"

"Well, Steve did say that she was blonde and good looking." Daniel answered. "But, its much too far from here to tell much about her, except that she s blonde."

"What about the man doing the carrying, any ideas?"

"Beats me!" Otis answered. "But, lets try to get a good…."

His last sentence was interrupted by the thunderous bark of a huge dog. The bark was promptly followed by a low guttural growl. Otis and Daniel turned about in time to stare into the exposed teeth of a very large and very unfriendly black dog.

"You take care of the dog." Daniel directed. "I'll try to get closer and get a good look at the man." Otis took a deep breath, closed his eyes, and began to concentrate. As he opened his mind and released his thought energy, the dog stopped barking. The telepathic impulses traveled in waves through the air and into the brain of the dog. The thoughts from Otis began to fill the dog's brain with nonverbal, yet totally understood commands. The big black dog tilted his head from one side to the other and gazed quizzically into Otis' eyes. The growling had stopped, but was replaced by a look of puzzlement, that crept over its face. He looked as though he were trying to figure out why he no longer wanted to kill the small creature in front of him. The dog then began to understand what the commands actually were. He was confused and unsure why, but he suddenly had the mad impulse to attack the larger man that was about to enter the vehicle.

Like a flash the large canine was in pursuit of the man that was walking toward the vehicle. Its eyes focused on the lower leg of the tall human. He was about to open the door, when the dog mad his attack. Its teeth were poised to clamp down hard around the man's ankle, but his efforts were stopped short. As the dog looked up, he saw the sole of the man's boot that was about to smash his nose. The pain was swift and intense. It attacked every nerve in the poor dog's body. He released a loud cry and fell to the ground, unable to focus and unaware of what had really happened. He shook his head and tried to clear the water from his nose and eyes. As the senses were about to clear, he received a message to the brain. It was clear and concise. There was no mistake in the command, attack again.

The dog rose to its feet in obedience, staggered slightly, and made another charge. He hit the side of the vehicle, just as the door slammed shut. The big engine fired to life, and the vehicle backed out of the drive. The dog was left standing, with a small trickle of blood oozing from one side of his nostrils. He turned and walked back to the side of the house.

Otis and Daniel stood waiting for their newfound friend to return. The dog limped around the corner and stood gazing at the two small men, with a somewhat stunned look. Otis began to communicate with the dog once again. He praised him for his obedience and patted him on the head. The dog enjoyed the attention and responded with a lick. The huge tongue caught Otis by surprise and washed his left arm and the side of his face with a generous supply of doggie saliva.

"Oh man!" Otis exclaimed. "I hate it when they get overly appreciative. Now look at this. I'll smell like dog breath the rest of the night." "He just likes you." Daniel said, with a distinctive chuckle. "He wants to be your friend." Otis raised one eyebrow and gave Daniel a cold glare and said. "Ha, Ha, very funny. How about I tell him to give you a nice big juicy lick right across the fact. After all, he is still listening to me, you know."

"Never mind. Never mind." Daniel said in a hurry. "No need to get mean now. Just tell him to go home and wait. We need to try and find that guy that just drove off."

Otis closed his eyes and told the dog to go back home and rest. He told the dog, that he would be back soon. The dog turned and trotted off into the darkness.

"Quick!" Daniel said. "Get the bird, we've got to follow that man if at all possible." Otis called the raptor from its perch and they climbed aboard. With several powerful thrusts of its mighty wings, they were once again airborne. "Which way did he go?" Otis asked.

"The same way we came in. Just follow that road until we find the vehicle. He can't have gotten very far." They followed the road out of the subdivision and onto tenth-street. "Which way from here?" Otis asked. Do we go back to town or toward the hills?"

"If I were leaving someone's house in a hurry with a bundle in my front seat, I don't think I would be headed into town." Daniel responded. "I think I'd take my chances on the back roads. Hang a right here."

Otis headed the bird in the direction away from town. The direction they knew, would lead into the hills surrounding the city. They had flown no more than a couple of miles, when they spotted the right vehicle. "Is that our man?" Otis asked. "I think so." Daniel answered. "Look he's going to make a turn. Get closer, we don't want to lose him now." The bird banked to the right and started to descend. As they approached the vehicle, Otis was able to see inside the passenger window.

"Yep, that's them." He said. "Lets follow." The hawk circled twice to regain its altitude, then followed the vehicle as it traveled through the night. They watched the headlights, as it made a couple more turns, before coming to a stop in front of a log cabin. Otis guided the bird to a large oak tree on the edge of the clearing that was the yard to the cabin. They sat on the limb and watched. It was too dark and too far away to make out any facial features. All that was visible was the man's camouflage clothing and the blonde hair of the woman in the blanket.

After stopping the vehicle, he ran to the cabin and unlocked the door. Moments later, they saw a light from inside the cabin, and the small dim porch light come on. The porch light was dim and barely able to shine through the winter night mist. He ran back to the passenger's door and opened it. He reached inside and pulled the limp blonde body out of the seat and into his arms. They could tell she was unconscious by the way he was carrying her. She was as limp as a rag. Otis wondered if she was dead, and the same thought passed through Daniels brain at the same time.

Otis looked at Daniel and said. "I don't think she's dead. I can't imagine anyone carrying a dead body into the cabin. If she were dead, I should think he would be looking for a place to bury the body."

Moments later the door closed behind him and the porch light went out.

"What do we do now?" Daniel asked. "Do we go down for a closer look, or do we go home?" "This guy means business." Otis said. "I think we'd better get back and develop a new plan. We know where he is, and I don't think he plans on leaving any time soon. I'm relatively sure he didn't see us. So, as far as this guy is concerned, he got away with only a dog as a witness."

"Good thinking." Daniel agreed. "Besides, I'm getting cold. Lets get home. It's getting late."

The bird dropped from the limb and filled its wings with wind. Several strokes later, it had gained the altitude necessary to sore effortlessly through the heavens. The wind whistled past their ears, as they glided toward home, home to Spelonia.

CHAPTER 21

Clayton Mills was just about to pour his second cup of coffee, when the phone rang. His deputy, Robert Ames, had not yet arrived for work, and he was beginning to get a little upset. That second cup of coffee was just the remedy his ragged nerves needed. He hadn't been sleeping well these last few nights, and it was beginning to take its toll. Indigestion was most likely the problem his dinner just wasn't going down like it should. He was up twice last night hunting for the Rolaids. And now, having to do everything this morning with out that lazy Ames wasn't helping the situation at all. The loud ringing of the phone caused him to shake just enough so that a small splash of hot coffee landed on his hand. "Ouch!" He shouted, as he sat the coffee pot and his cup down on the desk. "The heck with it."

His hand was still burning slightly, as he reached for the phone. "Sheriff's office." His voice was stern and all business. The level of his irritation could definitely be noticed in his tone. "Sheriff Mills speaking."

The voice on the other end of the line was unfamiliar to him, but it spoke in a calm and clear tone. "Sheriff, my name is Michael Davis. I'm the manager at Pizza Inn, here in town."

"Yes, Mr. Davis. How can I help you?"

"Well Sheriff, it seems that one of my employees has failed to show up for work today. Now I know that isn't normally that unusual, but Cindy is one of my most dependable employees, and this is the second day she's been out. I've called her house and there is no answer. Her friends haven't seen her, and no one has heard from her. I went by her house, but it was locked. The car was in the drive, but no one came to the door. I'm very concerned Sheriff, and I would appreciate it if you would go by her house and check it out."

"My deputy is on his way in right now, sir. I'll head out there as soon as he gets in."

"Thanks Sheriff."

Clayton Mills replaced the receiver and once again turned to examine the burn on the back of his hand. It was already beginning to turn red. Without thinking, he turned his right hand over and gazed at the scar that covered most of it. The sight of the scar kicked the access memory of his brain into rewind, and the night he acquired that burn flashed onto his memory screen.

The call came in at about ten-thirty. There had been a horrible auto accident out on highway 52 heading east out of town. He drove like a maniac to get there, almost loosing control of the patrol car on more than one occasion. When he arrived, there were several people standing around. The ambulance had not yet arrived, and he knew it was all up to him. He threw the gear shift into park, while the car was still moving, and it came to an abrupt halt rocking back and forth. He opened the door without waiting for it to stop moving and ran to the two vehicles that were now welded together at the radiators.

"Over here Sheriff!" A voice screamed from behind the back car. "I'll be right there." He shouted. "There's a woman in this car." The front car was a light blue Chrysler K-car, with a young woman trapped behind the wheel. The steering column had collapsed against her legs and pelvis, but she said that she was not in any severe pain.

Her seatbelt and shoulder strap had prevented her from becoming a human projectile and traveling through the windshield.

"Sheriff! Get over here now. There's a baby in this car, and I smell gas."

The sheriff raised his head and looked in the direction of the voice. It was Ralph Wheat, a farmer that lived nearby. "Hurry!" Ralph shouted then disappeared behind the car. Clayton ran around the cars where Ralph was waiting. There was a small child, a little girl about two years old, sitting strapped in her car seat.

"Where is the driver?" He shouted. "Who was driving this car?"

"The mother is lying over there Clayton." Ralph said. "She's cut up pretty bad, but I think she'll make it. Its this baby that I'm worried about." The baby was in the back seat and the car was smashed together from the impact. It was a two-door model, and the font seat was jammed against the back seat, making it impossible to get to the baby. Clayton could reach the seat and touch the baby's leg, but could not get to the harness and release the child. He too could smell the strong presence of gasoline.

"Wait here with the baby Ralph." He said. "I'm going to my car to get the hydraulic hack. Maybe we can jack this seat up enough to get me inside."

Just as Clayton turned and headed toward the patrol car, he heard the noise. It sounded like a huge clap of thunder. It was less than a second later, that he felt the heat surround the back of his neck. The hair on his head was blown forward about his face, and he fell forward onto the ground. A quick glance at the two cars, brought the horror of the situation to him with a sickening reality. There were flames leaping out from under the hood of both cars, and it was spreading.

Clayton got to his feet and started toward the cars, when a violent scream changed his direction. Ralph lay several feet away from the cars. He was engulfed in flames. The sheriff reacted on pure instinct and dashed to his aid. He grabbed Ralph's feet and ankles and began to roll him on the ground, in an attempt to extinguish the flames. He looked over his shoulder at the young girl standing frozen with fear, as she watched him roll the burning man on the ground.

Clayton screamed at her from the top of his lungs. "Quick, go to my patrol car and get my coat out of the back seat. Hurry!" The girl stood motionless for a brief second, as though the sound waves traveled much slower in the heat of the situation. When the command finally registered in her brain, she made a dash for the car and grabbed the jacket, and not a moment too soon.

Clayton was able to extinguish the fire that had threatened Ralph's life. He left him lying on the ground with the jacket over his shoulders, and ran to the Toyota. There was no time to get his jack from the car. The flames were moving toward the interior and would soon be inside swallowing the little girl. He had but one option. The .357 magnum revolver slid effortlessly from its holster, as Clayton grasped it firmly in his hand and drew it over his shoulder. With all the strength he had, he brought the butt of the gun down against the side window. His arm vibrated as the gun bounced off the glass causing no visible damage. He changed his angle and brought the gun down again. This time it was almost at a 90 degree angle, but again proved to be useless. What now, he thought. The glass was much stronger than he had expected, and time was running out. The final option flashed into his mind, as he moved to the back of the window. He carefully aimed the .357 through the rear side window at the back of the driver's seat. The air was shattered by the explosion from inside the chamber of his Smith and Wesson revolver, and the glass from the side window fell into thousands of pieces. The butt of the gun made a perfect hammer, with which to remove the remaining bits of glass that clung tenaciously to the rubber seal.

With his gun securely holstered, he climbed into the back seat of the Toyota. In the background, he could hear the unmistakable sound of the ambulance sirens approaching. Thank God, he thought, the cavalry is on the way. The windshield was still holding most of the flames at bay. There were a few brave tongues of fire trying to advance around the edge of the doorway and secure a foothold inside. He had precious little time, and he knew it. The child was conscious, but obviously in shock. She did not move or cry, she only stared at him.

The car seat had done its job and held her securely in place, but the force of the impact on her small body was obvious. Without some immediate help, she wouldn't last much longer. He released the harness, which surrounded her head and shoulders. He eased it back over her head, careful not to do any further damage to her. He eased her forward, and she fell lifeless into his arms. He gently lifted her from the seat. The windshield was still holding, but Clayton instinctively placed the little girl against his chest, with his back to the approaching inferno.

He thought later, that God must have been doing the thinking for him that night, for no sooner had he pulled her firmly against his chest, than then car was shook by the implosion of the windshield. He was surrounded by heat, and he knew that the flames would be biting at his heels soon. As he moved closer to the window, a voice from outside brought him peace of mind.

The paramedic standing by the window with outstretched hands was screaming. "Hand her to me quick." Clayton passed the small child through the broken window and into the waiting hands of the paramedic. As soon as they were away from the window, he dove through the opening. The dive did not exhibit the grace of an Olympic diver, but rather the force and effort of a man in fear of his life.

He hit the ground with a thud and began to roll. He was still lying face down when the gas tank of the Toyota exploded. The rear tires leapt more than a foot off the ground before settling back to the ground. They were already on fire and starting to melt. Two other paramedics had removed the girl from the K-car, only moments before the explosion. It was no small miracle that no one died that night. Ralph suffered third degree burns on about 20% of his body, but he was alive. It was not until Clayton had checked on the condition of each person involved, that the paramedic noticed the severe burns on the back of his right hand and arm. He had undoubtedly received the burns, when he was trying to extinguish the flames that covered Ralph.

"What's up chief?" Deputy Robert Ames said, as he slammed the office door behind him. The sudden loud noise brought Clayton back from the past to face the current reality. "Where in the Sam Hill have you been? This is the third time in two weeks you've been late, and I've got work to do. You'd better get your act together, Ames, or there will be one more in line at the employment office, and a job opening in my office. Now stay here and catch the phone. I've got some investigating to do." The anger in Claytons voice was obvious, as he stormed out of the office and got into his squad car.

Sheriff Mills settled back into the seat of the patrol car and took a deep breath, letting his temper subside. I've got to get a grip on this stuff, he thought, I let all this get to me way too easy.

The huge 454 cubic-inch engine roared to life at the command of its operator, and pulled out onto the highway. The thought suddenly occurred to him that in his anger and frustration, he had forgotten to get a description of the girl, nor did he know where she lived. I can't believe this, he thought, I'm slipping. Looks like I'm the one that had better get his stuff together. I'd better go by the Pizza Inn and get the info I need from that manager.

"She's blonde, about five-four or five-five, twenty-two or three. She is a very attractive young lady." Michael Davis explained to Sheriff Mils, as he carefully noted the information. "Has she had any arguments or disagreements with anyone lately?"

"Heck no! Not Cindy, she gets along with everybody. All the customers like her. That's why I have her working the register line. She talks and smiles at everyone, and between you and me, she brings in a ton of repeat business. No, definitely not, no one had anything against Cindy."

"Now, where does she live?" Sheriff Mills asked.

"Out on Wood Tick Road. I think the number is 338, but I'm not totally sure. It's a little white house with several large trees in the front yard. Her car will be sitting in the drive. It's a little red Geo, I think." He answered.

"Thanks." Clayton said. "I'll check it out and let you know what I find. By the way, where do her parents live? She's not from around here is she?"

"No." Michael answered. "She's only staying here while she finishes her college studies. I think her home is somewhere in East Tennessee. Seems like it was around Knoxville. I'm just thinking out loud, but I can find out for sure if you need me to."

"Why don't you do that, and I'll get it from you later. Thanks for your help." Sheriff Mills folded the flap on his notebook and turned to leave the restaurant. The smell of the freshly baking pizza made its way to his nose, and it made him realize that he was suddenly a little hungry. I'll get a bite on the way, he thought.

The bright red Geo Metro was parked in the drive of the small white house on Wood Tick Road. The snow had all but melted, and the yard was left wet and soggy. The morning sun beamed down, warming the temperature into the high forties. The cool, but comfortable morning air felt good, as Clayton opened the door and stepped out of his patrol car. He looked around the area and noticed that the nearest neighbor was a good two hundred yards away. The house was barely visible from the road, and he was certain that it would not be seen from the front porch. This was, after all, not the classiest neighborhood in North Ridge.

He surveyed the ground, as he walked toward the house. The water saturation level in the ground was so full, that it had washed any traces of footprints into oblivion. The only tracks in the drive were those of the Geo. The front porch was clean except for a few small smudges of mud. Several loud knocks on the door produced no response. There was no door bell available, indicating that the house must have been built in the late fifties. I guess that people back in the fifties didn't need a doorbell." He chuckled.

He stepped off the edge of the porch and began searching the ground around the side of the house. There was a set of steps that led to the back porch. The steps had small smudges of soil that could have been footprints, but were not clear enough to be of any help. After several loud hard bangs on the back door gained him no answer from inside, he decided to turn the handle. The door slid open effortlessly.

"Anybody home? This is Sheriff Mills. Hello! Is anybody here?" Again he got no answer. He pushed the door open and stepped inside. He found himself in the kitchen area, and it was dark and quiet. An odor suddenly reached his nose. It was the stale odor that develops, when something is shut tight for a time. But, there was another odor mixed with the staleness. It was something stronger, more acrid and harsh to his senses.

There was part of a pizza sitting on the kitchen table. It was dry and hard, and the aroma that had made it so appetizing had long since disappeared. The cheese that was once hot and stringy was now brown and hard as the box on which it sat. He passed by the pizza without a backward look. The hallway was dark and quiet. He glanced down the hallway toward the bedrooms. A survey of the living room was useless, as it was as empty as the kitchen.

The hallway was dark and stale, and filled with an odor that crept up the walls and into his nose. His brain tried to match the smell with something familiar, but no match could be found. He pushed the door to the bathroom open. It made a faint squeak, as it swung back on its old hinges. The bathroom was empty. Only the slow drip of the shower greeted Clayton, as he stepped inside for a closer look. Satisfied with the search so far, he proceeded down the hallway and peered inside an empty bedroom. The last room at the end of the hall was the last room to search. The door was shut tightly, keeping secret anything that was happening or might have happened behind it. The knob turned with ease in his hand, but the door refused to surrender its prize so easily. He held the knob firmly in his hand and leaned his shoulder against the door. The doorjamb, which had swollen slightly from being closed, popped and cracked, as it released its grip.

A small amount of light filtered through the tightly closed blinds. Narrow bars of dusty light painted streaks of white across a motionless body. In the faint light, Clayton was unable to tell if she were asleep or dead. He shouted. "Hello! Miss, this is the Sheriff. Are you alright." He got no response. With a flip of the switch, the room was filled with light and horror. As the light fell across her face, it became obvious to the Sheriff, that she was not asleep. The odor was much stronger now, and it rose to grip his throat. A sickening feeling stirred in his stomach. He approached the bed with dread and apprehension.

She was only partially clothed, but the sheet had been pulled over her left leg and covered most of her back. Her eyes stared into an empty space. They were glazed and frozen in time, never to enjoy the light of day again. His fingers loosely closed around her wrist. It was cold and limp. He raised her arm and released it only to see it fall effortlessly to the bed beside her body. Clayton Mills was no forensic specialist, but the dark pools of settled blood, that had collected on the back of her arms and along the side of her legs, was a clear indication, that she had been dead for several hours. Rigor mortis had already set in, served its purpose and diminished, leaving the body once again limp and lifeless.

He sat on the edge of the bed staring into the once lively face of the beautiful young girl that now lay wasted. The word "why" kept flashing across his mind. Why would anyone want to destroy such a beautiful young girl, with so much left to offer? She was only slightly older that his own daughter, who would be twenty on her next birthday. This could just as easily be here laying here, he thought, and a cold chill started at the base of his spine and continued upward until his entire body shuddered at the thought.

Clayton knew that there was a mother and father somewhere that he would have to call. How do you ever tell a parent that their little girl is dead? Where would he ever find the right words? He didn't know her parents, but his eyes began to burn for them at the thought of their great loss.

He stood up and wiped his eyes. Glancing around the room, he saw the phone. As he reached to pick it up, his investigative sense kicked in and told him to stop. "Fingerprints!" He muttered to himself, better not touch a thing in here. He walked back to the patrol car and radioed the office. Deputy Ames answered on the first call, which surprised the Sheriff. After giving the deputy orders to contact the coroner and give him the location, he leaned back against the car door and took a deep breath.

He looked at the burn on his hand, which was still tender, and said. "Well, might as well start looking for clues, cause I don't think he's gonna find this to be a suicide." He grabbed his camera, and made a pass around the house pausing at the back steps. The mud smudges on the porch could have easily been footprints. He took several shots of the smudges then went back inside to the bedroom. More light was necessary, so he opened the blinds and turned on the lamp beside the bed. He would wait for the coroner before examining the body. For the time being he could concentrate on the rest of the crime scene. Everything seemed to be in its proper place. There was no sign of any struggle, as a matter of fact, it appears as though she simply fell asleep and never woke up.

A search of the closet and dresser revealed nothing unusual. Even the small rocking chair beside the nightstand appeared to be in its normal place. He sat down in the rocker to think, staring at the body and trying to imagine what might have happened. As his gaze traveled along the edge of the bed, something caught his attention.

He immediately fell to his knees and lifted the ruffle edge of the bed. Lying there just behind the dust ruffle was an empty plastic sandwich bag. He removed the ink pen from his pocket and slid it inside the bag. It was an ordinary sandwich bag, but what was it doing under the bed? Maybe she was eating in bed, he thought, but thee was no sign of breadcrumbs or food of any type inside the bag.

What the heck, he thought, might as well take a whiff. The odor was familiar, but he could not identify it for sure. Another whiff was no help. He knew the smell, but could not place a name to it. He laid the bag on the nightstand for the coroner to see then lifted the dust ruffle to take another look. The search produced only some dust bunnies and an old pair of slippers. Funny, he thought, I guess the dust ruffle didn't do its job. They had better change its name.

His thoughts were interrupted by the sound of someone knocking at the front door. "Who is it?" He shouted.

"Its me, Leon Kennedy, the coroner. Is that you Clayton?"

"Yea, come on in Leon. I'm in the back bedroom, all the way down the hall."

Leon joined him and began his examination. He took several photographs and dusted for fingerprints, but none were found. Together they examined the body. There were no sign of any bruises or marks anywhere on the body. "I'll swear." Said Clayton. "It looks like she just fell asleep and died."

"Yes." Leon agreed. "That's what it looks like, but look here." He was using a pair of tweezers to remove something on the sheet just inside her thigh.

"What is it?" Clayton asked. "It's a hair." Said Leon. "And it doesn't appear to be that of our victim. My guess is that it probably came from the last person to be with her, and probably the person responsible for her death. We'll know more after we get her back to the lab and do the autopsy. I'll run DNA test on the hair and see what that tells us. Clayton handed him the sandwich bag and said. "I'm anxious to find out what was in here." "Me too." Leon agreed. "I'll let you know as soon as I can."

They strapped her body onto the cot and loaded her into the back of the coroner's van. As Leon drove away with Cindy's body, Clayton turned out the lights, closed the door, and drove in silence back to his office.

Inside the house where Cindy had died, in the room where Cindy had died, under the pillow on which Cindy had died, the washcloth lay waiting. The last of the chloroform had all but evaporated. It waited to be found.

CHAPTER 22

"Good morning, Mr. Farley." Ruby said, with a smile, as Horace walked blankly past her desk. "Did you hear about that young girl that was found dead in her house? I think it was out on Wood Tick Road someplace. Isn't that terrible. Who would want to do such a thing to a sweet young girl like that, and here in a small town like North Ridge? I just think...."

"Yes!" Horace barked. "I've seen the paper already, and yes it is a terrible shame. Now, would you please bring me a cup of coffee?"

"Certainly, Mr. Farley. I didn't mean to upset you."

"Thank you."

Horace stared blankly at the floor, as he trod past Ruby's desk toward his office. He closed the door behind him and leaned against it. A large breath of air filled his lungs, and his shoulders slumped forward. Why, he thought, why would someone do something like that to such a sweet girl? I just don't understand it.

Ruby knocked gently on the door before saying. "Mr. Farley, I have your coffee. Mr. Farley?" Horace leaned forward and opened the door.

"Thank you, Ruby." He said. "I'll be working on the computer, and I don't want to be disturbed. Is that clear?"

"Very well, Mr. Farley, I'll hold all your calls."

Horace sat the coffee on his desk and picked up the morning paper. The story about Cindy was on the front page. The column heading read: "GIRL FOUND DEAD IN BED. POLICE SUSPECT FOUL PLAY AND POSSIBLE SEXUAL ASAULT." The story was short and rather sketchy. It was obvious that the Sheriff's department had very little information on which to proceed. The paper did say that there was no sign of robbery or a break in. They are working on the premise that the victim knew her assailant.

He laid the paper down and brought the hot coffee to his lips. He gave the hot liquid a complementary cooling blow, then took a long slow sip and leaned back in his office chair. They didn't even give her name, he thought, maybe they haven't notified her parents. Poor Cindy, why would someone do that to her? I'll bet someone came in after I left her and did that to her. If only I had stayed longer, I might have been able to save her life.

He remembered how he had loved her that night, and the warm sweet smile on her face as he covered her and left. Horace sat staring blankly at the computer screen most of the day. He did manage to type Cindy's name on the screen several times just to read it. He sat most of the day trying to imagine who could have done such a horrible thing.

Sheriff Mills leaned over Cindy's body, as the medical examiner completed his autopsy. "Well, Chuck, what do you think happened?" He asked. "Did she die of natural causes or was she murdered?"

"Well!" Dr. Charles Albright began. This is a tough one. It appears as though she suffocated. The lungs appear to have been starved of oxygen for enough time to cause the brain to die. But, there is no sign of any external force that might have caused it. There is no hemorrhaging of the tiny blood vessels in the eyes that indicate any external trauma."

"How about a pillow or something like that?" Clayton asked.

"Nah, I thought of that, but there is usually some sign of fiber residue in the mouth or nostrils, and she has no sign of any fibers anywhere. Nope, I don't think she was smothered by a pillow."

"Maybe drugs, a pill, or a shot of something. Did you find any signs like that? The Sheriff continued to question the Dr's work.

"I already checked all that out, Clayton." Chuck said, with some obvious irritation in his voice. "Its all negative. I probably won't know any more until I get the results of the samples I sent to the University of Tennessee Medical Lab in Knoxville. The lung tissue and stomach content samples should provide the information I need to give you a more definitive answer. I should hear from them by tomorrow or the day after. "I'll call you as soon as I hear anything."

"Thanks, Chuck." Clayton said. "I appreciate everything you've done. Sorry if I came across a little critical a while ago. You know I trust your work with out question."

"Forget about it." Dr. Albright answered. "That just means you take your work seriously."

Clayton nodded his head, and asked. "Can I use your phone?"

"Sure, help yourself. Its over there by the suction machine."

"Yuck!" Clayton said, as he picked up the phone. "I'm not even going to ask what you suction with that thing."

Chuck laughed, and then returned to his work on Cindy.

"Sheriff's Office, Deputy Ames speaking."

"Ames, this is the Sheriff. Do I have any calls?" "Heck yeah." The deputy answered. "The phones been ringing off the wall with questions about that girl. I ain't said nothing though. All I tell them is that they will have to wait until we finish the investigation. Is that alright?"

"You did fine." The sheriff said, in a somewhat condescending tone. You just keep doing what you are doing. I'll call you when I get to the crime scene." He hung up the phone and said to Chuck. "See ya later Chuck."

Sheriff Mills was on his second trip around the house, when he paused at the side of the house leading to the back steps. The ground was still somewhat wet and soft from the previous melted snow. The soft bed of leaves and winter grass seemed to be undisturbed at first glance. He bent down to examine it a little more closely.

If I wee going to sneak into this house, he thought, I would hide one of two places to wait and this is one of them. I would be out of sight, if someone were on the back porch, yet close enough to climb the steps without being seen from the highway. The other logical place would be below the porch at the back of the steps. "Better check there again." He said aloud, as he stood and stretched his back. The ligaments and tendons of his nee joints loudly voiced their protest and sent their pain of resentment to be registered in the brain. At the same time that persistent pain that began to appear more often in the small of his back decided to make an appearance also. Must be getting old, he thought, I'll have to break out the old Ben-Gay tonight.

The leaves and grass below the steps provided no better clue, as to whom, if anyone, might have waited there. After a careful search, Clayton climbed the steps and once again began gleaning the house for anything that might help. No fingerprints had been collected other than those belonging to Cindy. He stood in the doorway of the bedroom where Cindy had spent her last night. The room was just as he had left it earlier. The bed was empty, and the sheets were wrinkled. The covers were lying back at the foot of the bed, where he and the coroner had left them

Everybody leaves some kind of clue, he thought, as he sat on the edge of the bed. The wrinkled sheets contained small pieces of what appeared to be cookie crumbs. "Well." He said. "I might as well cover the bed. I see no point is leaving it open to the world." He pulled the blankets forward and lifted the pillow. There atop the wrinkled sheets was a white washcloth, which had been folded neatly into a small square.

"Uh Oh!" He said. "What do we have here? Did someone get a little careless?" It appeared to be nothing more than a simple washcloth. But why, he thought, why would she have had a washcloth under her pillow? Oh well, better get it to the lab and hope for something. He carefully placed the cloth in a plastic bag and left.

"It looks like chloroform residue." Chuck said. "The unknown test indicates that the cloth contained heavy amounts of the stuff. There's your murder weapon, Sheriff. Whoever killed this girl used the cloth filled with chloroform to cover her mouth and nose. It would only take a few seconds to put her to sleep. It's quite obvious that she inhaled it for much more than a few seconds. I'll even wager, that when the lung tissue results come back, they'll say the lungs contained massive amounts of chloroform. "I don't think I'll take that bet. I know a sure thing when I see it." Clayton chuckled. "But, that only tells us how she was killed. We still have to figure out who and why."

"Sorry, I can't help you there my friend, but my job is only to determine how. You will have to handle the why and who."

"You're right." The sheriff said. "Its at times like these that I wish I were a school teacher."

Ruby sat behind her desk at the Ramco Corporation reading the newspaper's latest account of the murder of Cindy. Valerie Beacon stood behind her reading over her shoulder. They were both held captive by the words. This is the most exciting thing to happen in North Ridge in years, and it was of the utmost importance to be as knowledgeable as possible, when it came to spreading the latest gossip. "Look here, Val, it says that she was most likely killed by suffocation. "I'll bet he smothered her with a pillow."

"That's not what I heard." Val quickly replied, which was the standard answer to indicate that she was about to reveal some startling news that only she knew. "I heard that he had placed a grocery bag over her head and held it around her neck until she quit kicking. "I'm leaving Ruby." Horace said, as he rounded the corner.

"Oh!" Ruby said, as she jumped and dropped the paper. "Oh my, I didn't see you come by, Mr. Farley. We were just reading; oh, never mind. You're leaving a bit early this evening, aren't you? Got a date with your little pizza girl again?"

Horace stared coldly into her eyes. The gaze entered through her pupils and burned past her retina and directly into the optic lobe of her brain. The stare seemed to last an eternity. It was finally broken by the simple word "No", and then he was gone.

"That's odd." Ruby said. "Two days ago he was so excited about seeing this young girl, now he won't even mention her. He called her his little pizza girl."

"Maybe she dumped him." Valerie said. "After all, he is a little on the weird side, in case you haven't noticed."

"No, he isn't weird. He's just quiet and kind of a loner. After all, he is a very bright man, and I enjoy working for him.

"Well, I'm glad it's you and not me." Val answered, as she turned and walked toward her office. "I'll see you tomorrow Ruby. Have a good night." "You too Val, I'll see ya."

Ruby returned to the paper. I'll finish this article before I go, she thought. Grocery bag! Ha! That's the dumbest thing I've ever heard. I don't know where she gets her information, but it certainly isn't very reliable. 'The body of Cindy Metcalf was found in her home by Sheriff Clayton Mills. The exact cause of death is not available at this time. Ms. Metcalf was employed at the Pizza Inn as a cashier. She is survived by …'

"Pizza Inn!" Ruby said, almost as a scream. "I wonder if she know the young girl that Mr. Farley was seeing? Why, he might have even known Cindy. I'll bet that's why he was so quiet and distant all afternoon. Poor Mr. Farley, I'll ask him about it tomorrow." She folded her paper neatly before turning out the lights and leaving for home.

Valerie had just finished making the morning coffee, when Ruby walked into the lounge. "Good morning Val." She said, with a somewhat detached note to her voice. It was not her usual cheerful good morning.

"Hi, Ruby, what's wrong with you? You sound like you're down in the dumps. Did someone kick your cat this morning?"

"No Val, its nothing like that." Ruby replied. "Its just that something is bothering me, and I can't get it off my mind."

"Well, for heaven sake, tell me what it is." Val answered with the same excited curiosity that killed many a cat.

Ruby began. "Its Mr. Farley. Do you remember how disturbed he was and how differently he acted yesterday just before he left?"

Yeah! So What?" Val answered. "I told you he was weird."

"I know, but that was really unusual. Listen. I read in the paper after you left yesterday, that the girl that was murdered worked at the Pizza Inn. And, Mr. Farley tells me just two days ago, that he was seeing a girl that he called his pizza girl. Do you just think I'm being silly about this Val? What should I do? Should I ask Mr. Farley about it? Maybe he was upset because he knew the girl or maybe it was the same girl? I just don't know what to do?"

"No." Val said. "I wouldn't worry about it. Its probably just his personality, or maybe he has a little PMS."

"Stop that!" Ruby said, with a slight giggle in her voice. "You know that's not nice. Besides, you'll embarrass me." Valerie gave her a big smile and started out of the lounge. "Just kidding." She said. "I've got to get to work. I'll talk to you later." Ruby stood staring out the window and sipping her coffee. I guess it's just me worrying too much, she thought, better get to work.

"Sheriff's office. Deputy Ames speaking. May I help you?"

"Yes deputy. My name is Valerie Beacon, and I have some information that the Sheriff might be interested in. Its concerning the Cindy Metcalf murder."

CHAPTER 23

The large hawk landed gracefully on the soft forest floor, with its passengers safely aboard. The magnificent bird lowered its body and Daniel and Otis slid off. With a single waive of his hand, Otis commanded the large raptor to fly away, and it obeyed. It cleared the tree line with silent effort. The quiet darkness of the forest was shattered by the unmistakable scream of the bird, as it soared over the treetops and bid them farewell.

"The outside world just doesn't understand what its missing, does it?" Daniel asked.

"Nope!" Otis exclaimed. "And, they wouldn't believe us if we told them. Lets go, we have much to report.

The lights from the cave bid them a warm welcome, as they made their way into the main hallway. "Here's Daniel and Otis!" Someone shouted, and a small boy jumped and ran, shouting. "I'll tell Sebastian and the stranger." The two men sat at the large table in the center of the hall. Otis' wife arrived carrying two cups of hot steaming coffee.

"Oh thank you, Elsa." Daniel said. "That's just what I needed." "Me too." Otis agreed. "I'm almost chilled to the bone."

"Would you like something to eat?" She asked.

"Sure would." Daniel was quick to answer.

"How about you Otis, are you hungry?" Elsa inquired. "Maybe I'll get something later." He answered. "Right now this coffee will do just fine." Sebastian approached with his usual broad grin and addressed the two weary travelers. "Well, men, glad to see you made it. Do you have some news to share with us?" Steve was at Sebastian's elbow waiting for some news. The four men sat at the table to discuss the night's findings. The anticipation in the air was as thick as the aroma of the hot coffee.

"Well, what did you find out?" Steve asked. "Is Sheila okay? Did she say anything? What about Jennifer, is she alright?"

"Hold on, my friend. Lets slow down a bit." Sebastian interjected. "We'll answer all these questions directly, but lets take it one at a time. Now Otis, tell us what you have discovered."

All ears were intent on every word, as Otis and Daniel relayed the events of that evening. The look of anticipation on Steve's face slowly faded only to be replaced by the unmistakable look of pain and worry.

"What re you saying?" The words were frozen in fear, as they fell from Steve's lips. "Was she dead? Was she unconscious? Can you find this place again?"

"I don't think she was dead." Daniel tried to ease his worry. "She appeared to be unconscious. I can't imagine him going through the effort to carry her around and bring her back to the cabin if she were dead. No, I'm quite sure that she was alive. Now, as for the location of the cabin, yes, I'm sure we can find it again. If we can't raptor can." Otis added. "But, your daughter was nowhere to be seen. Is there somewhere your wife might have left the little girl for the evening?"

"Yeah, my mothers house. Jennifer loves to stay with my mother. She probably left her with mom." Steve answered.

"Now, Sebastian began. "Is there anyone who might want to do you or Sheila harm for any reason? Have you offended anyone, or made any enemies, that you can remember."

"No! Nobody! We haven't done a thing to anyone. I can't imagine why anyone would want to abduct Sheila. It just doesn't make sense." Steve said, then turned and asked Sebastian. "How soon can I return to normal size? I've got to get to town, and find out what's going on. I have to find Sheila. She needs my help."

"I understand." Sebastian said in a calm soothing manner. "I'll have Isabel examine your shoulder in the morning, but I don't expect you will be able to stand the transformation for several more days. In your weakened condition, the change could easily kill you, and if the shoulder is not completely healed, it could disrupt the healing process altogether. You were just lucky you made it the first time, but I had no choice in the matter at that time. Besides, the second transformation is much harder than the first, and more painful. The third is almost unbearable, and you know what happens during the forth. So don't get your hopes up."

"Then I'll go like this. I'll go as a Spelon. If Otis and Daniel will go with me, I'm sure we can handle this guy." The fire was evident in Steve's voice. Sebastian replied. "I admire your courage and ambition, Steve, but I'll ask you to put aside your emotions and listen to me with your head, not your heart. I know how much you love your wife and the worry that consumes you now. But, a wise warrior never attacks adversary without having full knowledge of him. We need to know about his strengths and weaknesses. We need to where and how to attack. My goodness, my boy, we don't even know for sure who this person is.

My suggestion is this. Otis and Daniel will go back tomorrow. They will get inside the house and try to make contact with your wife. They will observe the man and the location, then return with the information. We can then plan our next move. We have more than forty men here who are willing to help you rescue your wife. But, first we must know what we need to know. Does anyone have any questions?"

No one spoke. The four men sat staring at each other. No words were necessary. It was evident, that when Sebastian spoke in that tone and with that authority, no one was expected to ask any questions. It was obvious why he was the leader of the group. Steve felt some comfort in his words, and for a brief moment began to feel that everything would be okay.

"Now, we must rest. Tomorrow we have much to do." Sebastian directed, as he rose from the table. "It's late and my eyes are weary. Good night to all."

"Good night, Sebastian, and thanks." Steve said. "I'll be along in a few minutes. I think I'll sit here for a little while."

"Very well." He answered. "But remember, the more you rest, the sooner you gain your strength."

Steve sat quietly in the near dark hallway, sipping slowly on his cup of cooling coffee. His thoughts were far away from the confines of the cave. It seemed like an eternity since he had seen his wife and daughter. Sheila's image, which was usually vivid and clear in his mind, was now cloudy and faint.

His quiet thoughts were suddenly interrupted, when a small hand came to rest gently on his healing shoulder. There was no pain, only the sense of soft pressure and warmth. He was not alarmed, and for some reason, he knew who it was. He could feel the presence without opening his eyes. With a near instinctive gesture, he brought his hand up to his shoulder and gently embraced the hand that rested there.

"You need to rest." Gabrielle's gently voice floated through the air to invade his thoughts. It was pleasant and inviting. The images in his mind began to melt away and were replaced by the vivid portrait of Gabrielle. He opened his eyes and turned toward her. She stood beside him with eyes, deep and blue, looking at him to soothe his worried thoughts.

"You will heal much sooner if you rest." She said.

"I know." He answered. "I was just sitting here thinking. So much has happened in the past few days. Much of it seems like a dream. Its hard for me to determine what is real and what is only imagination."

She consoled him saying, "I heard the news that was reported by Daniel and Otis. I know how worried you must be, but at least your daughter is safe, and soon your wife will be safe too. Daniel and Otis are good man and will do whatever is necessary to rescue her."

"I know, and I can't thank them or any of you enough for all that you have done for me. I'll never be able to repay my debt to this community. It's just that I feel that I should be there with them. I feel so helpless sitting here waiting."

"As I said, you need to rest. Mother said you were healing nicely, and you should be at full strength in only a few more days."

Steve interrupted. "I may not have days. I have no idea what this man has done or will do. He is obviously one sick individual, and for all I know he may have already killed her. That's what makes the waiting so hard, not knowing."

He looked into her eyes and realized that he was still holding her hand. Her hand was soft and cool in his. Her fingers were small and delicate, and her skin was the color of ivory. He stood staring into her eyes, drowning in the two liquid pools that left him totally helpless. He could neither speak nor move.

"Come!" She said. "I'll walk you back to your room. We have a very busy day tomorrow." She turned and led him from the hall into the corridor. They walked side by side, still holding hands. Steve was in no hurry to release the comfortable grasp of her hand.

"Sleep well, Steve Mason." She said. "May only happy dreams fill your night?" She leaned forward and kissed him on the cheek, then turned and left. He watched as she disappeared into the darkness of the cave. Her sweet fragrance lingered for several minutes after she had vanished from his sight. Lying in bed, he realized how tired he really was, and sleep overtook him. He dreamed. Gabrielle. The following morning Steve awoke to the familiar sound of Sebastian's form and commanding voice. "Time to arise my friend. Otis and Daniel are about to leave, and I'm sure you will want to wish them God Speed on this journey."

"Sure thing." Steve answered. "I'm on my way. I'll be right there." He dressed quickly and dashed into the hallway. A large group of Spelons was milling about performing various duties in preparation for the days activities. Sebastian waived to him from the far corner of the hall.

Otis and Daniel were with him, dressed for the outdoors and obviously ready for their journey. Steve made his way across the large hallway amid a barrage of good mornings and hellos from most, if not all of the busy spelons.

As Steve approached the three men, he paused and said. "Otis. Daniel. I can't express to you how much I appreciate what you are doing for me. You are truly brave and courageous men."

"Not so loud." Daniel joked, with a sly grin. "The rest will hear you, and we'll have a reputation to live up to. Besides, we are doing absolutely nothing that you would not do for us. That is if I am any judge of character."

Steve replied. "I just hope I am able to repay you someday."

"Otis quickly interrupted. "Lets hope you never have to repay anything. Come Daniel, we must be on our way. We have much ground to cover and our ride is waiting."

As they emerged from the cave opening, a frosty winter wind filled their lungs, and the bright winter sun filtered through the barren limbs of the majestic oaks and bathed the forest floor in broken light.

"Ah!" Sebastian roared. "Nothing like filling your lungs with clean forest air. It makes a man glad to be alive on a morning like this."

"Right." Daniel said. "But, remember, that it will be about twenty-five degrees colder up there in the air, than it is down here."

"You've got that right." Otis agreed, as he settled himself aboard the back of the large Redtail hawk. "So Lets get going." The two men were whisked away on the wings of the raptor, high above the maples, the tall poplars, and the mighty oaks, toward the city of North Ridge. They were unaware of the danger that awaited them and unaware that the mighty bird would return with a much lighter load.

From his perch on the limb, Otis could see the vehicle parked in the driveway of the cabin. It was still early, and there was no sign of any movement inside the cabin. The smoke from the chimney circled lazily above the cabin and disappeared into the branches that hovered over the small house. The building was no more than thirty feet by twenty feet, and the front porch ran the length of the cabin. The steps to the porch were on the side, but from their location, Otis and Daniel could not see if there was a back porch or even a back door.

"Do you think he's awake?" Daniel asked.

"It doesn't appear as though anyone is awake yet, but lets not take any chances. You wait here and keep a lookout." Otis said. "I'll try to get a look inside. We make no noise from this point on. We will communicate with our minds, so keep it clear."

"You got it." Daniel said with a grin. "My mind is a total blank."

"Very funny!" Otis chuckled. "Your mind is a total blank most of the time. Now keep your eyes open."

Otis climbed back onto the bird and gave it the proper instructions. The bird obeyed. Moments later he was dismounting on the ground below the back porch. He listened carefully, but not a sound could be heard from inside. Otis moved with the stealth of a cat in search of its prey, and made no sound, as he made his way up the stairs and onto the railing. He settled for a spot beside the back window. The location gave him a fair view of the inside kitchen area.

It was dark and quiet. The only light was from the windows. A table sat in the center of the room, with a bottle of catsup and a saltshaker claiming their ownership of the entire tabletop. Two chairs sat empty beside the table. The chair closest to the window had a shirt hanging on the back. It was a brown man's shirt with two pockets.

"Are you getting all this? Otis thought. "Its very quiet inside."

"I understand." Thought Daniel. "Just be careful. Everything is still quiet out front."

"There's a window on the back side." Otis thought. "There is also a plant hanger beside the window. I think I can rope the hanger and get a look inside. I'll let you know when I get there. He swung the rope over his head and released the lasso. It landed surely and swiftly around the flowerpot hanger beside the window. Ah ha, he thought, the old boy's still got it. He began his climb up the rope.

From his perch beside the window, he could see into the small room. It was obviously a bedroom with one small bed against the wall. There on the bed was the woman they had seen being stuffed into the vehicle the night before.

"She's here." He thought. "She's lying on the bed."

"Is she alive?" Daniel thought.

"Can't tell." Otis answered. "She isn't moving, and the window is too dirty to tell if she is breathing. I don't see any sign of the man. I think I'll wait here for a few minutes. I want to see if she moves. There is no point in trying to save the life of a dead person."

"Good idea." Daniel answered. "I'll keep an eye on the front."

Otis had just positioned himself comfortably in the support arm of the hanger, when he heard a noise from inside the bedroom. He sat motionless and watched. A man walked into the dark bedroom and stood beside the bed. His back was to Otis, preventing him from seeing his face. He was dressed in brown pants and a brown shirt. He leaned over the bed and placed his hand along the side of the woman's neck, as though he were checking her pulse. After several seconds, he removed his hand and lifted the woman's arm. He reached into his back pocked and removed a pair of handcuffs. He locked one firmly around her small wrist, and the other he attached securely to the bedpost. He stood motionless for several seconds, then bent and kissed her on the forehead. He left the room without looking back. She never moved.

"Daniel, did you understand that? She is alive. He has her cuffed to the bed, but can you believe this guy, he kisser her on the head. I think he has stolen himself a bride. This guy is one sick ticket." Otis thought.

"I understand." Daniel replied. "What do you suggest we do now?"

"I'm not quite sure what our next move should be. Lets give it a few minutes and see what he does first. She isn't in any immediate danger. The guy kissed her, for heavens sake, so I don't think he's gonna come in and kill her any time soon. Let's be patient."

They waited. Daniel sat perched in the fork of the tree watching the front of the house, while Otis rested patiently on the support arm of the pot hanger and watching the woman on the bed. She lay motionless for several minutes. Just as Otis's leg was about to fall asleep, she began to move her head from side to side. Her free arm came to her head and she began to rub her eyes. As her hand came away, Otis could see that her eyes were open, and she was looking around her new cell.

"Daniel, listen. She's waking up and looking around. She just now realized that she was handcuffed to the bed. She's trying to sit up. Nope, not going to make it. She laid back down, must have gotten dizzy. Wait! I think I hear him coming. Just listen. He's saying something to her, but I can't make out what it is. She's starting to cry and shake her head. He's leaving."

She sat on the side of the bed with her head resting in the palm of her free hand. Otis could see that she was crying, but he was unable to help or console her. All he could do for now was to watch.

"Wait, Daniel, he's coming back. Oh, this guy is a real sweetheart. He's bringing her some breakfast. It looks like some super thick oatmeal. She's turning her head from side to side. Its pretty clear to me that she isn't going to eat that crap. I can't blame her for turning her head; I wouldn't eat it either. That creep! Forget it she isn't going to eat. Good, he's giving up and leaving. I guess we can wait a while longer."

Otis noticed his shadow against the side of the cabin, as the morning sun shown over his shoulder. He watched his shadow slowly slide down the rustic brown logs, as the sun rose higher in the sky. Minutes passed.

"Here he comes again, Daniel. I wonder what he has planned this time?" The man entered the room, again with his back to the window. But, Otis could see his hand behind his back, and gripped firmly in his hand was a small white cloth.

"What's he going to do with that?" Otis thought.

"With What?" Daniel asked. "What's he got? What's happening now? Speak up man, I can't follow your thoughts."

He's got a small towel in his hand, and he's folding it behind his back. I have no idea what he plans to do. We'll just have to wait and see. No sooner had Otis completed his thought transmission, than the man grabbed the woman behind the head and pressed the cloth firmly over her face. His large hand filled with the cloth completely covered her nose and mouth. She began to struggle, kicking and grabbing at his wrist with her free hand, but her efforts were useless. He was much too powerful for her, especially in her already weakened condition. The struggle lasted no more than twenty or thirty seconds. The woman's free arm fell limp to her side, and her head fell back into his hand. Her mouth was open and her eyes were half closed. He eased her back onto the bed.

Otis watched as the man removed the handcuff from her wrist. He checked her pulse and placed his hand beneath her nose to make sure she was still breathing. He gently let the back of his hand trace a line against the soft curve of her face and down her neck. He ran his fingers through her hair, then leaned forward and lightly kissed her on the lips.

"Daniel!" Otis screamed. "This monster is trying to kiss her. He thinks she is his bride. Oh, man, I can't take this Daniel. I'm going in. This guy is a dead man."

"Hold it Otis, hold on." Daniel thought. "I know how you feel, but you're no match for him. Not now, not yet. There is nothing we can do. We have to wait for the right time and the time is not now." Otis shook his head. He knew Daniel was right. He had no other choice but to wait. He sat quietly on the pot hanger with his fist in his mouth to keep from screaming, as he watched.

After what seemed an eternity, the man rose from the bed and left the room. Otis sat on his perch and watched. A tear rose to the edge of his eye and spilled over onto his cheek. The sorrowful droplet slowly traveled down the rough and furrowed face only inches, before his hand came up and wiped it away. His hurt for her was replaced by anger for the evil man. He had never hated a man as much as he hated this man with no face.

"Otis! Otis! Can you hear me?" Daniel asked. "He's coming outside. He is stepping off the front porch and heading toward the vehicle. He has a cap on so I can't see his face, but he is getting into the vehicle."

The sound of the engine as it roared to life echoed off the trees and shattered the quiet of the winter morning. A small trail of dust boiled up from the tires, as the vehicle sped down the narrow roadway that was the entrance to the cabin.

"He' gone Otis. What do you want to do now?" Daniel asked.

"I don't know how much time we have." Otis replied. "Lets move fast. I'll climb down from here. You summon the bird to get you, and we'll meet on the back porch." "You got it." Daniel replied.

Moments later the two small men were standing on the back porch of the cabin discussing the best plan for gaining entrance. "If I throw a rope over the doorknob, I can lift you up so you can open the door." Otis suggested.

"Sounds good to me." Daniel replied. Its time to do the cowboy thing." Otis tied a large knot in one end of his rope and sailed it over the doorknob, then lowered it back to the floor. "There you go!" He said. "Just like they do it out west. Now tie this around your chest, and I'll raise you up to the knob." Daniel secured the rope under his arms and snugly around his chest. He gave the rope a good tug, then looked at Otis and said. "Okay, pull when you get ready."

Otis began to pull on the rope, in an effort to lift Daniel to the knob. It was much harder than he had expected, as the rope did not slide easily over the neck of the doorknob. "You could help a little by trying to climb." Otis exclaimed. "After all you're not exactly as light as a feather you know."

"I'm trying." Daniel grunted. "But there's nothing to grab onto."

"Move over to the edge of the door and use the logs as a foothold. It should give you some leverage. Daniel obliged, and with a little effort, was able to begin his ascent. Soon he was able to reach the knob and give it a turn. Much to their surprise, the door opened with little effort. "How lucky was that!" Daniel said, as he slid down the rope and onto the porch.

"Quick!" Otis said. "Lets find the girl and see if there is anything we can do before he gets back." The two men swiftly made their way through the kitchen area and into the room where Sheila lay unconscious. With the agility of a mountain goat, both men were able to climb onto the bed. They stood beside her face staring at her.

"Any suggestions on how to wake her up?" Otis asked. "Not yet." Daniel answered. "Lets see if we can shake her and get some kind of response." Daniel tapped her on the cheek and lips, while Otis lifted her eyelid. "Forget it." Otis said. "Stay here with her, I'll be right back." "Where are you going?" "Out back into the woods. There must be some 'Rats Vein' out there. I think it might bring her around a bit sooner." "Go for it." Daniel said. "She's in good hands."

Otis leapt from the bed and onto the floor. In a flash he was out of the room and into the forest searching for the plant that might help the woman. He was so intent on his search, that he never heard the vehicle, as it approached the cabin. Daniel waited inside, patiently stroking the forehead of the unconscious woman. This must be Sheila, he thought, she is every bit as lovely as Steve described her. I can certainly see why Steve is so very anxious to get you back. His thoughts were interrupted by the sound of the front door slamming shut. "Oh no." He thought. "Otis, do you hear me? Otis! The man is back. He's in the house. We must hide now."

Daniel leapt from the bed onto the floor and scurried under the bed. No sooner had he dashed from sight, than the man entered the room. He stood beside the bed, which afforded Daniel an excellent view of his boots. They were black combat boots. The toes were scuffed and scratch, from many days of use and abuse. This guy has been into some heavy thickets with these boots on, he thought.

"Daniel, Daniel. Are you okay?" Otis thought. "Yes. I'm under the bed looking at the biggest pair of combat boots I've ever seen. This guy has a foot like a bear."

"Just stay out of sight and wait for an opportunity to get out. Maybe we'll get lucky and he'll leave again."

Daniel sat patiently waiting and wondering. Wondering what the man was doing just standing by the bed. Moments later the man turned and left the room. He had no idea where the man had gone. It was obvious that sitting and waiting was his only option. The quiet time gave Daniel an opportunity to think about his family back in Spelonia. He had never married, so Sebastian and Isabel were his only family. He loved Gabrielle like a daughter. He had often thought about marriage, and goodness knows he had several opportunities, but he just never took the plunge. He supposed that someday he might marry, but for now he was satisfied. After all, he was only sixty years old, and that's a spring chicken by spelon standards.

Click! The front door opened. He waited and listened. It seemed like an eternity, but finally the door slammed shut. "He's gone." Daniel thought. "I'm going to make a run for it. Otis, did you understand?" Daniel did not wait for a reply from Otis. Instead he made a quick dash from under the bed toward the kitchen. As he rounded the corner and scurried through the living room, he saw no one. He slipped quietly into the kitchen. The door was less than ten feet away, but something was wrong. It was closed. He distinctly remembered leaving the door open for a quick escape, and he knew that Otis would not have closed it.

A sick feeling began to creep into the pit of his stomach. He had obviously made an error in judgment. His only hope was to return to the safety of the bed, where he could hide and wait. As he rounded the doorway into the living room, his worst fears were realized. He was staring directly into the toes of the large black combat boots. Their sudden appearance caused him to pause for only a second, but that pause was long enough to cause disaster.

In an instant a loud crash came down around him, causing him to flinch and close his eyes. When he opened his eyes, it took a moment for him to realize what had happened. The owner of the boots had placed him inside of a small animal cage. He looked up, and for the first time was able to see the face of his captor.

"Otis!" He shouted in his mind. "I'm caught in a trap. Flee while you can. Go for help now. Run Otis." Otis heard his cry, but his instinct was not to run, but to return and fight for his brother. He called for the bird, and she came to his aid. He climbed aboard her broad shoulders and away they flew. He guided the hawk close enough to the back door for him to make a jump for the doorknob. The bird turned at just the right moment and Otis jumped. His arms landed firmly around the knob, and his chin hit with enough force to send a few stars flying past his eyes. Got to hold on, he thought, can't let go and fall from here. After shaking his head several times, he twisted the knob and opened the door. He was able to grab onto the door edge and slide down to the floor. As he charged into the kitchen, he had no idea what to expect, or how to handle the situation. A quick glance into the living room brought his worst fears to reality. Standing there was a huge man holding Daniel in a cage and staring at him through the wire mesh. Otis quickly thought. "Hold on Daniel. I'm going to try something." He summoned the raptor and told her to attack. The bird obeyed without question or fear and flew directly in through the open kitchen door. With uninterrupted flight, she chose a direct path to the man's face. It was her instinct to attack the eyes of any large prey. She knew that without his eyes, the man would be helpless. Her razor sharp talons were poised and ready to bury into the soft tissue of the man's face and rip the eyes from their sockets. But, just as she was about to make contact, the man ducked. Her weapons landed on his scalp, knocking him backwards. He dropped the cage and it fell to the floor with a thunderous bang. Daniel was thrown to the bottom of the cage with such force, that he was knocked unconscious.

The man hit the floor and rolled away to avoid another attack from the deadly bird. Otis decided to let the bird handle the man, while he tried to free Daniel. The cage door was wired shut, with a wire much too stiff for Otis to bend. The veins in his neck and arms bulged to the point of bursting, as he strained the free his brother.

His concentration was broken by the piercing scream of the hawk. The scream was followed immediately by the sound of a loud blast from the 10-gauge shotgun now in the hands of the man. The bird turned and made a dive for the door, just as the pellets of buckshot slammed into the wall beside the door. Otis heard the unmistakable sound of the pump on the gun, as it threw another shell into the chamber. He looked away from the wire in time to see the man turn his attention and his aim toward Otis. He knew he would not be able to help Daniel now. His only hope was to escape and return with help.

He jumped as far and high as he could in the direction of the door. The blast from the gun made his ears ring, and the splinters of wood sprinkled his face, as the buckshot buried into the pine wood floor. Otis hit the floor running and never looked back. As he ran, he called to the bird. Faithful to his command, she was waiting for him at the edge of the steps. He leapt the last few feet like a long jumper in the Olympics and landed squarely on the back of the bird. He looked back over his shoulder, as her wings began to fill with air. He could see the muzzle of the shotgun pointed directly at him, but no shots rang out. He didn't know if the man was out of shells, if the gun jammed, or if the man simply decided not to shoot. He would never know.

As he guided the huge bird back toward Spelonia, he thought of Daniel. He had to get help. He had no way of knowing how long the man would let Daniel live.

CHAPTER 24

Horace was awakened from a semi-sleep by the sound of his doorbell ringing. The echo of the ringing bell had barely left the air, when the sound of a fist banging against the door began. "Just a minute." Horace shouted. "I'm coming. Hold your horses." Horace glanced at the clock above the TV, and saw that it was 11:30. "Dang", he thought "I must have fallen asleep while watching TV again. Who could be banging on my door at this time of night?" His bathrobe gaped open from the top down to the cord that loosely bound it around his waist. He was still rubbing the sleep from his eyes, as he opened the door and peeked out past the safety chain.

"Are you Horace Farley?" The man standing outside the door asked. "Who wants to know?" Horace answered, with a distinct air of resentment.

"I'm Sheriff Clayton Mills, Mr. Farley, and I'd like to talk with you for a few minutes, if you don't mind."

"Why? What's this all about? I ain't done anything wrong."

"No one said you did, Mr. Farley. I just want to ask you a couple of questions. Now, may I come in?"

"Well, alright." Horace grumbled. "But make it fast. It's getting late, and I've got to get to bed. Some of us have to work for a living you know."

"I'll be as brief and to the point as I possibly can." The sheriff answered. "Now can you tell me where you were on the night of December fifth of this year?" "Yes I can." Horace answered with certainty. "I left work late, stopped and got something for dinner, then came straight home. Why? What going on?"

"Where did you stop for dinner, Mr. Farley?"

"I don't remember for sure, I think it might have been Pizza Inn. I eat there quite a bit. I like pizza."

"Do you remember a young girl working at the cash register? She was blonde, about five two, very attractive girl by the name of Cindy. Does that ring a bell for you?" The sheriff's tone was still pleasant, but Horace could tell he meant business.

"Sure I remember Cindy. I spoke to her a time or two. She seemed like a very nice girl. She had a nice smile and a pleasant personality. Why? What's this got to do with me?" Horace asked.

"Did you ever go out with Cindy, or ever ask her for a date?" The sheriff questioned.

"NO!" Horace blurted out with a force that surprised even him. "I mean no. We never dated. I only talked to her as I walked through the line. Why? What's wrong? Did something happen to her?"

"You mean you don't know." Sheriff Mills asked. "Haven't you been reading the papers, Mr. Farley? Cindy is dead. She was murdered, and we're just following up on as many leads as possible. Do you mind if I have a look around your apartment, Mr. Farley?" "Absolutely not." Horace objected. "You have no right to come in here and start prowling through my home and personal belongings. I've told you everything I know about this girl, now I'll kindly ask you to leave."

"Suit yourself." Clayton said. "But I can get a search warrant, and I tend to get a little messy when I have to go through all that trouble and make a second trip out here to see you. I'm much neater, when I just have a look around. Now, how about it? Mind if I have a look around? I'll be as quick as possible."

"Well, go ahead." Horace agreed. "But make it quick. I told you I have to get to bed. Six o'clock will be here soon, and I need some rest." Clayton Mills walked about the room casually looking at the furnishings, but always looking for anything unusual. Horace sat at the table with his hands folded across his lap. "Is this the bedroom?" The sheriff asked. "Yes!" Horace stammered. "But all that's in there is my clothes and my bed. Besides, the room is rather messy."

"I'll just have a quick look anyway." The sheriff said. "It won't take a second." His words trailed off into the darkness, as he searched for the light switch. His hand found the switch, and a simple flick of his thumb filled the room with bright light. He slid the door to the closet open and stood looking at the rod full of clothes. He saw suits, shirts, ties, pants, but nothing out of the ordinary. Everything looked clean and tidy. He was about the close the door, when he noticed a green garbage bag stuffed in the corner. Hum, he thought, what do we have here? He pulled the large bag out of the closet and into the bright light. A red twist tie held its contents safely inside.

The sheriff opened the bag and pulled out a camouflage hunting suit. He laid it on the floor and examined the knees. They were definitely soiled, and the stains were still somewhat damp. It looked like mud and grass stains, but he couldn't be certain. He slid his hand inside the breast pockets and found nothing, but when he placed his hand inside the deep pocket located on the leg, his fingers encircled a small glass bottle. Sheriff Mills withdrew the prize and read the label. 'Chloroform' "Bingo." He said. "Looks like we've found our man."

"What man?" Horace's voice interrupted the silence and caught Sheriff Mills by surprise. He jumped as he turned to face Horace. "Mr. Farley, it looks like I'm going to have to ask you to come down to the station with me for some more questioning."

"Why?" Horace asked. "I've told you everything I know about this girl. What more do you want."

"What I want, is for you to come with me to my office." Clayton said with a much sterner voice. "I've found something in you hunting suit that you will have to explain. Now we can do this the easy way, or the hard way. It really is up to you."

Horace stood firmly and said. "I'm not going anywhere. I've told you everything I know and that's the end of it."

The sheriff stood up and looked Horace squarely in the eyes and said. "I'm afraid that's not the end of it, Mr. Farley. I'm placing you under arrest for the murder of Miss Cindy Metcalf. You have the right to remain silent. If you give up that right, anything you say may be used against you in a court of law....." Horace was escorted out of his apartment and taken to the jail. A puzzled look was frozen on Horace's face, as the cell door slammed shut. He sat on the bunk staring at the floor. He still couldn't figure out why he was in jail.

The next morning Ruby sat at her desk at the Ramco Corporation. She was reading the paper and shaking her head. "It can't be true." She said. "Mr. Farley couldn't have done something like that. He just couldn't."

"What's it say about him?" Valerie asked. "Does it say how he did it?"

"It says here, that he used chloroform to put her to sleep, but he got carried away and gave her too much. She died from the excess chloroform. This just can't be true. He just wouldn't do something like that."

"That's sick." Valerie said. "How could anybody do something like that? Was this some kind of sick perverted love affair he had with her? Well, if he did it, I hope he gets what he deserves." Valerie finished her comments, as she walked down the corridor toward her office. Ruby sat at her desk for most of the day with the paper in her hand, shaking her head.

CHAPTER 25

Jennifer Mason sat beside her grandmother in the front seat, as the car came to a stop in the driveway of Sheila's house. "I can't imagine why your mother hasn't answered the phone, Jen." Mrs. Mason said, as she put the car in park. "Maybe she's still sleeping." Jennifer answered. "She has been really tired lately." "Well, we'll find out in a minute." Said Mrs. Mason. "Come with me. Let's go see what's wrong. Jennifer hopped out of the car and held her grandmother's hand, as they walked up the steps and rang the doorbell. After several rings, Mrs. Mason began knocking on the door and calling Sheila's name. She called several times and got no response. After several moments of waiting, Mrs. Mason turned the doorknob, only to find it locked.

"It's locked." She said. "Now what do we do?" "I know where the extra key is." Jennifer said confidently. "Mommy hides it on the back porch. Come with me Grandma. I'll show you where it is." They hurried around the house to the back deck. A large flowerpot sat in the corner near the house.

"There!" Jennifer said. "Its under that big pot. Just move it over and you'll see." Mrs. Mason tilted the pot back and removed the spare key from its hiding place. The back door opened effortlessly, and she and Jennifer stepped inside. She shouted several more times, as she walked through the house. There was no sign of anyone. The house was dark and quite, as she passed through the kitchen and dining area into the living room. She made her way down the hallway toward the bedroom, still calling for Sheila, as she walked.

The door to the bedroom was only slightly open. "That's mommy's room." Jennifer yelled. "Lets to see if she's still in bed." Mrs. Mason eased the door open and switched on the light. The bed lay empty, and the room was in perfect order. The bed was still made, and it was quite obvious that no one had slept there last night.

"Something's wrong here." Mrs. Mason said. "Lets go Jen. Lets get some help." She hurried into the kitchen and picked up the phone. "Hello, Sheriff's office. This is Sheriff Mills speaking."

"Hello, Sheriff. This is Harriet Mason. I'm Steve Mason's mother.

"Yes, Mrs. Mason." The sheriff answered. "Your son is the one that has been missing for several days. What can I do for you, Mrs. Mason?"

There is something terribly wrong here sheriff. I'm at my son's house, and his wife in nowhere to be found. She left my house about dusk yesterday on her way home, and now I can't find her. It doesn't even appear that she has been here. Her bed is still made, I'm certain she never made it home last night. This is so unlike her, sheriff, but what is more troubling, is that her car is still in the driveway. I think you should come out here right away. I'm terribly worried."

"Sure thing, Mrs. Mason." Sheriff Mills answered. "I'm on my way. Would you wait for me there until I arrive?" "Of course." She answered. "But please hurry." She hung up the phone and pulled Jennifer closer to her. Jennifer put her arms around her grandmother and began to sob. "What's happened to mommy? She asked. "I don't know yet sweetheart." Harriet said, in an attempt to console her only grandchild. "But the sheriff is on his way out right now. He'll be able to help us. Now don't cry. Everything is going to be okay."

The sheriff arrived fifteen minutes later, and knocked on the door. "Mrs. Mason, I'm Sheriff Mills. May I come in?" Clayton Mills followed her into the living room and sat on the couch. He asked her several questions about where Sheila might have gone, or if she had any other friends. "What about her parents?" He asked. "Could she have gone to see her parents?"

"No, I'm afraid both her parents are dead." Mrs. Mason answered. "I'm the only parent she has left. And as for friends, she would not have gone anywhere without letting me know where she was going."

"Thank you Mrs. Mason. Do you mind if I have a look around the house?" The sheriff asked. "Of course not." She answered. "Look all you want."

He made his way down the hall and stopped at the bathroom first. The shower curtain was open and the tub was empty. There was a towel on the floor that appeared to be slightly damp. The sheriff picked the towel up and confirmed his suspicions. Someone had used this towel within the past twelve hours. Everything else in the bathroom looked untouched. He left there and went into Sheila's bedroom. Mrs. Mason and Jennifer followed behind. The bed was as she had said. It appeared as though it had not been slept in. He bent over and picked up the pillow from beneath the covers. The previous day's investigation was still fresh in his memory, but a quick glance under the bed produced nothing. The closet door was slightly ajar, but everything inside looked undisturbed.

Everything in the house appeared quite normal, especially the bedroom. He turned and looked at Mrs. Mason, who was standing in the doorway with her arm around Jennifer's shoulder. "Are you certain she didn't leave with a friend and maybe just forgot to call. Nothing here looks out of the ordinary, Mrs. Mason, and I can't file a missing person's report until she has been gone for 48 hours. Lets give it a little time before we get too upset.

"Do you really think she's alright, sheriff? It doesn't sound like Sheila to do something like that, especially not since my son's disappearance."

The sheriff replied. "If she doesn't turn up by this evening, I'll start an official investigation. How's that?"

"That's fine." Mrs. Mason answered, as she turned and started from the room. As they left the room, Clayton turned to flip the light switch, and something caught his eye. There on the dresser, hidden in plain sight, was an empty sandwich bag. Again, the previous days investigation danced through his mind. He used the pen from his pocket to carefully pick up the bag. He brought it to his nose and gave it a whiff. There was only a faint odor, and he was unable to determine exactly what it was. He retrieved an evidence bag from his coat pocket, and placed the sandwich bag inside.

Mrs. Mason and Jennifer had already left the room, and didn't see anything that the sheriff had done concerning the bag, and that's the way the sheriff wanted it. There was no use getting them upset until he had something more to go on.

"Why don't you take Jennifer back home with you." He suggested. "I'll call you if I find anything new, or of I get any calls about Sheila. "Thank you, Sheriff. Let's go Jen." Grandma said. "We've got things to do." She took Jennifer by the hand and walked to the car.

Sheriff Mills did take a few minutes to have a look around the yard before leaving, and noticed a set of footprints at the edge of the driveway. There was also a set of dog prints in the still moist soil. The shoe print was familiar. It appeared to be a large hunting boot; it reminded him of the print found outside Cindy's house.

He drove back to town and stopped by the lab the first thing. "Check this out for me, when you get a chance, Chuck. I think I might be on to something." Chuck took the collection bag and opened it. A quick sniff, and he glanced at the sheriff. "I know what you're thinking, Clayton, it sure smells like the same stuff. What's up? Have you got another victim?" Chuck asked.

"Looks like we might, but I can't be sure, since I don't have a body. Just let me know what you find out from the bag. I'll be in my office."

Deputy Ames's chair almost flipped backward, as he hurried to get his feet off of the sheriff's desk. The door slammed behind Clayton, and the sound of his footsteps echoed through the office. "Making yourself at home aren't you deputy?" He asked. "Uh, no sir, I was just finishing some paperwork." Ames mumbled. "The prisoners are fine sheriff. No problems, I have everything under control."

"Give me the key." Clayton said. "I want to talk to Farley." The key turned with a loud click that echoed off the barren walls of the old and musty jail cell. The heels of the sheriff's boots announced his approach, as they struck the concrete floor with solid force.

Horace Farley sat up on his bunk and waited for whoever was walking down the hall. He hoped it might be a friend to visit, but his hopes faded, as the face of Sheriff Mills came into view.

"I've got a few more questions to ask you, Mr. Farley, if you don't mind." The Sheriff began. "I've already told you, I don't know anything about Cindy's death. I barely even knew her. We only spoke…."

"Its not about Cindy." Clayton interrupted. "This is about something entirely different. Do you know a lady by the name of Sheila Mason?"

"Of course I do." Horace answered. "She's the wife of a good friend of mine, Steve Mason. You know him. He's the man that has been missing for several days. I think he was on a hunting trip with Tom Phillips. Why? What's wrong with Sheila?"

"Oh nothing as far as I know. I just wondered if you knew her. Do you have any idea where she might be right now?" Now?" Horace exclaimed.

"How in the world would I know something like that? I'm in jail for heaven's sake. Or have you forgotten?"

"Oh no!" Mills said. "I haven't forgotten, and that's where you will stay for quite a while. I just thought you might have seen her lately. Never mind, Mr. Farley, I appreciate the conversation. "Anytime." Horace laughed. "Its not like I'm going anywhere." Horace heard the outer door slam shut. It was an ominous sound that hung in the air for several minutes only to remind Horace exactly where he was.

CHAPTER 26

Sheila awoke several hours later to the sound of her heart beating fiercely through her temples. The single light bulb in the center of the room made large circles about the ceiling, as she opened her eyes. Her right wrist met with an immovable force, when she tried to bring it to her face. It was then that she realized that she was still handcuffed to the bed. She relaxed the muscles in her right arm and brought her left hand up to cover her eyes. Her large brown eyes began to burn with warm tears brought on by her fear and despair.

Several deep breaths later, she was able to open her eyes and once again survey her surroundings. The room was barren except for a single chair in the corner. It was an old wooden ladder-back chair, the kind her grandmother used to have sitting on the front porch of her home. There were no curtains on the dirty windows, and the wooden floor was littered with dust. The large boards that made the floor failed to fit together snugly, and the cracks were filled with months of dust and dirt.

The muscles in the back of her neck burned as though she had a hot branding iron pressed against her flesh. The burning grew more intense, as she strained to sit in an upright position. Her feet came to rest softly on the floor, and her head once again started to spin. She laid her head to rest in the palm of her free hand. The temperature outside was barely forty degrees, and the air in the cabin was rather cool. Despite the cool temperature of the room, tiny beads of sweat began to form on her forehead. She wiped her brow with the corner of the sheet that covered her. After several more deep breaths, the spinning began to subside somewhat, and the room took on a more stable position.

She could see outside into the main room of the cabin. It was quiet and dark. Only the bright rays of the sun filtered through the window and bounced off the floor. She could see the tiny dust particles dashing about in the bright sunlight. Sitting here like this was accomplishing absolutely nothing, she thought, and decided to try standing. At first her legs were wobbly, and the spinning head didn't help matters any. She had to hold onto the bed to keep from falling. After several seconds, the circulatory system regained its balance, and the proper amount of oxygen finally reached the brain. She became stable.

The bed was close enough to the door, that Sheila was able to lean forward and see even more of the main room. It too was dark and empty. What the heck, she thought, I might as well drag the bed a little closer and get a good look. With a firm hold on the headboard, which was a light weight metal tubing, she was able to drag the bed several feet across the wooden floor. Lying on her stomach, she was able to see most of the living room. Nothing! It was empty; not a person in sight. "Hello!" She shouted. "Is anybody there?" She really didn't expect an answer. It was obvious that the house was empty. "Hello." She shouted a second time.

She raised herself to one knee and was surveying the living room for a possible means of escape, when she heard a faint moan. "Who's there? Who are you?" She shouted. "Why do you have me in here? What do you want?"

No one answered. Only silence answered her questions. Then, again the slight moan, followed by a small voice clearly saying, "Oh my head."

"Who's there?" She asked. "Who are you?" She waited for an answer.

"My name is Daniel." The voice replied. "Who are you?"

"I'm Sheila Mason. Where are you? I can't see you."

"I'm down here." Daniel said weakly. "I'm here in this cage."

Sheila pulled again on the bed and was able to move it a few more inches. It was enough for her to get her head around the corner of the doorway. There in the living room, beside the door leading into the kitchen, was a small animal cage, and trapped securely inside was Daniel.

Sheila rubbed her eyes and shook her head. "This can't be real." She declared. "I've got to be dreaming." "No." Daniel answered. "You're not dreaming. What you see is very real. I'm a full-grown man, but I'm only ten inches tall. Please don't be alarmed. The reason I'm here in the first place is to rescue you, but as you can plainly see, things did not go exactly as expected."

"What do you mean rescue me?" Sheila asked. "How did you ever know I was here? And, why are only ten inches tall? Wait! This is crazy. I'm losing my mind."

"Listen to me." Daniel began to explain. "Lets not waste time trying to explain who I am or why I'm here. We have to decide how to get out of here. "I agree." Sheila said. "But how? I'm handcuffed to the bed, and you're in a cage. Now what do you suggest?"

"I don't know yet, let me think a minute."

Daniel took a forceful grip on the thick wire that firmly secured the latch to his cage. He pulled and twisted with all the strength he could muster. "This is more than just soft wire, he said. "It must be some kind of spring steel. I don't know if I'm going to be able to open it."

"The cage has holes in the bottom." Sheila said. "Can you scoot the cage over here? Maybe together we can bend the wire."

"It's worth a try." Daniel answered with a grin, and began to push on the side of the cage. It moved less than an inch. "I don't know." He said. "At this rate it will take me a few weeks to get there. Is there something in the room that you can use as a weapon?"

"No, nothing." She answered. "Just the bed and one chair, and its solid wood. What are we going to do? I'm scared. I'm afraid he's going to kill me. I was unconscious, but I still know what has happened to me. You've got to get loose and help me."

"I'll do the best I can, but let me reassure you. I was not alone in my attempt to rescue you. My friend Otis was with me. He obviously escaped the clutches of this madman, and is right now in route to our community to get help. Your husband included."

"My husband!" Sheila screamed. "What do you mean my husband? Steve has been missing for several days now. What do you know about my husband? Where is he?"

"Well, Mrs. Mason," he began. "It's hard to explain, but take comfort in knowing that Steve did not die from the gunshot wound. He is alive and well and living in our community in the forest several miles from here. He himself would have been here to save you, but he is still mending and was not at full strength. But I'm sure that help is on the way. It is just a matter of time." "But I'm afraid that time is something we don't have." She answered. "And do you realize how ridiculous your story sounds. I find it hard to believe, and I'm looking at you. Anyway, how are we going to get out of here?"

"Well." Daniel said. "This maniac is no doubt in love with you in some twisted perverse way, and you must use this love to your advantage. I suspect he will want to keep you alive as long as possible. I, however, am a different story. The idiot certainly doesn't love me. As a matter of fact, he probably hates the very sight of me. So, I venture to speculate that if either of us is to meet our maker any time soon, it will probably be me. Now if you will excuse me, I am going to try and twist this wire one more time."

Daniel stood for several moments pondering his situation, then said. "You know, it's amazing how certain events in our life change our whole perspective on things. For example, right now all I have left to live for in this world is removing the wire from this latch. My entire existence for the past sixty years has come down to this. If I am able to untwist this thread of steel, I obtain my freedom and my life continues. But, if I am unsuccessful, and the beast returns before I can open the latch, then it's over. This is the first time in my life I have ever faced the possibility of death on such certain terms.

Oh it's one thing to soar on the back of a hawk, or swing over a ravine on a rope, but those are calculated risks. This has been calculated for me. My choices are obvious, and I choose to live." Again, his muscles strained, as he pulled against the steel wire. The veins in his neck swelled to near bursting, as the end of the wire in his left hand slipped over the twist in the other end of the wire. "Yes!" He shouted, and released a loud grunt.

"Did you get it?" Sheila asked, with joyful anticipation. "Are you free?"

"Not quite." He answered. "But I did manage to get one twist undone. I'll catch my breath then try again. I believe I can do it, if he stays gone long enough."

Sheila began to worry about the possibility of the man returning and finding her bed pulled over to the door. "I think I'll move my bed back against the wall." She said. "If he returns and finds me like this, he just might fall out of love in a hurry."

"Good idea." Daniel agreed. "As soon as I am free, I'll come in there and help you get loose. We can then get out of here and find a place to hide until help arrives."

She strained and pushed the bed back against the wall, ten collapsed in exhaustion on top of the wrinkled dirty sheets. It was evident just how weak and tired she was. Within seconds, she was nearing sleep. Her conscious mind gained control a split second before she drifted off. Her eyes fluttered and she shook her head. Can't fall asleep, she thought, got to stay awake. Daniel will escape soon and will need my help. She sat on the edge of the bed and waited.

Daniel's hand slipped on the wire, as he strained to release the second twist. His arm caught on the corner of the cage and tore a large gash down the length of his forearm. "Aaahh!" He screamed, as blood began to seep from the wound. "This is all I need." He moaned, grabbing for his handkerchief hanging from his back pocket. He wrapped the cloth around his arm and pressed firmly. A second look revealed that the cut was not too deep and the bleeding was beginning to subside. He held one end of the handkerchief in his teeth and pulled on the other end. With the bleeding problem abated, he returned to the task at hand.

Daniel took another firm grip on the wires then cleared his mind. I have to focus all my energy on this wire, he thought. I must center all my force on the wire. The flow of blood from his arm began to increase as he strained. He did not ease his efforts, but continued to pull with all his strength. At the moment he felt he could pull no more, the second twist came free. That leaves only the last and most difficult, he thought. Daniel let go of the wire and fell to the floor of the cage exhausted.

"How about it?" Sheila shouted. "Are you free?" "Well, I'm a lot closer than I was ten minutes ago." He said, as his breath continued to rush in and out of his lungs. "I have one more twist to conquer and freedom will be mine. It's only a matter of time."

"Did you see him leave?" She asked. "How long has he been gone?"

"Haven't got a clue." He answered. "I've been out since the idiot dropped the cage to the floor with me in it. The last thing I remember as I fell was seeing the hawk attack his head. I know she nailed him once, but I think I heard a gunshot after that. Things got a little fuzzy then. Anyway, I'm working as fast as I can. With my luck, the creep will come in just as I get the door open."

Large drops of sweat began to fall from Daniel's brow, as he strained against the final twist of steel. It moved less than a millimeter before he had to release his grip. "I don't know how much more I can do." He sighed. "My arms are getting really weak."

"Please keep trying." Sheila sobbed. "Please don't stop. I'm so afraid."

Daniel wiped the palms of his hands against his trousers to dry the sweat then grasped the wire firmly. It moved slightly with his first thrust then stopped. As he felt his strength slipping, Daniel wrapped his wounded arm around the piece of wire to gain some leverage. Blood from the bandaged wound seeped out from under the cloth and ran down the wire. The warm red liquid acted to lubricate the point where the two wires made contact. They slid only slightly, but he could definitely feel the movement. Daniel took a deep breath and pushed. His eyes closed, sweat poured, blood oozed, and muscles bulged.

"Well, I see you're awake." The voice boomed through the quiet room like a clap of thunder. Daniel released his grip and opened his eyes, only to see the man standing in the doorway. His right hand was holding the door and his left hand was holding a large green bag. Daniel released his grip and collapsed to the floor of the cage.

"Glad to see you awake my little friend." The voice echoed. "I think it's about time you and I had a little talk." The floor of the cabin seemed to bounce under the weight of his feet, as they struck the pine boards. His huge hand grabbed the handle of the cage, and Daniel was lifted into the air. From this height he was able to see Sheila lying on her bed, as they passed the doorway to the bedroom. The cage came to rest on the small wooden coffee table that sat in front of the couch. The man sat on the couch and leaned forward, his face only inches from the cage.

"Oh, I see we've tried to open the latch. Not bad." He said. "You almost had it open, didn't you? That's tough wire too; you must be a pretty stout fellow for your size. What's this? Blood? Did you hurt yourself? There was an obvious chuckle in his voice that only served to enrage Daniel even more. Daniel said nothing, but sat gazing into the face of the man waiting to regain some of his strength.

"What's your name?" The man asked. Again, Daniel said nothing.

"Now listen to me little man. It would be in your best interest to cooperate with me, but more important, it would be in the best interest of the young lady in the bedroom. Her life expectancy depends on your cooperation. Do I make myself clear?" He asked.

"Very well." Daniel said. "I'll talk. Just don't hurt her anymore. She has done nothing to you."

"Good!" The man said. "Let me begin by finding out a little about you. Who are you and why are you so small? Are you a dwarf of something?"

"Yes!" Daniel said. "I'm a dwarf, and I live in a home for dwarf's just outside of town. I was walking through the woods when I heard....."

"Cut the crap, little man. I'm no idiot. I saw your friend in here with you, and I also saw him fly away on the back of that hawk. Now, I know that dwarfs don't fly on hawks. So do you want to try again? This time I suggest you tell me the truth, or would you like to see the little lady loose one of her fingers?" The man pulled a large hunting knife from the sheath on his hip and slammed it down with force into the table. Daniel could see the tip of the blade as it buried deep into the wood. He knew then that the man was serious about cutting off one of Sheila's fingers.

"Alright! Okay, you ...., I'll tell you who I am. My name is Daniel, and I live in a community several miles from here."

"A community?" He asked. "You mean there are more like you out there?"

"Yes." Daniel replied. "We have about 120 men women and children living in our community."

"And just where is this community located?"

"We live in a cave network in the center of Jacob's woods, near the edge of the county line. There, are you satisfied?"

"This is unbelievable." The man said, scratching his head. "Imagine a whole group of one foot tall people."

"Now, let me ask you some questions." Daniel interrupted. "Why do you have that woman held captive in here? What do you plan to do with her?"

"Captive!" He exclaimed. "She's not a captive, she's my wife. It's just that she has been a bit unruly lately, and I have to teach her a lesson. There's nothing wrong with that is there?"

"Not at all, but I don't think Sheila is your wife. I believe she is the wife of Mr. Steve Mason." Daniel replied.

"And just how do you know Steve Mason?" The man asked.

"Steve was shot while hunting in Jacob's woods several days ago. The leader of our community found him shortly after he was shot, and brought him back to our home. The wife of our leader has been tending to his wounds since then. He is healing nicely, I might add."

"Wounded?" He shouted. "You mean he didn't die? But it was a heart shot. There is no way he could....."

"What?" Daniel said in surprise. "So you are the filthy creep that shot him and left him for dead. What manner of person are you, and why would you want Steve Mason dead in the first place? Steve is a wonderful man, with possible harm could he have done you?"

"What is between Steve Mason and myself is none of your business, but I do appreciate knowing that my work is not yet finished. And trust me, I always finish my work."

"But what about Sheila, what do you have planned for her?" Daniel voiced his concern.

"Worry not about her, little man, she is what I wanted. You see, I am a man who gets what he wants, when he wants. And I wanted her. Now I have her, and I will have her for as long as I wish. I love her. I've loved her from the moment I first saw her. It was just a matter of removing one simple obstacle. Once Steve Mason was out of the way, Shelia was mine for the taking. Now we can be together for as long as I desire. She will soon grow to love me as I love her. I really am a nice guy, once you get to know me.

"I understand what you are saying, Mister, but all I can say is that you need some serious help." Daniel added.

"I don't need anything." The man shouted. "Except for you to shut your trap and keep quiet. I'm tired of talking and I'm tired of listening to anything you have to say. Besides, you had better enjoy life, as your days are numbered."

With that, he picked up the cage and slammed it down hard against the table. Daniel fell crashing to the bottom and was dazed for a moment. He realized that this monster was losing control, so he decided to fake unconsciousness and lay still. The man leaned over and looked inside the cage at Daniel. He mumbled something under his breath then rose and left the room. Once his back was turned, Daniel opened his eyes and watched him leave.

The man walked into the bedroom where Sheila lay resting. He said nothing, which made Daniel think that she was pretending to be unconscious also. From Daniel's location, he could see only her hand, the one that was cuffed to the bed, and her right foot. The man checked the pulse in her wrist then bent over her. He was checking for breathing, Daniel thought, either that or he's giving her another disgusting kiss. The man rose and started out of the bedroom. Daniel closed his eyes.

He was mumbling under his breath, as he walked busily about the cabin. Daniel was only able to pick up a word here and there, but it was enough to send a cold chill over his entire body. The man was definitely saying something about dynamite and Jacob's woods. Daniel needed to hear no more. He knew that this pathetic excuse for a human being was going to dynamite the community of Spelonia, which would mean certain death for everyone inside.

"Blasting caps." The man mumbled. "I have to go to the shop to get those, but first, better take care of things here." Daniel kept his eyes closed and lay motionless watching the man. He gathered several pieces of equipment. The one that frightened Daniel most was the electrical triggering device for setting dynamite charges. The man packed his equipment carefully in a large green duffle bag then securely tied the top.

Again he turned and walked toward the bedroom, but paused long enough to push his face only inches from Daniel's lifeless body. "Sleep tight." He said. "It will soon be over." Then, he left.

Quietly, Daniel changed his position to afford a better view. The man was back in the bedroom standing beside the bed. He bent over and Daniel knew he was going to give her another kiss. He heard Sheila scream aloud. "Stop that. Leave me alone. Why are you doing this to me? Leave me alone, please." Daniel saw the man rise up with his hands on his hips and glare down at Sheila. He then screamed at her. "You lied to me. I thought you loved my. You will love me. You'll love me if it kills you." He stormed out of the bedroom and into the kitchen. Moments later he returned carrying a white cloth and a brown bottle. He reentered the bedroom and poured the contents of the brown bottle into the cloth. Daniel could see the man move his hand toward Sheila's face. He could hear her muffled cry, and knew that the man's hand was covering her face.

The screams and moans got lower and more faint. Soon, they stopped altogether. Daniel was afraid she was dead. He hoped she was asleep, but he was still afraid. He saw the man move toward the door and slam it shut. Daniel lay there motionless, praying for her safety and believing that she was still alive. He had no idea how long the man was in the room with Sheila, but it seemed an eternity.

He heard the squeak of the doorknob first then the sound of the door opening and his footsteps pounding against the pine floor. With his eyes barely open, Daniel could see the man as he left the bedroom and walked toward him. He paused in front of the cage and peered inside. His voice was like a foghorn as he yelled. "I'm sure you are awake, little man. Its time to rise and face the music." Daniel slowly raised his head and looked in the man's direction. He watched as the dark man placed a shell in the breech of the shotgun. The sound of the gun being slammed shut was followed by the unmistakable sound of the hammer being cocked. That one simple lonely sound sent a chill through Daniel. He knew his time had come. Daniel could only watch as the man brought the weapon to his shoulder and took aim.

"Its been nice meeting you, little fellow, but I'm afraid its time for you to say good bye. Ha, he laughed, but don't worry, you will soon be joined by your entire little community. I an personally going to see to that."

The air molecules in the room began to vibrate at a deafening rate, as the shotgun exploded. Daniel had only enough time to dive to the floor of the cage and cover his head, before the first of the buckshot arrived. It buried into his back and legs. Several pellets were embedded under his skin, but a few of the more stubborn ones made their way into his lungs and muscles. As the air molecules slowed their vibrations, the blood began to seep from the open wounds on the back of his shoulders. The small man lying on the floor of the cage in the cold and empty cabin was helpless. Daniel heard the door to the cabin slam shut and knew that the man had left the room. Once again the cabin was quiet. Daniel was lying in an ever-increasing pool of blood, and Sheila lay quiet and motionless in her room. The cabin was dead quiet.

CHAPTER 27

The phone rang with a loud incessant blast that shook deputy Ames out of his semi-sleep, where he had lulled most of the afternoon. His feet hit the floor, as his hand came to rest on the receiver. "Sheriff's office, deputy Ames speaking."

"Ames, this is Chuck Albright, at the medical examiner's office. Is Clayton there?"

"No, he isn't, Chuck. Is there a message I can give him?"

"Yes there is." Chuck answered. "Tell him that the bag he left here contained residue of chloroform. It looks like whoever is using that stuff is getting pretty loose with it."

"I'll tell him." The deputy said. "He should be back any time." He hung up the phone and leaned back in the sheriff's chair, pulled his cap over his eyes and nodded off to sleep.

"Dad burn boy!" Sheriff Mills blasted, as he stormed into his office and found deputy Ames asleep at his desk. "Is that all you do is sleep? You'd better lay off the late night running around and start getting some sleep. You know that an unemployment check is only about half of what you make here. Now, do I have any calls?"

"Yes sir." Ames stuttered. "The medical examiner called. Lets see, I think he said that the bag had chlorophyll in it."

"Chlorophyll! You idiot. You mean chloroform."

"Yeah, that the stuff. Chloroform. The bag had chloroform in it. What does that mean sheriff? Are we looking for a serial killer, boss?"

"No!" Sheriff Mills barked. "Not a serial killer, just a guy with a problem, but I think we're about to solve his problem for him. I'm going over to Steve Mason's house to have a look around. Stay here and catch the phone. Oh, yeah, if I walk through that door and catch you asleep again, I'll lock you up for vagrancy. Got it?" Deputy Ames nodded his head and kept silent.

Sheriff Mills walked cautiously around the outside of the Mason house searching for anything that might securely tie Horace Farley to the disappearance of Sheila Mason. The yard at the north end of the house appeared to be somewhat disturbed. There were obviously dog tracks, but another set of tracks was clearly visible. They were small and very faint, but appeared to be almost human in shape, but miniature.

"Beats the heck out of me." He said to himself. "But whatever made those tracks is not my killer." He was about to open the door to his cruiser, when he noticed a chunk of mud on the pavement. It looked as though it might have come from a shoe. He bent over on his hands and knees to examine the smudge of mud and grass. It had a definite pattern, but it was only the front part of the print. The heel of the print had caught in the grass and disappeared.

He opened the trunk of his patrol car and removed the Polaroid camera, which was always handy. The snapshot came out quite well, he thought. Maybe this will be of some help. From there he drove to the mall and pulled the patrol car into a parking space in front the Payless Shoe Store.

"Looks like some kind of hunting boot or combat boot print." The sales clerk said. "It's hard to tell from this photograph."

"But can you identify any particular brand or trademark from this pattern?" The sheriff asked.

"No, I'm sorry." The clerk said. "I wish I could be more helpful, but if it is a combat issue boot, the guys over at the Army Surplus can help with that." "Thanks." Clayton said. "You've been a big help."

The owner of the Army Surplus was definitely more helpful. "I can tell you that the boot that made this print is, without a doubt, an army issue boot. Now, that doesn't mean that the person wearing it is in the army. I sell the same boot here, so he could have just as easily bought it from me. Sorry. The owner said. "Wish I could give you more to go on."

"Oh, you've been a big help." The sheriff explained. "I thank you for your time and information."

The door to Horace Farley's apartment was locked, but his set of keys was part of his personal items collected during his arrest. Clayton noticed that the apartment was quiet but also had a sterile emptiness to it that almost made him sad. The atmosphere of the apartment alone made him feel that this man was a very sad and lonely person. The only sound was that of the door as it squeaked on its hinges. A heavy odor hung in the air like a thick fog on a rainy night. That's funny, he thought. I never noticed the smell before. It was an odor of stale food and dirty clothes. It was quite apparent that very few, if any, females had ever been in this apartment.

He clicked on the light in the bedroom and opened the closet door. The closet was packed with clothes and boxes, but there were no boots anywhere. He leaned over and checked under the bed and found nothing. "Dang!" He said. "Those boots have to be around here somewhere." A fruitless search of the bathroom only served to raise his level of frustration. The only room left was the kitchen. I can't imagine anyone leaving combat boots in the kitchen, he thought. But, I've come this far, and besides, we're not dealing with your normal run of the mill bachelor.

The space under the counters was filled with pots and pans, a few Tupperware bowls, and two chipped corning saucepans, but no boots.

He opened the door to the small pantry that was nestled in the corner of the kitchen, and a broad grin began to spread across his face. The plastic garbage bag was sitting on the floor with a twist tie securing its contents. Clayton pulled the bag out and sat it on the floor. The tie came off easily and the bag fell away to reveal a pair of black army issue combat boots. He picked one of the boots up to look at the bottom. The pattern sure looked like the photo, he thought. He put them back into the garbage bag and headed back to the office.

The bag containing the boots made a large thump, as the sheriff sat it down on his desk. "Now Deputy, lets do a little detective work."

"What ya got there, sheriff?" Ames asked.

"This, my boy, might be what we need to tie Mr. Farley to the question of what happened to one Sheila Mason. If the pattern on the sole of this boot matches the one in the photograph I took in front of the Mason house, he just might be in double trouble."

Mills removed a small magnifying glass from his desk and began to examine the photograph. His concentration shifted back and forth between the boots and the picture. After several passes between the two, he raised his head and looked the deputy in the eyes and said. "Call the D.A. I think we've got a case." Deputy Ames was still dialing the D.A.'s office, as Sheriff Mills opened the door to the cellblock, where Horace was waiting.

"Well, Mr. Farley. I've found your boots, and they match the pattern left on the sidewalk outside Steve Mason's house. You left the chloroform bag on the dresser in the bedroom, and that's only the beginning. Now, I'm here to give you some advice. Things will go a lot easier on you, if you tell me where Mrs. Mason is. If she is already dead, you had better tell me where I can find a body. But, if she is still alive, you had better do yourself a favor and tell me where to find her."

Horace sat motionless on the cell bunk. He stared at the floor, his head resting on his hands.

"Do you hear me?" The sheriff said, as he moved his face closer to Horace's ear. "I'm only trying to help you here, son. Now why don't you cooperate?"

The silence that followed seemed interminable, as Sheriff Mills waited for some response from Horace. The silence was broken, when Horace slowly raised his head and looked deeply into the eyes of Sheriff Mills. Clayton Mills' heart was touched slightly, as he saw a single tear fall from the cheek of his prisoner. For a brief moment a shadow of doubt passed over his brow. "I don't know anything about Sheila." Horace said in a weak and fragile voice. "And I loved Cindy." He lowered his head and the sheriff left the room.

CHAPTER 28

The big hawk came to a soft landing in the leaves, just outside the cave opening. Normally, Otis would not have landed so close to the opening, but today was not a normal day. Today, it was more important that he get to the cave as soon as possible. He paused just for a moment, before releasing the bird and watched. The mighty raptor flew to a large limb of a nearby white oak and began preening itself. She carefully brought each flight feather through her beak to make sure each plume was smooth and firm. The curved beak that could so easily mean death to a mouse or rabbit now becomes a tool for grooming. Otis admired the magnificent beast, as she prepared her wings for the next flight. He felt a special love for the bird, since she had most certainly saved his life today, and if Daniel were still alive, he owed his life to her also.

She finished her grooming, then looked at Otis through bright yellow marble shaped eyes. He could swear he saw the hawk wink at him just before she lifted from the branch and flapped her way out of sight. He turned and entered the cave filled with a sense of peace.

A young boy, named Amos, was standing sentry as Otis removed the cover from the entrance. "Its me, Otis." He shouted. "Go tell Sebastian and the visitor I'm here." The ruddy lad was off in a flash. He dashed through the main hallway in full gallop. As he climbed the steps leading to the hallway where Sebastian lived, he began to shout.

"Otis is here, Otis is here. Sebastian, Otis is here." His words faded in concentric echoes through the hallway, as he sped down the corridor toward Sebastian's residence.

"How does this feel?" Isabel asked Steve, as she rotated his shoulder. "There is still a little stiffness." He Said. "The pain is all but gone, and I have a lot more range of motion than I had a couple of days ago. This is amazing. Where did you study medicine?"

"The medicine I practice here in Spelonia has been handed down through many generations and some of what we know has been through trial and error. We've learned much from the animals. They are very smart when it comes to caring for themselves and healing their wounds. But, what has helped you is your own mental power. You have a burning desire to get well, and your mind is telling your body to heal itself. The mind is a powerful tool for doing good as well as evil. For you it has brought about healing."

"Listen to what she says." Sebastian said. "She is a very wise woman. Almost as wise has her learned husband." All three reeled in laughter, as the young boy, Amos, burst into the room shouting and jumping up and down. "Otis is back!" He exclaimed. "He just returned and asked for both of you come immediately."

Sebastian led the way as all three jumped to their feet and ran toward the hallway. Otis was sitting at the large table enjoying a well-deserved cup of coffee, as they hurried into the room. "Otis!" Steve shouted. "What happened? What did you find out? Where is Sheila? Is she alright?"

"Easy, my friend." Sebastian interrupted. "Let the man answer one question at a time. Now, Otis, tell us what happened. We are all anxious to know."

Otis began. "We found the cabin with no trouble. The man's vehicle was there, so we decided to take a look around.   I was able to secure a vantage point on a plant hanger on the back of the house. From there I could see the woman lying on a bed in the back room."

"Sheila!" Steve shouted. "Was it Sheila? Is she alright?"

Sebastian securely fastened his hand about Steve's wrist, as he grabbed Otis's shoulder. "Wait! Steve." He said. "I know you are anxious, but give him a chance."

"Yes, it was Sheila." He continued. "But, she has been heavily sedated, and was unconscious on the bed. We saw no one else in the cabin, but we knew he was there. After more than an hour, the man left the cabin. It was then that we decided to make our move. It required a bit of fancy climbing and acrobatics, but we managed to get the door open. We were trying to wake Sheila, when the man returned. I was outside looking for some plants to help revive her, and Daniel was inside waiting with her. From that point everything happened so fast, much if it is still a blur.

The man came into the cabin and caught Daniel by surprise. He somehow managed to capture him in an animal cage. I broke into the cabin in time to see him drop the cage to the floor. The cage hit with such force, that Daniel was knocked unconscious. I summoned the bird, and she came to our defense. She attacked the man, while I was trying to free Daniel, but it was useless. I remember seeing her dive at his face with her razor like talons aimed for his eyes. He moved and she got him with a glancing blow that knocked him to the ground. He regained his footing and grabbed his shotgun. My ears are still ringing from the sound of that blast. He shot at the bird, but she did some fancy flying and avoided the buckshot. He then turned his attention to me. I made a dash for the door and jumped, as I heard the hammer of the gun click. The buckshot pellets blasted the floor below my feet, but I was able to make it out the door. The hawk was waiting for me outside. I leapt on her back and away we flew. I could see the man pointing the gun at me, as I flew from sight. For some reason he never fired another shot.

I don't know the condition of Sheila or Daniel. I can only pray that they are both still alive. I am sorry, Steve, that I have no more encouraging news than that. All I can say is that Sheila was alive when I left."

"Thanks." Steve said, his voice heavy with worry. "Its good to know that she was still alive when you left. Maybe we can get there in time to save them both." He turned to Sebastian, his anger burning inside, and said. "I must return to normal size, as soon as possible. I can't fight this monster as a spelon. He's too powerful. I have to go back."

"I understand." Sebastian said, as he looked toward Isabel. "What do you think, Mother, can he stand the transformation?"

"He is a very strong man." Isabel answered with a smile. "If anyone can make that journey, he can." "Very well." Sebastian said, standing at the head of the table. "We will make the transformation first thing in the morning. Tonight we will organize our plan for rescue. Otis, we need a sketch of the cabin, both inside and out. We need to know what was inside the cabin that we might use to our advantage. Were there any tools outside that might help us, anything that might be used as a weapon?"

"I understand." Otis said, as he leaned over the table. "I'll need some paper and a pen. Sketching the cabin will be easy, but as for the furnishings, it was pretty vacant. Any weapons we use will have to be brought with us."

"Otis!" Isabel shouted. "You're bleeding."

All eyes turned to look at Otis, as a look if surprise spread over his face. "What? Where? I don't feel anything." Isabel bend down on one knee and lifted the bottom of his trouser leg. A tiny trickle of blood was oozing from a small wound on the back of his left calf. "It looks as though one of those nasty buckshot pellets just missed taking away part of your leg." She said. "But, you always were the lucky one. It only cut you enough to make it bleed. If you're lucky and handle it just right, you might get a little sympathy from this." Everyone standing nearby chuckled at Isabel's comments.

"Oh, I feel faint." Otis leaned the back of his hand against his forehead and pretended to fall. Steve burst forth with a loud laugh and caught him as he fell. They all laughed, and laughter was what everyone need at that time. They all felt better.

"Now." Sebastian said, bringing everyone back to reality. "Lets get to work."

Steve's sleep that night was fitful and sporadic at best. He could think of nothing but returning to his normal size and rescuing Sheila. His short dreams were of his family. Jennifer was at the lake playing in the water, while he and Sheila sat on the shore watching. Their life was happy and comfortable. As he lay on the shore watching his daughter play, he heard a noise behind him. The sun was to his back, as he turned to see what was responsible for the disturbance. All that was visible was the silhouette of a man against the sun. His face could not be seen, but he was no doubt laughing. Steve started to get up, but froze as his gaze fell on the man's boots.

"Steve! Steve! Wake up, you're screaming." Gabrielle shouted, shaking Steve and trying to wake him. Steve woke with a start and sat upright in the bed. "The boots." He said. "The boots. I keep thinking about the boots. What is it? Why can't I get them out of my mind?"

"I don't know." Gabrielle said, with a soothing voice. "But your screams would certainly wake the entire community."

"I'm sorry." He answered. "But it's just those dreams. They've haunted my sleep almost every night."

"Are you alright now?" She asked. Steve's heart began to race, as he came to realize that he was holding her soft hand. She had tried to touch his face, but he seized her hand and would not release it.

"I must go now." She sighed. "You need to rest. Tomorrow will be an eventful day." Her hand slid from his, as she rose and stood beside his bed.

"Thank you." He said. "You truly are a good friend." She left him alone in the dark room. Alone with his thoughts, and again his mind turned to the man in the boots. Sleep did not come easily.

The morning air was cool and brisk, as the men stepped from the cave entrance. "This is good." Sebastian said. "The cool air will make the transformation somewhat easier. Come follow me. You need to lie down during the process. This bed of leaves will do nicely." Otis and several other men followed Sebastian, as he prepared Steve for his journey.

Steve sat on the bed of leaves and took the cup from Sebastian's hands. "You'd better remove your clothes." Sebastian said. You'll rip those threads completely apart once the transformation begins."

"Gee!" Steve said. "I never thought of that. You mean I have to lay here naked in front of all you guys, while I transform?"

"No, No, No." Sebastian chuckled. "No one wants to see you naked. I have a blanked to cover you, and Isabel repaired you other clothes. I have them here for you to put on once you regain your original size." Steve looked inside the cup, and a frown came over his face. It was the same green liquid garbage he remember from the first time I had to drink it. He stared at it, and it seemed to stare back at him. He looked at Sebastian and said. "As I remember this stuff, it taste pretty much worse than it looks, right?"

"Oh heavens no." Sebastian said, with a sly grin. "That first batch was some I had to make in a hurry. This brew has had time to age. It has much more, how would I describe it, mellow flavor." Everyone laughed.

Steve moved the cup to his mouth and drank it down. "Drink it all, and drink it fast." Sebastian urged. Steve finished downing the dark green liquid, then turned to Sebastian and said, with a raspy voice. "You LIED!"

The fire came first, followed immediately by the intense pain. His bones and muscles were grinding and stretching. The pain was unbearable. He felt as though his body would explode in pain, but just as he thought he could stand no more, darkness. He was consumed in sweet blissful darkness. The pain was gone, and he remembered nothing.

More than an hour later, Steve became aware of the buzzing in his head. It was loud and incessant. He opened his eyes. The crowd of men was standing around him, but they were not standing still. They were flying about his head in large looping circles. The trees were also flying. He closed his eyes and tried to bring his hand to his face. His arm and legs were still numb, as the nerves had not fully returned to their normal operation. In the distance he heard a voice. It was Sebastian. "Stay still. Wait a few more minutes. It takes some time for all the body cells to return to normal. Keep your eyes closed and breathe deeply. The fresh cool air will speed up the process." He rested, closed his eyes and slept briefly.

Several minutes later, he felt the cool splash of water on his lips. One eye opened to reveal Sebastian standing beside him, with a small pail of water in one hand and a dipper in the other. "You can probably open your eyes now." He said. "Enough time has passed."

Steve opened the other eye and waited for the trees to start flying again, but nothing happened. 'You will have to sit up on your own." Sebastian said. "I'm afraid you are much too big for me to be of any assistance." As he raised his arm, he was aware that the feeling had returned. He rubbed his eyes and face and felt the tingling under his skin. He managed to raise himself up on one elbow and look around. Several deep breaths later Steve was able to sit up and actually felt quite well. "Well." He said. "That wasn't so bad. I think I made the trip quite nicely. Now someone hand me my clothes." They all laughed.

Steve finished dressing then looked at Otis with a raised brow, and said. "Hey! I just thought of something. How are we going to get to town? We can't all ride on that hawk." "Fear not." Said Otis. "We have all our bases covered. I've called several animal friends to our assistance. We shall soon have ample transportation."

"Yea, that's okay for you." Steve said. "But what about me? I can't ride on a fox or a bird. How am I supposed to get there?"

"Well." Otis began. "I took it upon myself to assume that you knew how to ride a horse. One will be here shortly."

"Lucky for you I can ride a horse." Steve chuckled. "Or else, we'd all be up a creek." "Wrong!" Otis laughed. "Its lucky for you, or you'd be the one walking." Steve was forced to laugh with the rest of the men.

Minutes later all the animals were ready. There were coyotes, hawks, owls, deer, foxes, and one eagle. A beautiful bay colored horse with four black socks and a black mane and tail had also arrived.

"Mount up and follow me!" Otis shouted. "Time is a wastin'."

Otis led the way as more than thirty men from the community followed. Steve brought up the rear astride the beautiful bay horse. The eight-mile trip took better than an hour. Otis brought the hawk to land at the entrance of the drive that led to the cabin. Minutes later all the spelons were there. "Is this it?" Steve asked. "Are we here?" "Yes." Otis replied. "The cabin is at the end of this drive, but we must spread out from here and surround the house."

"Why don't I just go up to the cabin and knock on the door like I'm lost?" Steve asked.

"I don't know who this guy is." Otis stated firmly. "For all I know he might know who you are and shoot you on sight. And, it would serve no purpose for you to get blown away the very first thing. Are we all in agreement?"

"Agreed." Steve said. "So what's your plan?"

"Okay." Otis began. "Here is how this is going to go down. Steve and I will slip around to the back of the cabin. There is a window there that will afford us a view of the inside. We will then decide if anyone is still inside. The rest of you will circle the house and wait for my command. Remember we will be communicating mentally, so keep your minds open and listen. Once everyone is in position, and Steve and I have evaluated the situation inside, we will adjust our offense. Any questions?"

Nothing was said, indicating that everyone understood and that all were in agreement.

"Good, lets go." Said Otis. "Steve, you follow me, and for goodness sakes stay low and try to be small." "Very funny." Steve laughed. "Don't worry about me, little man, just take care of yourself."

They all moved out swiftly and silently, with the speed and silence of a cat in search of its prey. If anyone were inside the cabin, they would have to look closely to see the small men moving about the surrounding forest. Once in place they each communicated their location to Otis. Steve stood behind the cabin, with his back to the wood. Otis sat comfortably on his shoulder, as they inched their way toward the bedroom window. Steve lifted Otis slightly allowing him to peek over the edge of the windowsill and into the bedroom.

"She's in there!" He said, with some excitement. "It looks as though she is still unconscious. She's just lying on the bed, but I don't see Daniel. He must still be in the living room. Steve, we'll have to move to the back porch and look through the door window. From there we can see into the kitchen area as well as part of the living room."

"You got it." Steve said. "Just hang on." Steve lowered himself to this hands and knees and began to creep around the edge of the porch. Once on the back porch, he was able to look through the door window into the kitchen.

"Empty!" Steve exclaimed.

"Sebastian." Otis thought. "The cabin looks empty. We're going in. Everyone move closer and be ready to move on my command. Be ready to move in a hurry if we need you."

Steve turned the doorknob slowly, waiting for the locked resistance to greet his hand. It turned freely, and the door swung inward slightly. "So far luck is with us." Otis whispered to Steve. "From here we move carefully and quietly." Steve removed his hunting knife from its sheath and pushed the door open. A slight squeak announced their presence. The sound echoed through the house, and Steve knew that the time had come to make a move. He pushed the door open and stepped inside. He stood momentarily looking about to make sure he was alone. Otis stood beside him with his bow and arrow in hand.

Steve quickly made his way to the doorway leading into the living room. His heart was beating as though it would explode at any moment. He eased his head around the doorway. The room was empty. There was only the couch and chair standing sentinel with the coffee table in the center. Below the table, he caught a glimpse of the cage. Before he could say a word, Otis was across the room and standing beside the cage. He shouted at the top of his voice. "Get in here now!"

Seconds later all thirty spelons were standing beside him. "He is still alive, but barely." Otis sobbed. "He's been shot. There are several wounds and they are still bleeding. We have to stop it." He looked squarely at Sebastian and said. "We need some verbascum. It will help stop the bleeding. There should be some growing out back in the rocky soil." Sebastian spoke not a word, but was gone in a flash.

Steve broke his gaze from Otis and looked into the bedroom. "Sheila!" He shouted and ran toward her. He knelt down beside the bed and took her hand in his. He stroked her face with his other hand and softly called her name. "Sheila, Sheila, can you hear me? Sheila, please talk to me. Sheila wake up. Otis! Otis! Come here quick. I think something is wrong."

Otis left the two men working to open the wire latch holding the cage door shut, while he came to Steve's aid. He climbed onto the bed where Sheila lay. His hand lay softly against her neck, but he felt no pulse. No breath entered or left her body. As a final act, Otis lifted her eyelid only to reveal the dilated glazed lens of a person past the point of no return. He turned to his friend and said. "I'm sorry Steve," as a tear streaked its way down his cheek and disappeared into the redness of his beard.

Steve fell back onto the floor and sat there staring. He just stared at Sheila. "How could she be dead?" He asked. "She was so young and alive. It can't be. You must be wrong. Lets start CPR, we have to try and save her." "I'm afraid it's too late for that." Otis said. "The that time has long passed." Tears filled Steve's eyes, as he took his wife into his arms and held her against his chest. He cried.

Sebastian returned shortly with a handful of soft pale green leaves. They resembled tobacco, only much smaller and covered with a soft white downy hair. Thomas and Silas were successful at opening the latch. Daniel had been removed from the cage and was lying on a mat on the floor. Otis began crushing the plant, until the thick fluid filled leaves released their medicinal sap. He rubbed the juice over each wound and replaced the red blood with a thick green paste.

"There is still some buckshot in the wounds." He said. "But we'll have to leave it there until we can get him back to the cave. The sap will harden and stop the bleeding." Daniel was turned over onto his back and his face was washed with water. Otis poured a small amount of water into his mouth and he began to awaken.

"Daniel, Its me, Otis. Can you hear me? You're going to be okay buddy. Just take it easy. We'll get you back to the cave, and Isabel can work her magic." Daniel opened his eyes and looked at Otis. The fear in his eyes sent a chill down Otis's spine. "What's wrong, Daniel? What are you trying to say?" Daniel was weak and barely able to whisper, but was able to say. "Man, dynamite cave, hurry!"

The hair on Otis's head tingled in fear, as he realized what Daniel had just said. He turned to Sebastian and stared blankly. "What did he say?" Sebastian asked.

Otis spoke. "The man has gone to the forest with dynamite. He plans to destroy Spelonia. He obviously thinks I'm the only one that can identify him and he plans to destroy man and the entire community."

"I'm calling the sheriff." Steve said. "We've got to stop him."

"No wait!" Sebastian interrupted. "Ws can't afford to tell the sheriff where he is going. If he knows about us, it will destroy our entire way of life. We'll have to do this on our own. Steve, we need your help."

Steve nodded his head. "You can count on me, but I need to call the sheriff and let him know about Sheila. He will have to bring someone out here to get her."

"Yes." Sebastian agreed. "But say nothing of us or what we are doing."

"Sheriff's office, Sheriff Mills speaking."

"Sheriff, this is Steve Mason, and I want to report a murder."

"Steve Mason!" The sheriff exclaimed. "Where in the world have you been boy? Half the county has been looking for you for more than a week. Murder? What murder? What are you talking about?"

"Its my wife, sheriff, someone has murdered Sheila. I just found her body in a cabin at the end of Pine Tar Road. It's out off route 293."

"I know where it is." The sheriff said. "Wait there for me. It will take me just a few minutes to get there."

" I can't wait for you sheriff. I've got to go after the guy that killed her."

"Don't waste your time, Steve. I've got the murderer right here in my jail. I'm afraid your wife is his second murder."

"In jail!" Steve exclaimed. "Who is it? Who do you have in jail?"

"Horace Farley." The sheriff said. "I believe you grew up with this boy. Now you just wait there for me, and I'll take care of everything."

"Horace Farley!" Steve said with a puzzled sound in his voice. "Hold on a minute." He cupped his hand over the phone and looked at Otis and asked. "Otis, what did this guy look like the one that shot at you and did this to Sheila. Was he in his late twenties, a little over weight, kinda bald in front, with sandy brown hair?"

"No." Otis replied. "This guy was dark headed, kind of slim, about six feet or so, and he wore black army boots." The word 'boots' caused Steve to freeze for a moment. His mind filled with the memory of that day in the woods, looking up at the silhouette of the man, then seeing the boots. "Hello Steve, are you still there?" Clayton Mills asked. The sound of the sheriff's voice brought Steve back to reality.

"Yea! Sheriff, I'm here. Tell you what sheriff, you come on out here and bring the ambulance. Take care of Sheila for me, if you would. I'm pretty sure you have the wrong man, but I'll let you know for sure soon." He hung up the phone before the sheriff could protest.

Daniel had been strapped to the back of the eagle and was being air lifted back to the cave. "Come!" Sebastian shouted. "We have work to do." '

"You go on ahead." Steve said. "I've got a couple of stops to make. I think we could se some reinforcements."

"What are you talking about?" Otis asked.

" Never mind. Just trust me." Steve answered. "I'll meet you at the cave, and don't worry, we'll get this maniac."

Less than a minute later, Steve was alone in the cabin. The spelons had vanished in the blink of an eye. He walked slowly to the bed where his wife lay. He took her cold hand in his and spoke softly to her with tears in his eyes. "Sleep my darling, sleep, know that I will avenge your death. I will not rest until this man is lying dead in the cold forest floor."

He closed the door behind him and mounted the bay horse. He knew where he was going he just hoped that Tom would be at home.

CHAPTER 29

The eagle came to a gentle landing near the opening to the cave. Daniel was strapped securely to the back of the big bird, while Otis held his head and guided the raptor. Seconds after the landing, they were surrounded by most of the returning Spelons. Someone brought out a stretcher made of wood and canvas, and Daniel was carefully placed upon it. The men were gentle, as they hoisted the stretcher and made their way into the cave with their precious cargo. Daniel was unconscious during the trip. His breathing was shallow and irregular. Otis could tell from his appearance, that he had very little time to spare.

He was hurriedly brought into the main room of the cave, and Isabel was summoned. There were two lead pellet holes in his back, one in his arm and one in his right leg. A single pellet had apparently grazed his head, leaving a visible gash in his hair and scalp.

Isabel went to work immediately, cleaning the wounds and struggling to keep Daniel alive. Otis turned to the group and said. "Lets go men. There's nothing more we can do here. Daniel is in the best of hands. We have much work to do, so round up your weapons and meet me outside in fifteen minutes." The men dispersed in a rush, each going in his own direction, but intent on one thing, and that was the protection of Spelonia and their way of life. Fifteen minutes later more than fifty men were gathered outside the opening to the cave. Each was carrying a small piece of dried river cane. It looked like a ten inch piece of fishing pole. The inside pith of the cane had been removed, thereby producing a perfect ten inch blowgun. Each man also carried a leather pouch containing several small feathered darts. The darts were made of bone, so that the semi porous tip could be coated with potassium cyanide, which had been extracted from the wilted leaves of the black cherry tree. The spelons used the darts to hunt small game and occasionally ward off an unwanted prowler. Once the dart would strike the animal, the body fluids would mix with the poison in the bone and the toxic combination would cause death to follow rapidly. But, today they were hunting a much larger and more dangerous prey.

Otis stepped onto a tree stump and gathered their attention, saying. "As I have explained, the man, as far as we know, is planning to set dynamite charges in this area and destroy our community. Steve has gone for help and will join us later. Now, this is our plan. We will encircle the entire area with a network of trip wires. All of the wires will be brought back here to me, where I will wire them to the master control panel. We can then determine if anyone is passing into the protected area. We will all communicate mentally, so keep your minds open. If anything trips a wire, the men in that area will investigate. If it is the man, we will all converge on him. Jason, you and Seth take a group and cover the North area. Raymond and Elijah will cover the East. Simon and Paul will have the South, and Aaron Adam and Zac can handle the West. Now lets move quickly, we don't have much time. I've given you a description of the man, so if you see him talk to me as soon as possible. Any questions? Lets go."

The spelons left with lightning speed, as Otis began working on the master control panel. He worked diligently, but his thoughts were with Daniel and Steve. They were all counting on Steve to return with help, and soon. The safety of Spelonia was at stake. He knew the man was coming.

Each pair of workers connected strands of copper wire, the thickness of a hair to trees, twigs, and vines. The wire was all but invisible. It was so fine, that the man would not even be aware of the wire if he walked through it. In less than two hours, each team had completed their assigned tasks and Otis was busily attaching the wires to the control panel.

"That should do it." He said. "All the wires are attached. Now all we have to do is wait. Each of you has your assigned positions, so lets go and stay alert."

Otis sat quietly beside the control panel. Only the master power light was on, indicating that all the lines were still intact. He waited. He waited for Steve to return. He secretly hoped that Steve would make it back before the man returned.

Less than a mile away, the man brought his vehicle to a stop at the edge of the woods. It was well hidden from the main road, a road that was seldom traveled, except during the hunting season. The large green army duffel bag in the back of the vehicle lie waiting with its deadly cargo carefully tucked inside. It was full, very full. A single stick of dynamite protruded slightly from the mouth of the bag. The early afternoon sunlight washed over the bag, causing bright diamond like sparkles to appear on the end of the dynamite stick.

The man opened the rear hatch of his vehicle and grabbed the bag. He threw it over his shoulder and began walking into the woods. He knew the woods very well and had a very good idea as to where the cave opening might be located. The dry leaves rustled, as the large black combat boots kicked their way through the forest.

CHAPTER 30

The sod flew from the hooves of the young stallion that carried Steve Mason through the back woods toward his house. It was near noon, and the sun was almost directly overhead. His horse cast a short shadow, as it hurried over the hills at full speed. If I can get home, he thought, I'll get the truck, find Tom, and together we'll hunt this killer down.

The subdivision was, for the most part, deserted during the middle of the day. Steve saw no one, as he rode the horse through the backyards of the neighborhood homes. At last he saw the back of his own house, standing silent sentinel to the horror that only hours before had taken place. He slid from the back of his steed and tied him to the porch rail. He ran up the steps to the back door and found it unlocked. He was unaware that it was his mother and daughter that had left the door open.

A dark silent house greeted Steve, as he swung open the door. He really didn't expect to find anyone home, but the anticipation still forced his heart to race. The hallway was dark and quiet. The bedroom door was only slightly ajar. Steve had to push it open with his foot. The bed lay just as it was the night Sheila was stolen. The bed was made and her house shoes were still sitting in the floor beside the bed where she always kept them. He could smell her perfume. The thought of her lying in the bed next to him talking, laughing, and loving, brought a tear to his eye. He took a deep breath and screamed out loud. "NO!"

Standing here thinking about her and feeling sorry won't bring her back, and it certainly won't help my friends, he thought. I've got to hurry. The keys to his Bronco were lying on the dresser in the tray where he always left his extra change. He grabbed the keys and ran out of the bedroom. With determination, he walked down the hall toward the garage.

The only gun he had was a 22.caliber rifle, and he always kept in the garage. The shells were stored in the kitchen junk drawer. Sheila was always afraid that Jennifer might find the shells and the gun, and she knew that accidents could happen. The shells were exactly where they were supposed to be, and the rifle was hanging over his workbench on a couple of nails. It was an old Model 1904 Winchester, that his father had left him, when he died. Steve had shot the gun several times as a child, but in the time he had owned it, it had never been fired.

He thought of is father, as he lifted the rifle from its resting place. The barrel had browned from years of exposure to the elements, and the wood stock was scratched and scarred. His dad had been an excellent shot. Steve remembered the times he had gone squirrel hunting with his father, and watched him shoot the squirrel from the tree with only one shot. The small rodent never knew what happened. It simply released its grip on the limb and fell to the ground.

The sound of the phone ringing in the kitchen brought Steve out of his brief daydream and returned him to the problem at hand. His hand trembled slightly, as he lifted the receiver to his ear. "Hello." He said.

The voice on the other end replied in a soft timed tone. "Who is this? Who is speaking please?"

"Mom!" Steve almost shouted. "Mom, is that you?" Steve's ears were greeted by the sweet sound of his mother calling his name.

"Steve. Steve son. Are you okay? Where have you been? Where is Sheila?"

"Mom, calm down. Yes, it's me, and I'm fine. Everything is okay. Mom, Is Jennifer with you?"

"Yes, Steve, she's here. She's okay, but she is very worried about you and her mother."

"Okay, Mom, tell Jenn that I'm okay, and that I'll be by to see her later today. Please, Mom don't worry, and please reassure Jennifer, that everything is going to be okay. Do you understand?"

"Yes, son, if you say so, but please be careful."

"I will, Mom. I've got to go now I've got a lot of things to do. I love you, Mom. Give Jennifer a kiss foe me. Bye." Steve stood staring at the phone for a brief moment. It sure was good to hear his mother's voice, and he felt better knowing where Jennifer was. That was one less thing to worry about. He picked up the phone again and dialed Tom's number. Tom's wife answered the phone. "Hello."

"Hello Judy?" Steve asked.

"Yes, this is Judy. Who is this?"

"Judy, this is Steve Mason. Is Tom there?"

"Steve!" She blasted. "Where in the world have you been? Do you know that people have been looking for you for days? What happened?"

"Judy, listen. I know that, but I haven't got time to explain right now. Is Tom there?"

"No, Steve, he's down at the mill. They're sawing some new logs today, you can reach him there."

"Thanks, Judy. I'll talk to you later. Bye." He pushed the receiver button and waited for the dial tone to return. The familiar buzz signaled him to dial the mill.

"Gregg Lumber Company." The voice said.

"Is Tom there?" Steve asked.

"Sure is, can you hold a minute?"

"Sure." Steve said. "But please hurry. This is an emergency." Steve waited impatiently for Tom to come to the phone. Minutes later he heard the familiar voice of his best friend. "Hello, this is Tom. What can I do for you?"

"Tom, this is Steve, I need your help as soon as possible."

"Steve!" Tom shouted. "Where have you been, son? I've been looking for you for days. Everyone had given you up for dead. What's going on?"

"I don't have time to explain over the phone, Tom, Just trust me. I need your help desperately." "You got it." Tom answered. "What can I do?"

"Great!" Steve exclaimed. "I guess all your guns are at home, right?"

"Sure they are. Why?"

"Cause we need them. How soon can you meet me at the house?"

"I'll be there in ten minutes." Tom said.

"Great." Said Steve. "I'll see you there." Steve hung up the phone and heaved a sigh of relief. He didn't know for sure why, but he just felt better knowing that Tom was going to be with him. Perhaps it was the fact that Tom was an expert marksman and a pretty darn good fighter.

Steve stood looking around the kitchen for several minutes. Sheila was everywhere. The little notes written to herself her apron hanging on the handle of the stove, but his heart nearly sank, when he saw her watch and rings lying on the kitchen counter. She must have taken them off before she took a shower, he thought. That was her usual routine. He glanced at the clock on the wall, and it reminded him of his meeting with Tom. He had little time to spare. Steve brushed away the past for now just long enough to take care of business.

He locked the door behind him, as he left the house. No point in making things easier for the thieves in the neighborhood, he thought. The Bronco fired up, and Steve wasted no time in backing out of the drive and speeding to meet Tom. Tom's house was less than ten minutes away, and he had not yet arrived, as Steve pulled into the drive. He decided to wait in the truck for Tom rather than trying to explain everything to Judy. He barely had time to get comfortable, before Tom came roaring into the drive beside him. He was out of his truck almost before it stopped moving. Steve jumped out to meet him. Tom grabbed him in a tight bear hug and lifted him off the ground. "You sorry thing." Tom roared. "You scared the living daylights out of me. Do you know that?"

"Trust me." Steve said. "I had nothing to do with it. These past few days have not been my idea of a great time. Lets start getting the guns and ammo, and I'll explain what has happened." They turned and walked into the garage, as Steve began to reveal the events of the past several days. Steve finished most of the story just as they were backing out of the drive with the guns and ammo on board. He had not brought himself to explain what had happened to Sheila, but Tom asked. "What about Sheila? Where is she?" Steve was silent. Tom continued. "Steve, buddy, what is it? What happened to Sheila?"

"She's dead." Steve's voice trailed off into a whisper, as, once again, tears filled his eyes.

"What?" Tom shrieked. "How? Why? What happened? Why would someone want to kill her? She wouldn't hurt a fly."

"I don't know why." Steve sobbed. "I don't even know how. All I know is where he is headed, and that's where we're going right now."

"Do you know who it is?" Asked Tom.

"Not for sure, but I am pretty sure he's the same creep that tried to kill me. Besides, we'll be looking for the only guy in the woods with a bag full of dynamite."

They drove the next several miles in silence. Only the roar of the tires against the pavement filled the cab of the truck. As they approached the edge of the woods, Tom asked. "Do you have any idea what area this idiot is going to be?"

"Well." Steve began. "I suspect that he has figured out by now that I was shot somewhere near the entrance to the Spelon's cave. So I would assume that he would start in that general area. My problem is that I'm not sure I can find the spot where I was shot."

"Leave that to me." Tom said. "I know exactly where I left you, and I figure you got shot somewhere near where we found your gun and tree stand. Ten inches, huh. That's really hard to believe."

"Actually." Steve answered. "Sebastian is ten and a half, and he is very particular about that half inch." They laughed.

"I'm going to get to meet these little guys, ain't I?" Tom asked.

"Sure." Steve said. "No problem. They're just like you and me, only ten inches tall, but they've all got a heart that is at least ten feet tall. These are the happiest and friendliest people I have ever met. I'm serious, Tom, living the life of a Spelon wouldn't be half bad."

"Park it here." Tom said. "We'll have to walk from here. It's a little over a mile from here. Tom lifted the 30-06 from the back of the Bronco and handed it to Steve. "Here." He said. "You take this one. It's an automatic. All you have to do is aim and pull the trigger. If you pull it six times, it will fire six shots, then you are through. If you haven't killed him with six shots, you'll have to beat him to death with the butt of the gun. Got it?"

"Very funny, Rambo, just don't worry about me. I'll kill him with my bear hands if I have to. You just lead the way." They walked side-by-side over the first ridge and deeper into the woods. The afternoon sun cast long shadows in front of them, as they made their way in an Easterly direction towards the spot where Steve had been shot. It was a spot where death was sure to occur.

CHAPTER 31

The man moved slowly and carefully through the woods. He picked his footing, as though his life depended on it, and it did. The bag across his shoulder became quite heavy, as he had carried it more than half a mile. He leaned the bag against a tree and sat down to rest. The large hunting knife was strapped securely to his leg just above the black hunting boot. He removed the knife and scarped several small burrs and seeds from the leg of his camouflage hunting suit then returned the blade to its sheath. The cold fresh winter air quickly dried the drops of sweat from his forehead. He stood up, rested and ready to continue.

As he continued through the woods, he thought about Sheila. It was truly a shame that he had to eliminate her, that was such a waste. He had loved her for such a long time, but it was from a distance. It was sad that his time to love her closely had been so short. But, it was the fault of those little people. If they hadn't entered the picture, everything would have been fine. It would have taken only a few more days, and she would have been able to return his love totally. Those dirty little people were the problem, and he was about to take care of that problem for good. Their cave should be over the next rise, he figured. He knew he had to be getting close. He could feel it. A golden ray of sunlight filtered through the trees and bounced off the thin thread of copper wire that was stretched between two small trees. A tiny glint of light caught his eye, just as he was about to step. The large black combat boot paused in mid-stride, frozen only inches above a hair-thin copper wire. The man slowly lowered his foot to the ground in front of the wire. "Ah!" He said quietly to himself. "Pretty smart for a bunch of little elves, but not smart enough." He bent down to examine the wire. It was the thinnest piece of copper he had ever seen. "I'll have to come back and collect some of this, when I'm finished." He carefully stepped over the wire and continued on his way.

Three hundred yards deeper into the forest; the man lay on his stomach with his binoculars against his eyes. Within the two circles of the glasses, he could see the redheaded little man kneeling over some sort of light panel. Master control, he thought. Those wires must be connected to that control box, and anyone, who trips a wire will be surrounded by a mob of little people. Pretty smart, he thought, but not smart enough.

He crawled back down to where the bag of dynamite was waiting. Using the compact military shovel, he dug a hole. Two sticks of dynamite were carefully placed inside. The electronic igniters were installed and the wire attached. "That's one." He said to himself. "About ten more and it will be the fourth of July all over these woods." Trailing the wire behind him, the man moved in a Northerly direction around the entrance to the cave. He dug similar holes and placed two sticks in each hole. Soon, he was back to near the original hole. The trailing edge of the wire was long enough to move the man more than fifty yards from the blast site. The small battery powered firing mechanism was in the bottom of the bag. He stripped the ends of the wire leads, exposing the bare copper wire. He wrapped the copper wire around the contacts of the firing mechanism. All was ready. One simple twist and the little people would cease to be a problem. He took the device in his hand and prepared to twist.

CHAPTER 32

"Hold it a minute, Steve." Tom said. "Over there is the tree where we had your stand. If my senses of direction is on track, and it usually is, the spot where you were shot is about three or four hundred yards directly ahead of us."

"Then lets get going." Steve said. "We're burning daylight."

"Not so fast." Said Tom, as he grabbed at Steve's arm. "This guy could be anywhere around here. I think we have a better chance of finding him if we split up and move at an angle from here. I'll head right toward the southeast, and you can go left toward the northeast. How does that sound?"

"You mean you trust me in the woods by myself?" Steve joked.

"Don't worry!" Tom reassured him. "This time we will be sure to stay within shouting distance. Now, if you find something or get into any trouble, fire two shots into the air. That should be enough of a signal to bring a crowd."

"You got it." Steve said. "I'm outta here, good hunting." He walked off in the direction of the man setting the charges. "Keep your eyes open." Tom shouted, as he watched Steve disappear into the forest. Tom turned and started walking in the direction where Otis and the other Spelons were waiting. Tom had walked over two ridges and started down the second, when he felt a slight pull against his ankle. A quick glance downward revealed nothing. Must have been a vine, he thought, as he proceeded cautiously. Less than twenty feet away Aaron and Adam were watching his every move. Aaron spoke to Otis with his mind saying, "Otis, a man has just broken through the wire."

Otis replied. "I see. It's showing up on the control panel. I'll summon several others to assist you. Keep out of sight and follow him. We'll join you as soon as possible." Aaron agreed, and he, Adam, and Zac moved swiftly and silently to keep Tom in sight. Minutes later they were joined by twelve other Spelon men. Aaron ordered everyone to form a tight circle around the man, and he would do the talking. As soon as everyone was in place, Aaron jumped out from behind the tree and shouted at Tom.

"You there. Stop. You are surrounded with a dozen poison darts aimed at your neck this very minute. At my command you will become target practice for my friends."

Tom jumped in startled surprise. He shook his head and rubbed his eyes, trying to convince himself that he was not dreaming. "Well I'll be!" He exclaimed. "Steve wasn't lying about you guys. You really are only ten inches tall. Howdy guys my name is Tom Gregg. I'm Steve's friend. I'm out here with him looking for this guy with the dynamite."

"Sir!" Aaron announced. "If you will kindly have a seat and wait, we will determine your identity as soon as Otis arrives."

"I appreciate you being cautious and all that, fellows, but you have to understand. I need to find this man who is going to try and blow this whole mountainside to kingdom come. Now if you want to come with me and help, that'll be fine. But, I really need to be traveling."

"Sir, as I told you before, Otis will arrive shortly to establish your identity. Until then, I must remind you that each man here has a dart dripping with potassium cyanide pointed directly at your neck. You might last two minutes."

"Dad gum!" Tom said. "You fellows are serious ain't ya? Well I guess I can wait a few minutes. Steve hasn't fired any shots for help yet. Lets just hope this Otis fellow gets here soon."

"I'll call him again." Aaron said. "I will find out how soon he will arrive."

"Call him?" Tom asked. "Where is your phone?" Tom sat watching in amazement, as the small man closed his eyes and sat motionless. He looked around at the other twelve. They stood like statues, blow guns ready and aimed at his neck. For some odd reason, he believed every word the little guy had said, and he did not doubt for a second that those darts would end his life in less than two minutes. Tom decided to wait.

Aaron raised his head and opened his eyes. He looked squarely at Tom and said. "Otis will be here in about five minutes. There was another break in one of the lines on the east side. He's waiting for someone to communicate with him about the break. So, we wait." Tom hoped that the wait would not be too long. He knew that time was running out.

Not more than a half a mile away, Steve had walked through one of the trip wires, causing a light to blink on the control panel. Otis sat waiting for someone to report back to him about the break. Steve was totally unaware that he had tripped any wires and continued his walk through the woods. The climb up the second ridge was steep and rough. He had the rifle slung over his shoulder, freeing both hands to grab for trees and rocks to help his climb. He pulled and tugged his way up the steep ridge.

With sweat pouring from his forehead and gasps of breath surging in and out of his lungs, like a racehorse, he finally reached the plateau. He stood holding onto a tree and taking deep breaths in an effort to regain his equilibrium. While he stood waiting, he surveyed the woods immediately surrounding him.

His breath caught in mid-gasp, as he looked at the narrow ridge off to his left. He could just see the back of a man. He was bent over working with something in the leaves. The man was wearing some sort of a dark green coat. It looked like one the forestry people wear. Must be someone from the state, he thought. I'd better check him out and see if he has noticed anyone suspicious.

Steve walked casually down the hill and onto the ridge where the man was working. As he approached, he shouted. "Hey there. How ya doin'?" The man jumped up with a start and turned in the direction of Steve's voice. Once the man turned around, Steve recognized him. "Why Dave Black, what are you doing in this neck of the woods?"

"Steve!" Dave said with surprise. "Is that really you? I thought you were dead. I've been searching these woods day and night for your body. What happened, where have you been?"

"Oh, it's a long story." Steve said. "I'll be glad to share it with you someday, but right now I'm looking for someone."

"Oh, Really?" Dave questioned. "And who might that be?"

"Well, to tell you the truth, I don't exactly know for sure." Steve said. "But, he's the no good snake that killed my wife and tried to kill me, and now he's going to try and destroy some very good friends of mine."

"Well, how are you going to know when you find him, if you don't know who he is?"

"Oh, don't worry." Answered Steve. "I'll know him when I see him, he has….." Steve paused in mid-sentence, as his gaze fell upon the black combat boots on the feet of Dave Black. His instant memory recall kicked in, and he was staring up at the silhouette of the man against the setting sun. As his eyes fell to the ground, he saw the boots. They were black combat boots. The toes were scuffed and heels were worn.

"Has what?" Dave asked. "What does this guy have that will identify him?" Steve took a couple of steps forward as though he were going to sit down, and brought the high-powered rifle from his shoulder. As he sat on the ground, he brought the barrel of the rifle around and aimed it squarely at Dave.

"What do you think you are doing?" Asked Dave. "Have you lost your mind?"

"Boots!" Steve snarled. "The lying coward had boots on his feet. They were boots exactly like the ones you have on right now. You're the one, aren't you?"

"I don't know what you are talking about." Dave assured him, as he leaned forward as though he were going to sit also.

"Hold it right there." Said Steve. "Don't you move a muscle."

"I'm only going to sit down. Just don't shoot me, we can figure all this out." Steve squeezed the trigger of the powerful rifle twice, sending two rounds into the air. The sound waves from the rifle traveled through the silent woods at mach one speed in search of Tom's ears.

More than fifty pairs of ears heard the two shots, the spelons began to converge. The two blasts gave Dave the split second he needed to grab the blasting mechanism and hold it up in front of his chest. "Now, my friend." He said. "I have the fate of all your little friends in my hands. One twist of this knob and this ridge will go under like the titanic. Now, put the gun down and lets talk."

Steve knew this maniac with his hand on the firing control was capable of anything. He had no choice but to comply. He laid the gun down on the ground in front of his feet. Dave leaned forward and grabbed the barrel. He pulled the weapon to his shoulder and aimed it at Steve. The firing control lay on a bed of leaves at his side.

"What do you want now?" Steve asked. "Why? Why me, and why Sheila?"

"Ah! Sheila." Dave began. "She was everything. She was my whole reason for everything. You see, I've loved her for quite some time. Granted, it was from a distance, but it was just a matter of time until I was able to figure a way to have her close to me. When you decided to go hunting, it was perfect. You would die in this horrible hunting accident, and I would be there to console her and take your place. But, somehow things didn't go exactly as I had planned. When I returned the next morning with the search party, I couldn't find your body. You were gone. I didn't know at the time who might have found you, or where you might be.

It was then that I decided that you might someday return. I had to move fast. I had to change my plans. I didn't know exactly how I was going to do it, until some local idiot in town gave me the answer. Some moron by the name of Horace Farley had slipped into this girl's house and killed her with chloroform. He was arrested and locked up. There was my answer. All I had to do was use a little chloroform to put dear sweet Sheila to sleep and take her with me. I left the chloroform bag behind to convince the sheriff that Horace had struck again. It worked. I think this guy is going to hang for both murders."

"But why did you have to kill her?" Steve asked.

"Well, that was mostly the fault of your little friends. If they hadn't tried to play the hero, she might well be alive today, but after that little encounter, I had no choice but to destroy her and them too. And that, my friend, brings us back to the task at hand. That will simply be to twist this little handle on the firing box and it's all over. Dave was so intent on his description of the past events that he didn't hear Jason, Seth, Ray, and Elijah approach from below the ridge. They had not seen Steve and Dave, when Ray said. "We must be getting close."

Dave caught a faint sound of the voice and turned looking over his left shoulder. Steve's response was more out of instinct than common sense, and he made his move. He had but one chance, and that was to grab the barrel of the rifle and pull it away from Dave in a single motion. He was midway through his dive, when Dave turned around. He brought the gun up and squeezed the trigger. The explosion from within the chamber of the 30-06 shattered the silence of the forest, and the lead projectile was sent speeding harmlessly through the naked branches of the forest canopy.

Steve landed directly on top of Dave and knocked the rifle loose from his grip. It fell to the ground, as the two men began to roll around, each trying to gain the advantage. Fists were flying in all directions and occasionally one successfully found its mark. Steve felt the impact of Dave's fist against the side of his head, and he thought for a brief moment he might lose it. But, the adrenalin in his system was high enough to keep him going. Steve brought his right fist down with all his might, and caught Dave squarely on the chin. His eyes opened wide, and he released his grip on Steve's arm. His hands fell to his side, and his eyes closed. Steve sat astride him staring down into the unconscious face of the evil man responsible for the death of his wife. The hatred boiled inside him, and it was all he could do to keep from strangling him where he lay. He sat there long enough to regain his composure then slowly rose. He stood beside man fight with his emotions. No, he thought, if I kill him like this, I'll go to jail, and who will be there to take care of Jennifer. As bad as I hate to I guess this will have to be handled by the authorities.

Steve turned to pick up the gun. The ejector was jammed open, and Steve pushed and pulled on it in an attempt to release the jammed device. Dave was as silent as a mouse, as his right hand moved slowly to the knife strapped to his leg. The ten inch steel blade slid from its sheath in total silence. He sat up slowly bringing the knife over his head. All he had to do was make one lunge and bury the knife in Steve's back. The muscles in Dave's legs and arms tensed, as he prepared t leap. Only the slightest noise made by the movement of his boot against the leaves signaled his approach. Steve had only enough time to turn around and see Dave flying through the air. The knife was raised above his head making its deadly path toward Steve's chest. He was helpless. He closed his eyes and waited for the knife to enter his chest.

For the final time that day, the violent explosion from within the muzzle of a high-powered rifle broke the peaceful silence of the pristine forest. The 30-30 bullet traveling at better than three thousand feet per second struck Dave Black in the side of the head just above the ear. It entered on the left side of his head and made a hole about the size of a quarter, but when it exited on the right side, it brought with it most of his brain and half of his scull. Dave Black came to rest on the lap of Steve Mason. The remainder of his brains was still seeping from the large gaping hole that was once the side of his head and collecting in a pool beside Steve's leg.

He shoved the body off and jumped to his feet. He was still in shock and not sure what had just happened. That was when he heard a familiar voice shout from a distance. "Hey! Are you okay?" He looked in the direction of the voice and saw Tom standing on the ridge about one hundred feet away. Otis and several other men were with him. As Tom and the others approached, Steve's legs began to shake. He sat down on a large rock and leaned against the huge old oak tree. Several deep breaths later, he felt the comfortable hand of his friend resting on his shoulder. Again that comforting voice asked. "Are you sure you are okay? I don't see any cuts and no blood anywhere." "No." Steve said, with a still shaky voice. "I've never felt better." Steve looked up and saw the smiling friendly faces of his new found friends. Fifty or so spelon men had gathered around Steve and the body of Dave Black.

"Well." Steve began. "What do we do now? We've got a dead man on our hands. I guess we'd better notify the sheriff."

"Yea. I suppose." Tom agreed. "But as far as I am concerned, I'd just soon kick this snake in a ditch and let the buzzards pick his bones."

"I've got a better idea." Steve said. "This creep never did anything good for anyone while he was alive, I say we let him do something good for someone now that he is dead."

"What do you mean?" Asked Tom. "I don't follow."

"Come with me." Steve said. "Lets drag him to the truck, and I'll explain on the way.

CHAPTER 33

"Are you sure about that Chuck?" Sheriff Mills asked.

"No doubt about it, Clay." Chuck answered. "The mason woman died of asphyxiation from the presence of chloroform in the lungs. Yep, I'd say the man that killed Cindy also killed Sheila Mason."

"Thanks, I appreciate your help." The sheriff said, before hanging up the phone. His concentration was broken as the door to his office opened and Tom Gregg and Steve Mason entered.

"Sheriff, I'm Steve Mason, and this is a friend of mine, Tom Gregg."

"A lot of things have happened since you disappeared, but I'm glad to see that you're okay." Clayton answered. "Now if you would like to explain that phone call, I'd like to hear it."

"Right Sheriff, but first, Sheila. Did you?"

"Oh, yes sir, Mr. Mason, and I am truly sorry about what happened. You wife's body is with the medical examiner. An autopsy was necessary to establish a cause of death. I'm sure you understand."

"Yes sheriff, I appreciate your concern and thank you for your help. Now, I'll be more than happy to explain the circumstances involving my wife's death, as well as the death of the other young girl you mentioned."

Steve explained everything that had happened to Sheriff Mills, who sat with his mouth open in disbelief. "So you see, Sheriff, my intend was to bring Dave Black in to you, after he admitted to me that he had killed my wife and the girl named Cindy. But I made the near fatal mistake of turning my back on him for a brief second. If tom had not been such a good shot, you might well be looking at my autopsy report also."

"I'll need sworn statements from both you and Mr. Gregg." The sheriff explained. "They will need to be read at Mr. Farley's hearing."

"Not a problem, Sheriff. We'll be glad to do what ever is necessary. Ma we see Mr. Farley for a moment?"

"Sure, I suppose that would be permissible. Follow me."

Together the three men walked down the naked corridor that led to the cell where Horace was being held. Surprise filled Horace's face, as Steve and Tom appeared in front of his cell door.

"Steve!" Horace shouted. "I thought you were dead. What happened? Where have you been and why are you here?"

"Thanks sheriff." Steve said. "We'll only be a couple of minutes."

"Just yell, when you want out." Clayton said, as he locked the cell door behind them and turned toward his office. "Oh by the way, sheriff, you might want to call the coroner. Black's body is outside in the back of my Bronco." Clayton shook his head walking down the hall to his office. He had a small grin on his face. Sometimes justice isn't blind, he thought. It gave him a good feeling.

Steve briefly explained to Horace what had happened. "So you understand, Horace, I don't know for sure what happened to Cindy, but I do know that you would not intentionally hurt anyone."

"I loved her." Horace answered. "I was with her that night, and we held each other, but I didn't kill her."

"Don't worry about it, buddy." Steve told him. "It will all be over soon, and then I need to talk to you about your future. Tom and I have to go for now, but we'll see you in a couple of days."

Steve shouted through the bars for Sheriff Mills to come and let them out. The cell door squeaked slightly as it swung open and Steve and Tom walked out. He glanced back over his shoulder at Horace sitting on his cot. Horace smiled.

"How soon can I have the Funeral Home pick up Sheila?" Steve asked.

"First thing in the morning." The Sheriff answered. "Chuck should be finished by then."

"Thanks Sheriff."

The ride back to Tom's house was mostly in silence. Much had happened that day and much had already been said. Now was the time to think. As he pulled the Bronco into the driveway, Tom asked. "Where are you going from here?"

"I guess I'll go over to Mom's house. Jennifer is there, and I can't wait to see her. I just dread telling her about her mother."

"I sure am sorry about Sheila, Steve. I wish there were more I could do."

"Hey!" Said Steve. "You have done more than enough. I owe you my life, and I don't know how I will ever repay you."

"You don't owe me a thing." Tom said. "I'll sleep tonight knowing that you would have done the same thing for me."

"Yea!" Steve agreed. "You're probably right, but with my shooting, I would have probably shot you instead of Black." Both men were laughing, as Tom shut the door to the Bronco. He waved as Steve backed out of the drive and disappeared into the night.

<hr>

The doorbell rang twice before Mrs. Mason could answer it. She was always a bit nervous about opening the door at night, but tonight she had too much on her mind to be nervous. Steve stood smiling, as the door opened. "Hi Mom." He said. "Got anything to eat?" The tears began to stream down the soft cheeks of his mother, as she pulled him to her. "Oh Steve." She sobbed. "I knew you would be back. Thank god you are all right. C'mon, get in here out of that cold wind, and I'll fix you something to eat. Oh my. Jennifer is in bed. Shall I wake her?"

"No." He said. "Let her sleep. I'll see her in the morning. Besides, we need to talk. I have a lot of things to tell you." Steve spent the next several hours explaining to his mother all that had taken place in the past several days. Her eyes widened in disbelief, as he explained the secrets of the Spelon community.

"Ten inches tall!" She exclaimed. "Oh pooh. I don't believe you. Quit pulling my leg."

"Believe me, Mom, its true, but wait, there's more."

Tears filled her eyes once again, as Steve explained what had happened to Sheila. She made the sign of the cross then leaned against Steve's shoulder and sobbed. "I loved her like my own daughter." She said, as Steve patted her head.

"I know you did, Mom, and she loved you. I don't know how I'm going to live without her, and I sure don't know what I am going to say to Jennifer." His mother raised her head and looked into his eyes saying. "We will manage. Just remember that God never gives us a cross that is too heavy to carry." Steve smiled and once again held his mother's head to his chest.

His sleep that night was peaceful. There were no dreams of boots or silhouettes. That night he dreamed only of Sheila. Steve was awakened the next morning by the sound of Jennifer shouting. "Daddy, Daddy, you're home. Oh, Daddy, I missed you." She came running into the bedroom and leaped into the waiting arms of her father. They held onto each other tightly, as the loved passed between them. Finally, Jennifer released her grip and looked him in the eyes and said. "Do you want some breakfast, Daddy? Me and Grandma have been learning how to cook. Do you want some cookies for breakfast? I made them."

Steve laughed and hugged her again. "I think I'll just have some coffee and a toast this morning. I'll eat some of your cookies later on in the day. Can you fix me some toast?"

"Yea boy." She said, and leaped from the bed. She barely missed colliding with her grandmother, as she darted from the bedroom down the hall to the kitchen.

"When are you going to tell her about her mother?" His mom asked.

"After we eat. I'll sit down and explain things to her. She's pretty smart for her age." Steve said. "I hope she can handle it."

Jennifer talked continually through breakfast, pausing long enough to take a bite of toast and drink her juice. "What are we going to do today, Daddy?" She asked. "Are we going to get Mommy? Where is she anyway?"

"That's what I have to talk to you about, sweetheart." He began, as he lifted her onto his lap. "Do you remember in Sunday School, when you learned about heaven. Remember we learned that someday everyone would get to go to heaven and be with Jesus? Do you remember?"

"Sure Daddy, I remember. Someday, when we get old, we will die and go to be with Jesus in heaven. That's what happened to Grandpa, isn't it Grandma? He's in heaven with Jesus right now, isn't he?"

"He sure is, sweetie." Mrs. Mason answered, as she fought back the flood of tears that were welling up inside.

"Well, honey." Steve continued. "Sometimes people die even though they aren't old. Sometimes Jesus needs them in heaven sooner than we expect. And that's what has happened to your Mommy. Jesus needed her to be with him in heaven, and now she is up there with Him and Grandpa."

"Is Mommy not coming home?"

"No, I'm afraid not, baby. She is in heaven." There was a long deafening silence, and Jennifer said nothing. Steve was starting to get worried, when Jennifer finally broke down and began to cry. She cried for several minutes, before pausing and looking up at her father. "Daddy, aren't we supposed to be happy for someone who has gone to heaven?" Aren't we happy for Grandpa?"

"Yes, sweetheart, we'll be happy for Mommy too."

Two days later, Steve and his mother were returning home from Sheila's funeral. Jennifer sat quietly in the back seat. "Mom." He said calmly. "I've made some very special friends in Spelonia, and I think that Jennifer and I could be very happy living there. If I decide to go, and I probably will, only you and Tom will know where we are. I'll arrange a line of communication, so that we will be able to stay in touch. When Jenn is older, she can decide for herself, if she wants to stay or return here to live."

"But why can't you go back and forth between the two places?" She asked. He explained. "I will be able to make the transformation only one more time. Any more than that, and it will do permanent damage to my body. It could even kill me. No, mom, this decision will be permanent."

"You now what is best for you and Jennifer." She said. "But I will certainly miss you."

"We will still be able to visit, it's just that I'll be ten inches tall." He laughed. As he stopped the car in the driveway to his mother's house, he said. "Would you watch Jennifer for a few minutes? I need to talk to Tom. I'll be back soon."

"Tom, you know where I'll be, if you need me for anything. The spelons know you and trust you, and you will be welcome anytime. Another thing, once Horace is released, take him to Nashville to get some help. I don't think he's dangerous, I just think he is confused. Who knows, someday, I may bring him to live with us in Spelonia."

"Don't worry about a thing." Tom said. "I'll take care of everything. I'll watch out for your mother too, so don't worry about her."

'Friends like you come along once in a life time." Steve said, and gave him a hug.

The next morning Steve and Jennifer left for the forest. Sebastian was waiting outside the entrance to Spelonia. "Are you sure you want this?" He asked. "You know that this will be permanent."

"I'm sure." Steve said. "This is where my family is."

ONE YEAR LATER....

Jennifer stood beside her newest best friends, Alaura, Alex, and Autumn, and watched her father. Steve's heart was once again alive, as he looked into her liquid blue eyes and said. "I Steve, take you Gabrielle....."

But that's another story.